A

Ryan Weller Thrillers:

Dark Water

Dark Ship

Dark Horse

Dark Shadows

DARK WATER

A Ryan Weller Thriller - Book 1

EVAN GRAVER

Dark Water

www.evangraver.com

ISBN-10: 1-7338866-0-5

ISBN-13: 978-1-7338866-0-4

Cover: Wicked Good Book Covers

Editing: Larks and Katydids

Proofreading: Gerald Shaw

Printed and bound in the United States of America

First Printed March 2018

Published by Third Reef Publishing, LLC

Hollywood, Florida

www.thirdreefpublishing.com

ACKNOWLEDGMENTS

I'd like to thank my wife, Becky, and son, Patrick, for putting up with the many hours I spent writing and editing this book. Thanks to my mother and father, Bruce and Susan, for the encouragement and motivation, my mother-in-law, Sarah Ansley, for graciously allowing me to spend hours writing in her coffee shop, Ths. Jitterz Coffee Company, in Kenton, Ohio. Thanks to the Davie Writers' Group in Davie, Florida, for listening to the story and offering much needed direction and advice.

I am grateful to all the men and women who are serving, have served, or will serve in the U.S. Armed Forces and the Coast Guard. I made many lifelong friends in the Navy and some of them appeared throughout this book in various forms. I served with the mighty Vanguard, HM-14, and love those big, smoky birds. During my time with the squadron, I was a line shack maintainer and then crossed over to work on the mine countermeasures gear. It was a job I truly loved.

CHAPTER ONE

Mustafa Wahib Abdulla sat in the driver's seat of the Toyota 4Runner. His finger rested on the detonator switch. He caressed it as he prayed. His lips moved as he stared straight ahead at the closed garage door of the old four bay auto repair shop. Abdulla rocked back and forth in rhythm with his holy pleadings. A smile played across his lips as he finished. He was ready to make the ultimate sacrifice, be received into Paradise and rewarded for his zeal.

"Mustafa, are you ready?"

The Pakistani looked up at the American he knew only as "Professor" with his long, white pony tail. Abdulla tried to hide his disdain with a nod. This American had been instrumental in helping them infiltrate the United States, sheltered them in the city, and provided materials and support for their cause, yet he was not a believer. Abdulla thought again how this was a means to an end. The end of the Great Satan. Allah would forgive him for taking the aid of a nonbeliever to destroy more nonbelievers.

Abdulla climbed from the SUV. As he closed the door,

he could feel its extra weight. The door shut with a satisfying *thunk*. They'd molded one hundred pounds of Semtex into the hood, doors, and quarter panels of the Toyota. Then they poured quarter-inch steel ball bearings a deadly, flying hail on top of the plastic explosives. The switch Abdulla had caressed would arm the device when he was ready to ram his target. He'd connected it to the front-bumper airbag sensor. An impact strong enough to deploy the airbag would also trigger the bomb.

"We will pray one final time," he replied to Professor.

Professor stroked his goatee as he watched Abdulla's men kneeling on their prayer rugs. Swarthy men from the Afghan and Pakistani mountains and smooth-skinned Saudi Arabians, all clothed in black combat fatigues. Each carried an AK-47 and wore a chest rig packed with extra ammunition and grenades. The men had trained relentlessly on a mocked-up target in a Syrian training camp to perfect their timing and coordination.

Abdulla knew he and his men were only pawns in a larger game orchestrated by his leader, Abu Bakr al-Baghdadi, and the leader of the Mexican movement, who had brought them to the US. He hadn't heard the name of the Mexican leader, nor dealt with anyone but Professor. Abdulla studied his contact again. He was of medium height with a slim build. Square glasses framed brown eyes above a wide nose and mustache. What Abdulla had found curious was the silver coin Professor wore around his neck on a matching silver chain. Professor had told Abdulla it was a symbol of his defiance of the Great Satan.

Professor glanced at his watch, then said, "Hurry up."

The arrogance of the man angered Abdulla. He wanted to break his neck. He closed his eyes and willed himself to remain calm. Then he walked across the stained and scarred cement floor of the two-story concrete block building that had once housed an auto repair shop. The structure stank of used oil and burnt rubber. Outside, garbage cluttered the gutters, rusty car parts leaned against the chain-link fences, and graffiti covered the walls. Abdulla abhorred the filthy garage and the rotten stench filling his nostrils with every breath. This was America, the land of milk and honey, yet the neighborhood was no better than the slum he'd been raised in outside Islamabad. He was ready to leave this awful place, the hard cots and the electric hot plates that warmed their food. He was ready for Paradise.

Abdulla knelt on his own prayer rug. In unison, he and his men bowed and prayed, consecrating themselves to the Prophet Muhammad and to Allah so their actions might bring glory and honor to their cause. When they were done, they rose and walked to where Professor waited.

Abdulla said, "We are ready."

Professor nodded and motioned for them to proceed. The fighters loaded into a Ford Explorer and a Honda CR-V while Abdulla sat in the driver's seat of the Toyota. He gripped the steering wheel at ten and two until his knuckles whitened. He'd prepared for this moment, yet he was still nervous. Abdulla muttered a prayer as he turned the ignition key. Ahead, the garage door slid open to reveal brilliant sunlight. It was a metaphor, Abdulla thought. They were about to step out of darkness and into the light. He would venture from this dreary world into a glorious Paradise.

The Explorer exited the garage and Abdulla fell in line between it and the CR-V. He slipped on a pair of sunglasses and turned onto the main road. He accelerated to keep up with the lead vehicle and he was thankful for the bomb's kill switch. All around him, Americans went on, blissfully unaware of the danger near them. Knowing he was about to destroy a sacred landmark, kill and maim leaders of the cult of consumerism, made him smile. They would die a scorching death and burn forever in the fires of Hell.

CHAPTER TWO

Rueben Morales, the man known as Professor, stepped out of his SUV in the parking lot on Lavaca Street at the rear of the Texas Governor's Mansion. He closed the door of the Dodge Journey, a vehicle made in Toluca, Mexico, and part of the reason he'd purchased it. Mexican hands had built the Journey for an Italian company that sold it to Americans who believed they were helping the Detroit economy by buying from the Big Three. He chuckled at the irony as he walked to the right rear passenger door and opened it. Morales leaned across the seat and turned on the video camera. Aiming it through the already open window, he turned it on and then positioned it for maximum exposure.

A ghost of a breeze wafted over him as he moved to the front of the Journey and leaned against the hood. They had chosen this day with care. The governor was hosting a luncheon for election campaign donors. They would mingle with the Republican state senators, representatives, and the governor's family. Morales had also heard a rumor that a sitting U.S. senator would attend. He smiled, hoping it were true. He watched the tall sycamore, pecan, and cottonwood trees around the white Greek Revival mansion sway with the breeze. A wind would help fan the flames. His gaze fell on the two vehicle entrance gates set in a white, concrete block fence topped with black wrought-iron spikes. Texas State Troopers patrolled the sidewalk.

"Let *la Revolución* begin!" Morales muttered. The peace these white mercenaries believed they held over their ill-gotten gains was about to be shattered. They'd stolen the Southwest from Mexico with their concepts of manifest destiny and by waging unjust wars on the Mexican people. It was time to take back Aztlán.

Morales's attention snapped back to the present as a Ford Explorer careened onto Lavaca and came to a screeching halt alongside the gates. Three men jumped from the vehicle. Two immediately shot the uniformed troopers and placed explosives to blow the gates open. The third ran to the guard booth where he shoved a grenade through the window before racing toward the patrol car sitting at the corner of Lavaca and West Tenth Street. He rolled a grenade under the car. Behind him, the detonation blew out the sides of the guard house and threw chunks of concrete twenty feet into the air. The second grenade blast lifted the trooper's Ford Crown Victoria off its wheels. Fire blew out from underneath, and when the gas tank exploded, it sent the trunk lid somersaulting through the air. Morales howled with delight.

Abdulla's modified Toyota 4Runner swept in from Tenth Street. He curved wide into the oncoming traffic lane and then shot through the now open gates of the vehicle entrance. Morales knew a carload of Abdulla's men would commence as assault at the front of the mansion, blowing up the patrol car on Colorado Street, breaking through the wrought-iron gates, and killing everyone they could find.

The 4Runner disappeared behind the wall. Morales blew out his breath and covered his ears. He could see the steps leading to the rear entrance under the porte-cochère. The Toyota reappeared and charged up the steps at full throttle. The massive tires bounced as they hit the first step, hung in the air for a moment, and fell back in slow motion. Then the four-wheel drive powered the vehicle up the steps. White light burst from the car as it exploded.

Morales felt the heat and shock wave roll over him. His mind couldn't take in all the details of what happened in those seconds after detonation. Later, he would play back the video frame by frame and see the ball bearings blast from the car, punching, tearing, ripping, and gouging anything in their path. The porte-cochère disappeared and the back of the mansion disintegrated. Fire spread from the Toyota's gasoline tank to the wooden siding and framing. A secondary explosion rocked the grounds as natural gas, spilling from a ruptured line, ignited in a scorching fireball.

Debris pelted the roadway more than a full block away. Morales ducked as wood splinters and ball bearings rained down all around him. Pride swelled inside him as he turned to run for cover behind a brick building. He discovered he was laughing.

CHAPTER THREE

Greg Olsen had never known his grandfather to show much emotion. The old man held his white cowboy hat by the brim and slowly turned it in circles. Clifford Olsen's cheeks shone with a trail of tears as he stared out the window at the docks holding Dark Water Research's collection of boats, barges, and ships necessary for commercial diving. He still had a full head of black hair, making Greg hope his own would look as good when he was seventy-five, and he wore his usual black slacks, a tan Western shirt with pearl snaps, and alligator hide cowboy boots.

Their feelings were still raw six days after the funeral for Allen and Denise Olsen. They had died in what the news had deemed a terrorist attack on the Texas Governor's Mansion. The sense of loss weighed heavily on each man, Greg for the loss of his parents and Cliff for losing his only son.

The two faced each other in the office that had once been Allen's. Responsibility for running what they all referred to as DWR now fell on Greg's shoulders, whether or not he wanted it. Time didn't stop because his parents were dead. It marched on. Bills needed paid, contracts negotiated and fulfilled, and the phone calls never ceased. Greg wasn't sure how much he could take. His own wounds were still fresh from the battlefields of Afghanistan. But he was a warrior. He would do what sailors always didhitch up their dungarees, square their white caps, and order another beer.

Cliff set the hat down on a chair, pulled a hip flask from his pocket, and unscrewed the top. He took a healthy slug and handed the flask to Greg. "Cures what ails ya, boy."

Greg took a sip. As he suspected, it was tequila, Cliff's favorite. And his own. He took another hearty swig from the flask and handed it back. The liquor burned in his mouth and throat, but damn was it good. *Nothing can cure what ails me,* he thought. First, the loss of his legs when shrapnel had severed his spinal cord, and now, his parents were dead.

Cliff pulled a pack of cigarettes from the left front pocket of his shirt and slid a lighter from his pants pocket. Greg pressed a button to turn on an exhaust fan built into the wall. Cliff tossed the pack and lighter on the desk and Greg helped himself to a cigarette. He'd given up smoking after leaving the Navy. The nicotine made his leg muscles spasm and dried out his mouth. He sparked the lighter and took a deep drag. Self-destruction didn't ease the pain, but it helped, or so he thought.

"Grandpa..." Greg's voice cracked as he spoke.

Cliff waved him off and leaned forward in his seat. "I know how you feel, son."

Greg nodded. Hot tears surged to the corners of his eyes. Cliff's tears had triggered his own. He squeezed his eyes shut so hard they ached and opened them to stare at the calendar serving as a desk blotter. Penciled on the small lines were jobs, deadlines, phone numbers, and notes in his father's neat handwriting. Everything reminded him of his parents. A tear fell from his cheek and dotted the neat paper.

"I want to come back to work and help you out," Cliff said.

Greg nodded again. He didn't feel he was ready to take over the multimillion-dollar corporation, and he really wanted to focus on the mansion bombing. Terrorists had killed his parents and he wanted revenge. He planted his elbows on the blotter and put the cigarette to his lips. He inhaled and exhaled before turning to Cliff. "What about Shelly? We can bring her in as chief operating officer."

"You sure you want to mix business and pleasure, son?"

"She'll do great. She's run her own crew, knows the work, and she has a master's degree in business management."

Cliff ashed his cigarette into a crystal ashtray and shrugged.

"Always scout the talent, isn't that what Dad said?"

Cliff nodded absentmindedly, focusing on something far away. The distance widened into a chasm. The two men didn't speak while they chain-smoked cigarettes to the nub. On one of the three flat-screen televisions across from Greg's desk, the twenty-four-hour news played images of the smoking rubble that had once been the Texas Governor's Mansion. Greg's parents had died instantly in the first explosion. They hadn't suffered, but Greg vowed to make those responsible for their deaths suffer.

"Next order of business," Greg said. He leaned back in his chair. "I want you to find a buddy of mine. A guy I was in the teams with. He lives in North Carolina. Wilmington, I think. His name is Ryan Weller. Don't tell him you're coming, just go find him and bring him back."

"What for?"

"Floyd Landis called me yesterday. He has a new job for us."

"Greg, you can't..."

"That's why I need you to find Ryan. Bring his ass back here."

CHAPTER FOUR

Cliff Olsen pulled the rental car to a stop on a side street in Kings Grant, a suburb of Wilmington, North Carolina. He climbed out, pulled a cigarette from his pack and lit it. He leaned against the side of the car and looked at the construction zone in front of him. The two-story home was clearly being remodeled with piles of discarded plywood, cut lumber, and deteriorating drywall in the side yard. Windowless openings in the second-story yawned at the street. The house wrap covering the plywood walls had peeled away at one corner. Three pickup trucks with bed boxes and ladder racks were parked haphazardly in the yard.

The screech of a power saw fighting through wood raked his ears, followed by solid blows of a hammer. He walked up the sidewalk.

Before he could reach the porch, a man leaned out the mouth of a second-floor window and yelled, "This is a construction site, no trespassing."

"I'm looking for Ryan Weller."

"Who's asking?"

"Clifford Olsen, I'm Greg Olsen's grandfather."

The man pulled back from the window and yelled, "Ryan, you got a visitor."

Cliff watched the window and a second man appeared. This one had two weeks' growth of beard and mustache.

The man slid safety glasses off his nose to rest on his head of shaggy brown hair. "What can I do for you?"

"I'd like to speak with you." Cliff dropped his cigarette butt to the ground and crushed it with the toe of his boot.

Ryan disappeared from the window.

He reappeared in the front door and walked onto the porch where he brushed sawdust from his cargo shorts and stomped his desert tan combat boots on the floor, knocking more dust loose. He grinned. "Man glitter." His six-foot-tall frame filled out his clothes with wide shoulders and a narrow waist. Years of constant physical exercise and activity had hardened and strengthened his muscles. His hazel green eyes searched Cliff up and down.

Cliff snorted and stepped up on the porch. He introduced himself as he extended his hand. "Can we go somewhere to speak in private?"

Ryan said his name and shook his visitor's hand. "Here's good." He bent to open a cooler and pulled out a bottle of water.

Cliff spotted the dark necks of beer bottles encased in icy water. "I'll have one of them beers."

Ryan tossed his water back in and extracted two longnecks. He cracked them open with a bottle opener tied to the cooler handle and distributed the bottles. He sat on the cooler. From a pocket in his shorts, he produced a cigarette and a lighter. Above him, work carried on with the sounds drifting down through the house.

Cliff eased his body down into a lawn chair beside the

cooler. He watched Ryan stretch his legs out and saw the purple scar on his thigh just above his left knee. Cliff stared at it. He knew the pain of a bullet wound. As a Navy SEAL in Vietnam, he'd earned a purple heart himself before calling it quits.

"What brings you East?" Ryan asked.

"We want you to come work for us at Dark Water Research."

Ryan took a swig of beer. "Long way to come to pitch a job. I've got work here."

"I won't lie to you, son," Cliff said. "We want you to be part of our operation. Greg sent me to bring you back to Texas. He needs your help."

"What's wrong with Greg?"

"Greg's having trouble..." Cliff scratched the back of his neck, searching for words. "You hear about the attack on the Texas Governor's Mansion?"

Ryan put down his empty bottle. It fell over, sounding hollow on the planks of the porch. He nodded.

Cliff paused a few minutes to steel himself for the next words. Just thinking about it made his blood run cold, and his body gave an involuntary shudder.

"Is Greg all right, Mr. Olsen?"

Cliff shook his head and tilted back his beer bottle until it was empty. He tossed it onto the floor beside the other empty. It made the same hollow sound as Ryan's. "When those ragheads blew up the governor's mansion, they killed Greg's father and mother." Cliff leaned forward in the chair and coughed. His voice trembled as he whispered, "My boy."

Ryan's shoulders drooped.

An overweight man sagged his body against the jamb of

the house's front door. "Hey, we got them windows installed. We're gonna take off now."

"Have a good night, guys," Ryan said as five men trooped past him.

The two men on the porch were silent until the pickup trucks had driven away. Nearby, someone push-mowed a yard, a string trimmer ran at full bore for a few seconds, and, further off, fences, hedges, houses, and passing traffic muffled a dog's bark.

Cliff broke the quiet. "We could use your help."

"Like I said, I'll think about it." Ryan stood and stretched.

"Travel, steady work, benefits, a new challenge every day," Cliff promised him.

"Sounds like the Navy's old slogan, 'Let the journey begin,'" Ryan retorted.

"You want back in the game without all the rules and other headaches, let me know," Cliff said as he stood.

He stepped off the porch. Halfway to the car, he stopped and turned around. Ryan was leaning against a porch post, cigarette in hand, watching him.

Cliff pulled out another smoke and lit it before returning to the porch. "Listen, son, Greg sent me to find you. He spoke very highly of you. We do clandestine work for the government. I did it, Greg's father did it, God rest his soul, and we wanted Greg to do it. You know he can't do what he used to. We need someone to run those operations. He named you specifically. I'm staying at the Holiday Inn on Wrightsville Beach for two days. You don't call me before I leave, I'll find someone else."

CHAPTER FIVE

Ryan Weller pitched the paperback across the cabin of his thirty-six-foot Sabre sailboat. The book landed on the settee across from him, tumbled down the back, banged against the cushion, and came to rest on its face. A bookmark fluttered to the ground. His restless legs carried him to his feet. His mind would not shut off.

Most nights after the crew left the house they were working on, he stayed to make lists of jobs to be finished, or to just deal with small jobs in solitude, enjoying the quiet, and the time alone.

Tonight, his mind had refused to concentrate on the mundane carpentry he normally took pleasure in. His visitor had unsettled him enough to cause him to make wrong measurements. In a fit of anger, he'd busted a piece of trim over his knee, and thrown it into the trash can along with the patience which usually allowed him to fit the jigsaw pieces of finished carpentry together. He'd stormed off the construction site and drove to the marina where he kept his sailboat.

The restlessness had gripped him as soon as he was on

the boat. He tried to stave it off by drinking a beer and reading a book. It hadn't worked, so he changed to surf shorts, a T-shirt, and running shoes. Pounding out the miles always purged his soul. Turning right out of the marina, he ran along Causeway Drive, over the South Banks Channel Bridge to the warm sands of Wrightsville Beach. He made a left, churning through the soft sand beside the frothing Atlantic Ocean, feeling his calves and ankles burn. When he reached Johnnie Mercer's Pier, he paused. The Holiday Inn, where the old man was staying, was further up the beach. He could run up there and tell Cliff he would help his former lieutenant, give Greg another kick in the ass.

Instead, he headed west, crossed Banks Channel again on the River to the Sea Bikeway and pounded past his parents' house on Pelican Drive. He showered in the marina restroom, letting the hot water rinse away his sweat, and walked back to the boat in just his shorts.

Ryan snatched the discarded paperback from the settee and paced from one end of the sailboat to the other, cleaning, straightening, and dusting. The chore took him twenty minutes, and when he finished, he dropped into the seat at the navigation table. He drummed his fingers on the polished wood.

When he'd first bought the storm damaged Sabre, as a sophomore in high school, it had already sat for two years and the interior was a rotten, moldy mess. Ryan and his father spent nights and weekends tearing it apart, rebuilding the thirteen-horsepower Westerbeke diesel, and remodeling the interior. They'd done away with the starboard side settee, built a custom navigation table, and extended the kitchen countertop to give him more storage. Over the years, he'd spent many hours sitting at the table, staring at navigation charts, plotting positions, and reading paperbacks.

Lifting the top on the nav table allowed access to the charts, sextant, and handheld electronics. A Walther PPQ M2, loaded with sixteen nine-millimeter hollow-point bullets, lay on top of the charts and a laptop computer rested beside it. He left the gun and pulled out the computer.

A minute later he was online and looking at the website for Dark Water Research. Established by Homer Olsen during World War Two to service and repair U.S. Navy ships stationed on the Gulf Coast, DWR had since grown into a worldwide conglomerate, providing a wide range of ship husbandry, oil-rig maintenance, underwater construction, infrastructure rehabilitation, along with design, inspection, maintenance, and technical services for all aspects of the commercial diving industry.

The company believed in service to its country and employed a wide range of former military members, from Navy SEALs to Air Force satellite geeks, to supplement the usual crowd of roughnecks, pipefitters, scientists, and able seamen.

What had Cliff said to him? "Call me if you want to get back in the game?"

What did it mean? Back in the game, back to work, back in the saddle. He had a job already, though he would enjoy going back to diving for a living and blowing stuff up. Life hadn't been a bang since he'd left the Navy and Explosive Ordnance Disposal a year ago, after ten years of service.

Since his return from his last tour in Afghanistan, he thought every trash can, bag, vehicle, and box could hold an improvised explosive device. He plotted how to strap his gun to the truck console for easy access and duct-tape magazines to the dash for quick reloads. Loud noises startled him more than he wanted them to, and he assessed his surroundings before settling down in restaurants, job sites, and the docks.

Even his parents' home needed a plan of extrication. He desperately wanted to feel normal or at least apply the skills he had. None of it was the life-and-death roulette wheel of combat. Construction was tedious compared to handling explosives. Carpentry wasn't the silent world beneath the sea requiring perfect buoyancy, steady hands, and complete focus to disarm a mine in pitch black water.

Could a job as a commercial diver fill any of those holes in his soul?

Some days he wondered why he'd quit the Navy, then he turned on the television and watched the news. He missed the job, the people, the camaraderie, and the sense of belonging to a greater purpose, but not the politics or the ever-changing rules of engagement that killed good men because politicians had bowed to political correctness and were too chicken to win the fight.

No, he didn't miss the 'pussification' of the military one bit.

The sailboat swayed in the gentle swell of a passing boat. He closed the computer and grabbed a beer before going topside. He stretched out in the hammock swinging from the Bimini top framework and lit a cigarette. He nursed his beer, paperback lying on his stomach, and stared out across the water.

His two gunshot wounds had entitled him to leave the Navy, and he'd taken the option. There were new EOD techs in the pipeline every day. Ryan had concluded the military was there before he arrived, and it would be there long after he left.

Greg Olsen had asked Ryan to join him then, but Ryan had turned him down, preferring to return to Wilmington and his family's business. Now, Greg had sent a recruiter to pitch him on a job running government ops for DWR. The fact Greg had asked for him, made Ryan feel good. He'd always gotten along with Greg, who had been a lieutenant while Ryan was a first-class petty officer. In the teams, the wall of separation between officers and enlisted often blurred and eroded as the men trained and fought side by side. Ryan and Greg had become good friends during their time together.

Ryan swung his legs off the hammock and reached for his cell phone. He was about to dial the number for the Holiday Inn when a man walked up the dock and stopped at the boat.

"Aye, da youth of America is rotten with dem electronics."

Ryan put the phone down and glanced up at Henry O'Shannassy, owner and manager of Wrightsville Beach Marina. He was a third generation Irish-American who liked to speak with a heavy brogue. The former Navy Senior Chief had given Ryan his first job outside of construction. Ryan had worked the gas docks and done odd jobs around the marina.

O'Shannassy had helped Ryan buy his Sabre and convinced Ryan's parents he would be fine sailing around the world at age eighteen instead of going to college. He was also a guiding force when Ryan had decided to enlist in the Navy.

"Hey, Henry."

"You look troubled, me lad."

"Got a minute?"

"For you, I've always a minute."

Ryan motioned for the man to step aboard, and Henry did so with ease.

He sat down on the bench across from the younger man. He dropped his brogue. "What's the scuttlebutt?"

"I've been offered a job at Dark Water Research."

"A nice outfit."

"They want me to work as a covert operative."

"I've heard rumors about them running some sort of shadow operation."

"How were you able to walk away from your Navy career and start a new life?"

"I won't lie, it was hard. Civilians aren't like us. The discipline and work ethic we have doesn't always gel outside the service. I wondered if you'd go back in or find another demolition job."

Ryan studied his mentor. At sixty-two he still stood ramrod straight at five-feet-ten inches and could work circles around most men. His hair had all turned gray, yet it was as thick as Ryan remembered it when the man was forty-five. Laugh wrinkles and scowl lines creased the leathery skin of his face. His big meaty hands were gnarled and veined. He'd lost weight in the last few years from a battle with pneumonia he hadn't quite recovered from.

"You're not happy here, Ryan. You need adventure. You always have. You want to see what's over the horizon, and there's nothing wrong with that. I get the itch myself. What I'm telling you is this: go."

Ryan nodded. He'd tested himself against the sea at an early age by learning to sail, scuba dive, and free dive. The Navy and EOD had been part of the adventure. Pounding nails into wood was dull in comparison.

Henry stood. "You're happy under a full sail on a big blue ocean. Don't regret not making the leap. You've always landed on your feet, you will now. If they say they need you, then they do."

"You remember me telling you about Greg Olsen?"

"He knew the risks and so do you."

Ryan gazed out at the forest of aluminum sailboat masts and the sea of gleaming sportfishers, trawlers, and cruisers. A handful of garishly painted offshore high-performance Cigarette-style boats hunched like sleek greyhounds at the starting gate. He loved the big go-fast boats, but for distance and cruising offshore, he'd take a sail any day.

"Thanks, Henry."

The brogue was back. "Ryan, me lad, you've nothing to thank me for. You already knew what you was doin'. *Ádh mór.*" He wished Ryan *good luck* as he extended his hand.

CHAPTER SIX

Stationed outside the door to DWR's inner sanctum was a well-dressed woman in her fifties. Muriel Johnson had worked for the company longer than any other employee, save for Clifford Olsen. She had started as a secretary at age eighteen and knew the ins and outs of the business almost better than the Olsens.

"Good to see you," Muriel said when Ryan walked up to her desk. "Greg is expecting you. It will just be a few minutes." Her warm emerald eyes flashed with amusement. She was a favorite of anyone who came through the company. She always had a smile and a welcoming greeting. "Have a seat." She pointed to the chairs in the waiting room.

Ryan stepped to the coffee maker and poured himself a cup of black coffee. He sipped at the steaming brew. It was strong and smooth. He carried the cup to a chair, took a seat, and pulled out his phone to look at his messages. There was a text from his brother, giving him grief for leaving the remodeling project when it was halfway done and forcing him to pick up the slack.

The phone on Muriel's desk buzzed and she answered

it. She glanced up at Ryan then hung up the phone. "Mr. Weller."

Ryan was already standing and had slipped his phone into the pocket of his suit jacket. He smoothed the tie of his dark blue Brooks Brothers suit and followed the secretary through a door and down a hallway. He hated this suit. He'd bought it for his sister's wedding and decided to wear it on this job interview. The tie felt like a garrote, threatening to suffocate him. He should have worn his cargo shorts and flip flops. This suit put an end to one of his favorite diving jokes. The only suit I have is a wet suit.

He searched for exits and possible threats. Old habits died hard.

Muriel opened a door and motioned him in. Ryan stepped into a well-appointed office. Dark hardwood flooring ran to floor-to-ceiling windows, which overlooked the docks fronting Industrial Canal. A large desk anchored the room at the far end. On the wall opposite the desk were three large flat-screen televisions. From left to right they displayed sports, news, and weather. The first two Ryan hadn't cared about in a long time, although he'd developed an affinity for college football since hanging around with Greg. Even then he didn't follow it with regularity. The weather was always important to a sailor. Two chairs faced the front of the desk and Cliff Olsen sat on a sofa opposite the windows.

Ryan walked over to Greg, who had wheeled out from behind the desk. The two men gripped each other's hands in a contest of strength. Ryan snorted to ease the pain in his hand. Greg had caught his fingers and was mashing them together. He grinned down at his friend. "You need to have your grandpa teach you how to shake like a man, LT." Ryan used an enlisted man's term synonymous for lieutenant.

"Hands like vise grips." Greg flexed his fingers. "How you been?"

"Ready for some action." Ryan glanced over at Cliff.

"Good. Sorry to keep you waiting," Greg said. "Not everyone in the shop knows we do clandestine work."

"No problem." Ryan held up his cup of coffee. "Your secretary makes some good joe."

"Grandpa trained her right."

Ryan observed his old friend. His brown hair was short to the scalp and his gray eyes shone with delight at reuniting with his fellow teammate. The man's shoulders and arms had thickened from constant upper body activity. His gray polo shirt had a brass diving helmet with the words *Dark Water* arching over it and the word *Research* under it. The shirt was taut across his torso and swelled around his biceps in what their dive instructors had referred to as "beach muscles."

Ryan turned to Cliff and shook his hand.

"Glad you could make it, son."

"Glad to be back in the game, sir."

"Sir," Cliff harrumphed. "I work for a living."

Greg said, "Let's go upstairs. I've got a couple of guys I want you to meet."

Ryan watched as Greg used his thick arms to propel his wheelchair across the room. The blue jeans he wore couldn't hide his atrophied legs.

At the door, Greg stopped and pointed to a picture Ryan hadn't noticed earlier. "Remember that shot?"

Ryan stepped over to the photo and looked at the EOD team in desert tan camouflage, wearing full battle rattle: eighty pounds of body armor, EOD kit, packs, helmets, ammunition, side arms, and rifles. Ryan picked out his own image, holding an M4 by the pistol grip with the collapsible stock resting on his hip. Sunglasses hid his eyes. Greg stood next to him with his gun hanging from a three-point sling across his chest. Around them, three more men and one woman squatted, kneeled, or stood holding their weapons. A bunch of smiling, cocky 'dirt sailors,' the nickname given to naval personal who served in the desert.

A sadness crept over Ryan. "Afghanistan, the day before you got hurt."

Greg nodded and shoved his chair out of the room. Ryan and Cliff followed him down the hall to an elevator.

"We added this when Greg came home," Cliff said as they gathered in the lift car. "About five years ago, we bought this hangar from the Corpus Christi Navy base. We moved it up here and turned it into a state-of-the-art management facility."

The elevator doors opened onto a rooftop deck. Several picnic tables sat under a canopy beside a large, outdoor kitchen.

Greg wheeled under the extended picnic table top. Ryan and Cliff sat down across from two other men. Greg made introductions. The first was Jerry DiMarco, a stout black man of medium height. His bald head glistened with perspiration and his massive arms made Greg's look puny. DiMarco was a former Navy SEAL who now ran DWR's diver training, utilizing a two-story dive tank built into a corner of DWR's building. He tested all divers on underwater welding, cutting, and fabrication to keep them current on certifications and procedures. He promised to bring Ryan current on qualifications.

The second man, Floyd Landis, was in his fifties. He'd let a once solid body go soft around the edges. He wore his steel-gray hair in a brush cut, and his watery blue eyes highlighted what was otherwise a bland face. Ryan suspected he'd bought his wrinkled suit off the rack at Macy's. Landis acted as the liaison between DWR and the Department of Homeland Security. DWR and DHS worked jointly on maritime security issues in and around the waters of the United States.

"Ryan," Greg began. "We called you in to help run our government-assigned ops. We get these little jobs because the government doesn't have the time or the means to investigate them. They fall into our laps, and since we like our legitimate government contracts, we do these favors for them."

Ryan nodded. He'd suspected something of this nature.

Landis cleared his throat. "When Greg informed me that he wanted you on board, I ran a background check. You're former EOD."

DiMarco's suspicious expression cleared as he listened to Ryan's credentials. He, like anyone who worked with special operations, understood that Navy Explosive Ordnance Disposal was one of the military's toughest programs, a grueling year-long course consisting of diving, ordnance disposal, parachuting, small-unit tactics, and firearms training.

Once through the course, the physical conditioning and the education continued so EOD techs could stay abreast of the latest technology and enemy tactics. They operated in the harshest environments to disarm and dispose of all manner of explosive devices, from car bombs to underwater mines.

"Yes, sir," Ryan answered.

Landis continued. "A silver star and two purple hearts. Then you got out and worked for your father's construction company."

Ryan pulled a cigarette from his jacket pocket and lit it.

He avoided talking about his battle scars. Sweat trickled down his back. The early May afternoon was in the eighties. From his vantage point at the table, he could see the five-mile-long dike extending into Galveston Bay, built to protect the Port of Texas shipping channel. Far off in the haze, in the other direction, he could see the Galveston high-rises.

"Am I boring you, Mr. Weller?" Landis asked.

"No, sir. I know what's in the file, so does Greg. If Mr. DiMarco wants to read it, let him."

Landis closed the file and stared at Ryan. "You and I will be working closely together, Ryan. We need to have a good rapport. For Jerry's benefit and for Cliff's, I was letting them know you're a highly skilled operative, and I, for one, am impressed. You worked on the Joint IED Task Force in Iraq to determine where the builders of the IEDs were obtaining their materials and then used those materials to track them down and put them and their pipeline sources out of business."

"Fat lot of good it did us," Ryan said bitterly.

"Why? Your record with the task force was superb. You guys shut down several major builders."

Ryan pointed his cigarette at Landis. "We busted our asses to get that intel. We'd put one guy out of business, and two more would pop up. It was like playing whack-a-mole. Notations in files and joint service ribbons and letters of accommodation mean nothing when those bombers are killing and injuring our guys."

"I know you were with Greg when he was injured," Landis said in a quiet voice. "He told me about your actions that day as well. You saved a lot of lives. We're not here to rehash old business or pick at scabs. Greg recommended you for this job. I've got no qualms about him hiring you, but if you can't keep a level head, you might be better off building houses."

Ryan took a final draw from his cigarette, pulling the cherry all the way to the thin blue line circling the paper just forward of the filter. He stubbed it out in an ashtray full of butts he knew were Cliff's brand of choice. "I'm capable of keeping a level head, Mr. Landis. I'm disgruntled with the politicians who feel the military-industrial complex is their personal play toy."

Landis nodded. "I was an Army Ranger, myself, back in the eighties. Jumped into Grenada. I left the Army and became a cop in Las Vegas, then worked my way up to detective and got noticed by the FBI. Later, I converted to Homeland. I understand your frustration all too well."

"What do you say, Ryan?" Greg asked. "You made the trip over here. Want the job?"

"What will I be doing? Sounds like you get the grunt work dumped on you. Are you the outhouse for the alphabet agencies?"

"No." Landis shook his head. "These are jobs we need done but for one reason or another, can't do ourselves. Take this one for instance." He opened another file folder. "There's been a rash of sailboat thefts in the Gulf of Mexico. They're taking place outside our maritime boundary. We have a treaty with Mexico to establish our individual boundaries in the Gulf; however, they're easily blurred. We try not to infringe on our neighbor's rights. In these instances, we send in people, such as yourself, to investigate the crimes. Mexico doesn't care about a little piracy in their waters."

"Are the sailors being killed or kidnapped?"

"Both, and we suspect the boats are being used to smuggle weapons or drugs into the country."

Ryan asked, "Do you have evidence of this?"

Landis turned the folder, so Ryan could see them. He continued while Ryan leafed through the pages and looked at the pictures. Landis reached over and tapped the picture of a sailboat. "The Coast Guard captured this guy in Bayou Sale Bay, headed for a little place called Burns Point Park in Louisiana. They found a hold full of guns, cash, and explosives."

"Any idea who's behind the thefts?" Greg asked.

"No," Landis said. "The men on the boat were Hispanic."

"What happened to the owners?" Ryan asked.

Landis shrugged. "No idea."

Greg cut in as Ryan lit another cigarette. "If Ryan takes this job, you'll be in luck. The man's an accomplished sailor. He spent two years circumnavigating the globe."

Ryan looked over at DiMarco, who hadn't said a word. "What's your place in this?"

"I helped Allen Olsen run government ops." His voice was deep, reminding Ryan of the actor Michael Clarke Duncan. "I'm available to help, but my focus now is on training"

Greg picked up on DiMarco's cue. "That being said, Ryan, I want you to look for a partner. Someone you're compatible with and has other skill sets besides what you bring to the table."

Ryan nodded. In the Navy, they'd operated in teams of two—swim buddies. It would be nice to have someone to cover his six. "I'll come up with a list."

"You haven't answered the pertinent question," Cliff said. "Will you take the job?"

All eyes swiveled to stare at Ryan.

"Yeah, I'll take it."

"Great!" Greg clapped his old friend on the back. "Now, let me have one of those cancer sticks."

Ryan pulled the pack of Camel Blues from his pocket and tossed it on the table.

Greg extracted one and examined it. He looked up at the other men. "I never smoked before joining the Navy." He shook his head in memory of a different time. "Cigarettes, Red Bull, coffee, and nonalcoholic beer got us through fourteen- to eighteen-hour days in Iraq and Afghanistan. I think everyone except the fobbits smoked or chewed."

Greg's use of *fobbit* drew blank stares from Landis and DiMarco.

"Fobbit," Greg explained, "is a guy who never leaves the safety of the FOB, or forward operating base. It's a cross between Tolkin's hobbit and... never mind." He waved a hand in dismissal.

"Sorry to interrupt you guys."

Everyone turned to see a woman in khaki capris and a dark blue DWR polo shirt walking toward them. She smiled at Greg, who gave her a grin. Ryan glanced from his friend to the woman and back again. It was clear Greg had fallen in love.

Greg motioned her over to the table. She stopped beside Greg and put her arm around his shoulders. Greg introduced her as Shelly Hughes, DWR's chief operating officer and his girlfriend. Ryan nodded to her.

Shelly pulled her brunette hair into a ponytail and asked Greg, "When did you start smoking?"

"A long time ago. I quit after I got hurt. I'm just enjoying one with our newest employee."

Shelly tilted her head and gave Ryan a look he translated to mean, *don't be a bad influence.* She patted Greg's shoulder and said, "I came up to start lunch."

"I almost forgot." Greg looked at his watch.

Shelly walked over to the grill and busied herself with cleaning and lighting it.

"Does she know about your DHS ops?" Ryan asked.

"Yes." Greg let smoke out of his lungs as he spoke. "When we made her COO, we brought her into the loop. She has to know when we allocate resources to certain missions."

Cliff stood and stubbed out his cigarette. "You staying for lunch, Floyd?"

"No. I need to get back to the office." He slid the file over to Ryan. "This is what we have so far. Keep me in the loop."

"Yes, sir," Ryan replied.

Landis stood. "Good day, gentlemen." He straightened his suit coat and headed for the elevator.

"I'm going to help Shelly with lunch," DiMarco said, rising from the table.

"I'll join you," Cliff said.

Ryan and Greg sat alone at the table, smoking.

Ryan broke the silence. "Sorry about your folks."

"Thanks." Greg stared off into space.

"Do you have an office I can work from?" Ryan changed the topic to avoid the uncomfortable subject of Greg losing both parents in such a senseless and tragic way. Compounded with his injuries, life had handed Greg Olsen the short straw.

Greg zoned back in and finished his cigarette. He pushed back from the table and called to Shelly, "Do you need help with lunch?"

"No, we got it," she replied.

Greg turned back to Ryan. "We serve lunch for our employees every Friday. Whoever's in port or around the office gets fed hot dogs, hamburgers, and brats. Just our way of showing appreciation, and it gets everyone together to network and socialize."

Ryan followed Greg to the elevator and stepped inside.

"Where are you staying?" Greg asked as the elevator descended.

"Holiday Inn Express on Galveston Beach."

"I have a house on Tiki Island. You're welcome to move in with me."

"I'd like to bring my sailboat over and find a marina near here."

"You could park it in DWR's marina," Greg said. He wheeled out of the elevator. "We keep a Hatteras GT63 there for sportfishing and running around the Gulf. We could clear a berth beside it for your boat. Like I said, until you bring it over, you're welcome at the house."

"Thanks," Ryan said.

"Dad ran DHS ops from a small, commercial, office space not far from here. I'll have you follow me there."

They maneuvered through the massive interior of the DWR hangar and exited into the parking lot. Greg led the way to a bright blue Chevrolet SS sedan. Ryan watched Greg throw his legs into the car and then slide into the leather seat. Greg removed the wheels and cushion from the wheelchair, tossed them into the backseat, folded down the chair's backrest, and drew the chair frame across his chest and into the car before resting it on the front passenger seat.

Ryan climbed into his rented Jeep Wrangler four-door. He followed Greg past DWR's entrance gate and waved to the security guard standing in the booth.

Ten minutes later, they parked outside a row of industrial office buildings. To break up the blank, gray, concrete block wall, each office had a door, a large picture window, and two tall narrow windows. Greg tossed Ryan a set of keys and motioned for him to open the door.

Ryan pulled the office door open and held it for Greg. The picture window looked in on the small reception area which contained two office cubicles divided by a low wall. Each had a desk, chair, and a computer. Ryan followed Greg into an office the size of the two cubicles. It had a small sofa against the far wall. Behind the desk were bookshelves loaded with binders, books, memorabilia, and pictures. The tall, narrow windows flanked a wall-mounted, flat-screen television.

Greg sighed. “This was Dad’s office.”

Ryan put his hand on his friend’s shoulder. He knew no words to ease the pain. He’d lost men in battle, but not parents.

“Sorry, man,” Greg said as he wiped his cheek with the back of his hand. He wheeled across the room and picked up a picture of his parents. He studied it for a minute, then set it face down on the shelf.

Ryan spied a bottle of Cazadores Blanco tequila on a shelf behind the desk. Beside it were two tumblers. He sat down at the desk and poured a finger’s worth of alcohol into each glass and handed one to Greg. “A toast to your parents.”

Greg lifted his glass and clinked it against Ryan’s. They tossed back the clear liquid and set their glasses on the desk. Greg motioned for a refill and Ryan obliged.

Ryan pulled off his tie, stuck it in the pocket of his suit jacket, and then hung the jacket on the back of the chair. He retrieved the file Landis had given him from his briefcase and flipped it open. “Have you read this?”

Greg shook his head. "No, Landis called me last week and said he had a new job for us. That's when I sent Grandpa after you. I was hoping he'd send us after those bastards who bombed the mansion. I'd like to send a few more of them to search for their virgins."

Ryan picked up the cover sheet. "Unless sailboat thefts are linked to a bunch of dirty terrorists, we're looking for pirates." He read the first line aloud. "To date, forty-three sailboats have disappeared in the Gulf of Mexico."

Two hours later, they'd read everything in the file.

"Well?" Greg asked.

"We've done more with less."

"What's your first move?"

Ryan said, "I'd like to talk to the company who insured the majority of these boats. Have you heard of them?" He picked up a paper and read the name, "Ward and Young?"

"They're one of the largest insurers on the Gulf Coast. We insure some of our boats through them."

"What's your agent's name?"

"Call Muriel and ask her. I'm sure she knows."

Ryan dialed Muriel's number at DWR. He asked her for the name of their Ward and Young agent. She gave him the number with astonishing quickness. Greg chuckled at the ease with which his secretary handled her daily tasks.

After hanging up with Muriel, Ryan dialed the number she'd given him.

"Ward and Young, Harry Ball speaking."

Ryan had to choke down the laughter welling inside him. Ball's gravelly voice fit his name.

Greg rolled his eyes and smirked before he leaned into the speaker phone and said, "Harry, this is Greg Olsen. How are you?"

"About the same, old, fat, and bald." Harry paused. "Sorry to hear about your folks, Greg. I really liked them."

"Thanks, Harry. I'm working on a salvage case, and the boat belongs to you guys. Who do I need to talk to about it?"

"Was it stolen, wrecked, or swamped at the dock?"

"Stolen."

"Do you have the hull identification number?"

"Yes." Greg read the HIN from the sailboat the Coast Guard had confiscated in Louisiana.

Harry said it would take a minute. They could hear him typing on a computer keyboard.

Ryan took out a cigarette and stuck it between his lips but didn't light it.

"Okay, Greg, I can't help you with this one. You need to call corporate. A woman by the name of Emily Hunt is handling those cases. Seems like she's got quite a workload."

"Do you have a number for her?" asked Greg.

"Yes, I do. It is... Okay. Ready?"

Greg said, "Yes," and Ryan wrote the name and number on a legal pad he'd found in a desk drawer.

"Where's corporate?" Ryan asked.

"Tampa," Harry answered.

Greg said, "Thanks, Harry."

"Any time."

Greg pressed the *End* button, and the phone went silent. "There's your first lead."

"I want to meet with Emily Hunt and review her files. Maybe I can spot something of value. I'll make flight arrangements." Ryan pulled a laptop from his briefcase and opened it up.

"You don't need to make reservations. I'll have Chuck fly you over."

Ryan looked up from searching the desk drawers for an internet password. "Who's Chuck?"

"Chuck Newland. He's our resident pilot. We've got a Beechcraft King Air."

"You must be doing well," Ryan said, surprise in his voice. He found the password on a scrap of paper taped to the bottom of the main desk drawer and typed it into his computer.

"Dad got it from a government auction site. We were the low bidder. Surprise, we were the only bidders." Greg glanced at his watch. "One more stop before I have to get back to the office. I didn't realize how much work it required to run this company. Come on, one last thing to show you and I'll leave you alone."

They walked out of the office and turned right. A door behind the second cubicle led into a two-story-tall garage space divided by a plywood-covered wall which didn't reach all the way to the ceiling. In the cool darkness, Ryan could smell oil, sawdust, damp concrete, and grease. To him it was a pleasant mix of odors.

Greg wheeled to the left side of the dividing wall, reached for a bank of switches, and turned on the overhead lights and an exhaust fan.

"Dad set this place up, so he could keep DHS gear separate from the other DWR assets. He spent a lot of time getting everything the way he wanted it. Matter of fact, he bought this whole office complex a few years ago. We operate it under a different name."

"No need to pay rent." Ryan lit a cigarette and walked to the right-hand side of the divided space. The space was open with an industrial roll-up garage door with an electric opener in the far wall. A variety of garden implements hung by hooks screwed into the plywood. Ryan wondered why Greg's dad kept garden tools at his industrial office.

The left side of the dividing wall was where Allen Olsen had built his workshop. A seven-foot-tall set of cabinets ran the length of the plywood dividing wall. At the back of the shop, the cabinets stopped at a concrete bunker built eight feet inside the original walls of the main building. The small room had a concrete roof and inset in the block was a heavy vault door with electronic security locks.

On the left side of the workspace, a fifteen-foot-long workbench ran from the bunker back toward the office. It ended beside a long bright red-and-chrome tool chest. From there, a set of shelves ran to the office wall, turned, and stopped at the door they'd just come through.

"Wow!" Ryan finally said.

"Dad went a little overboard. Let me show you the coolest part." He wheeled to the vault door and told Ryan what code to tap into the electronic lock.

The door swung open and they ventured inside.

Ryan's eyes went wide as he looked around the eight-by-fifteen room. Around the bottom of three walls were cabinets equipped with either sliding drawers or doors. Above the cabinets, Allen had mounted long guns on Pegboard hooks. There wasn't an empty slot on the wall. Ryan tried to name all the firearms he saw: FN SCARs, Tavor SARs, Armalite M4s, Sig Sauer MPXs, Heckler & Koch MP5s, UMPs, Springfield Socom Model 16s, and two M32 six-shot grenade launchers. The ones he couldn't name were an assortment of sniper rifles in a variety of calibers and configurations.

Greg opened a drawer to reveal neat rows of pistols. He said, "There are three more drawers of handguns. The rest is ammunition, cleaning kits, targets, and battle dress."

Ryan shook his head in dismay. "I don't think I've ever seen a gun locker like this anywhere, even in the military."

Greg grinned. "We're quite proud of our collection. Dad formed a corporation to get a Federal Firearms License so we can own full auto guns and silcncers." He opened a drawer and showed Ryan a variety of the round suppressors.

Ryan turned and pointed at the wall on his right as he entered the gun locker. "What's behind there?" He'd noticed the gun locker wasn't quite as large as the bunker's outside dimensions.

"On the other side is a compressor for filling scuba tanks. It's accessible from the other garage bay."

Ryan nodded and stepped out of the gun locker. Greg closed the door behind him. Ryan looked at the cabinets and saw two lockers labeled *Jerry* and *Allen*. He opened both to find an assortment of diving gear and other personal items.

"What do you want me to do with your dad's gear?"

"Keep what you want and take the rest out to their house. My sister, Anna, and I have to get rid of their stuff." He wheeled over to the workbench where a Poseidon Se7en rebreather was awaiting assembly. He pulled a lighter from a drawer and lit the cigarette dangling from his lips.

"What are you and Anna going to do with their things?" Ryan asked.

"I think we'll have an auction after we take what we want. Just sell everything and be done with it."

Ryan leaned his backside against the workbench and lit his own cigarette. "I've never met your sister."

"I'm keeping her as far away from you as possible."

With mock sincerity, Ryan pointed to himself and said, "But, I'm a nice guy."

Greg snorted. "And pigs fly."

"Come on, buddy. Send her by, I need a secretary."

"No," Greg said emphatically.

Ryan laughed. "You know I'm joking, right?"

"If you were joking, you'd say, 'A horse walked into a bar and the bartender said, why the long face.'" He was stealing a line from one of their favorite movies to watch while on deployment, *Hot Shots! Part Deux.*

The ringing of Greg's cell phone interrupted their laughter. He pressed *Answer* and put it to his ear. Ryan listened to Greg's side of the conversation. Finally, Greg said, "I'll be there in fifteen minutes." He hung up and slipped the phone back into its holder. "I've got to get back to work. Call Chuck and let him know when you want to fly to Tampa. I'm sure Dad left a list of numbers in his office. If not, call Muriel and she'll get you what you need."

"Thanks, Greg."

"For what?"

"For asking me to do this job."

"No problem, buddy. You gave me a kick in the ass when I needed it and I'm doing the same for you. Anything else you need?"

A shy smile curled the left side of Ryan's lip. "A corporate credit card?"

"You joke but see Muriel and she'll give you one."

"Does she run the whole company?"

"Pretty much. I gotta go. Bring your gear by the house tonight and we'll set you up."

Ryan watched Greg get in his car and drive away. His stomach rumbled, and he scrolled through internet listings on his phone to find a number for a sandwich shop that delivered and ordered lunch. He went back to the office, picked up the legal pad and continued to the workshop. He began inventorying all the gear in Allen's personal locker.

By the time his sandwich arrived, he'd gotten through what was there. Ryan also collected the pictures and mementos Allen had spread throughout the office and shop and put them in a cardboard box. This was his office now and he didn't want Greg to be reminded of his parents every time he stopped by.

Between bites of his Italian sub, he turned on his office's desktop computer. It was password-protected. He called Muriel and asked her if she knew the password. She gave the code to him, and he unlocked the screen. He was glad Allen had shared the information, and he told Muriel he would leave it as it was and got off the phone.

He swiveled around in the chair and looked at the row of notebooks on the bottom shelf. One was a three-inch thick, three-ring binder with all DWR's personnel and vendor contact information. The others were operations manuals, warranties, and parts lists for all the equipment, guns, dive gear, and computers in the shop.

Back at the computer, Ryan found a file containing a complete inventory of all the gear in the shop. He printed it out and flipped through the ream of paper. The military had instilled in him a need to inventory his tools before and after every dive. With the inventory list for the workshop, he would know if anything was missing and exactly where everything was located.

The clock on the wall told him it was almost two in the afternoon. Time seemed to be flying by. He picked up the phone and dialed the number for Ward and Young's corporate headquarters and asked for Emily Hunt. After answering a series of questions to get past the gatekeepers, he got her answering machine. He left a message, hung up, and took his inventory list to the garage.

CHAPTER SEVEN

Ryan had researched Ward and Young before Chuck flew him to Tampa. Ward and Young dated back to the early 1900s. They began covering automobiles, boats, yachts, and houses when rich young industrialists started making their way to Florida to escape the dreary northern winters. Their business was tied to the booms and busts of Florida's economic cycle, and Ward and Young almost folded in the 1930s. Post-World War Two prosperity, the invention of air conditioning, and the interstate highway brought an influx of new residents to the state. Ward and Young once again flourished, quickly expanding into other Gulf and Atlantic states to become the number one boat insurer in the country.

He'd pictured the company in a downtown Tampa Bay high-rise with stale cigar smoke deeply ingrained in worn, leather sofas, dark wood paneling, and snifters of brandy on oaken sideboards. When the cab pulled up in front of Ward and Young's corporate headquarters, Ryan saw a tall, modern, glass-and-steel building in the suburbs. Inside, minimalist styling dominated with steel-armchairs, glass tables, sculptures, art, and plants.

At the reception desk, Ryan asked for Emily Hunt. The receptionist tapped a series of buttons on the phone and spoke into her headset. He'd made this appointment three days ago when Emily had returned his phone call, telling her he was investigating the recent rash of sailboat thefts and disappearances in the Gulf of Mexico. He outlined his search parameters based on the boat the Coast Guard had found in Bayou Sale Bay.

Emily Hunt appeared as the elevator doors slid open. She was a striking figure in white slacks and a pink blouse. She wore open-toed flats, allowing him to see her toenail polish matched her fingernails. Her layered blonde hair, the color of ripe harvest wheat, fell just past her shoulders, and her eyes were cornflower blue. She extended her hand and introduced herself. Ryan reciprocated.

They rode the elevator in silence, staring straight ahead at the blinking light telling them what floor they'd passed, until the doors opened on fifteen. Ryan appraised her out of the corner of his eye. She stood just two inches under his six-foot height. Her skin had a golden glow, and her long limbs showcased athletic prowess.

She moved with the grace and ease of a model along a window-lined hallway, past rooms full of cubicles, with representatives chatting on headphones, to a conference room. On the table were two stacks of files, both about eight inches high. Some files were much thicker than others.

Emily set a hand on each pile. "These are all the files I could gather pertaining to the information you asked for. I've handled many of these cases myself."

"Thanks for doing this."

"I don't know what you're looking for, but I hope you find it. I have work to do. If you'll excuse me."

He nodded, and she left the conference room. After pulling out a chair, he sat down in front of the files and sorted through them. There were more than he'd expected.

Ryan had been working steadily for several hours, drinking Pepsi from a machine in the lobby and lost in concentration, when Emily came in and sat down across the table from him.

"Any luck?" she asked, taking in the neat rows of files lined up on the conference table. Each was open to a different page with a sticky note pasted on it.

"I concentrated on larger boats, thirty-five-foot and above. I'm just trying to connect the dots to see if something ties all the thefts together." He swept his hand over the whole pile.

She shook her head. "There are thousands of boats stolen each year. Most are stripped for their gear, especially fishing boats. Generally, we never find them. Some show up when other people find them adrift or sunk."

"What happens if you find one of the stolen boats?" He leaned back in his chair, soda can in hand.

"Usually, we've already paid out on the insurance claim and the boat is ours. We sell them at auction. If someone finds a boat and brings it back, we negotiate salvage rights and they can have the boat to deal with as they please. They either fix them up for resale, part them out, or demolish them for scrap. If the boat suffers loss or damage caused by theft, vandalism, or malicious act, we replace or repair the stolen or damaged items. We have separate values for hulls, motors, sails, trailers, and other items on the boat.

"In these cases," Emily continued, pointing at the files, "we look at the police report, if there is one, and I, or one of our other investigators, take the case. Like I said, if, and I mean this is a big if, the boat shows up someplace, we own it and we can sell it for salvage, scrap, or have it demolished."

"It says here, some of your boats have shown up—two in the Bahamas, several down in the Keys and one in Tahiti."

"Yes, we even had one turn up here, in St. Petersburg."

"What happened to that one?"

"We'd already paid out on it, so we sold it to a local company that fixes them for resale."

Ryan took a swig of Pepsi and looked out the window at the sun-dappled waters of Old Tampa Bay. "You ever go down to the Keys to look at these boats?"

"No. We don't go look at sunken boats. We have them moved if they're blocking shipping lanes or present a navigational hazard. Why, what do you think you'll find?"

He shrugged and got up from the chair. Emily remained seated, looking at her fingernails as if his questions bored her.

"I'm just trying to cover all the angles. I guess you're familiar with boats."

"This is my job," she snapped. "And I live in Florida."

"Just making sure. I want to look at the wrecks."

"Why? They're a bunch of sunken boats."

"You're a former cop, Emily." He caught the look of surprise in her eyes at knowing her background. "Let's look at this as a crime scene. That's what we have here. Each boat has a story to tell, and in order to interpret that story, we have to look at the crime scene, and put together the pieces of the puzzle."

Emily nodded and watched him sip soda and study the files.

"Find anything unusual?" Kyle Ward, the company CEO, asked as he stepped into the room. Ryan had seen his picture on the company website. The man was in his thirties and well-groomed, from his tailored suit to his polished shoes and close-cropped black hair.

"Mr. Weller wants to look at two wreck sites of our stolen sailboats," Emily said.

"What are you looking for?" Ward asked.

"Anything to tell me why these particular boats were stolen and who stole them. Really, any piece of the puzzle that will bring us closer to capturing the thieves and saving you some money." Ryan flipped a file closed and stared at Ward. "That's the bottom line."

"I like this guy already. Get him what he needs, Emily." He laid a hand on Emily's shoulder and smiled at Ryan. "Nice to meet you and good luck with your search." Ward left the office, closing the door behind him.

"Do you dive?" Ryan queried his new associate.

"Yes, recreationally. I'm not a big-shot commercial diver like you."

"Good." He ignored the barb and stretched his whole body, feeling his chest muscles tighten as his arms extended back and above his head. When he relaxed, Ryan asked, "Do you have your own gear?"

"Yes."

"There are two wrecks I'd like to look at, one in the Dry Tortugas, the other near Marathon. They're close and they may give us some clues. Like I said earlier, it's a crime scene. Do you know any dive operators down there?"

"You can't throw a stone without hitting a dive operator in the Keys, but we charter a boat when we need one."

"Get one out of Key West. We'll fly down there in the morning."

Her sarcasm was clear when she asked, "Do you want me to book airline tickets, too?"

"No need." Ryan grinned. "I'll have Chuck file a flight plan from here to Key West."

"You have an airplane?" Emily asked, dumbfounded.

Ryan nodded while gathering the files he wanted and stacked the others neatly in a pile. He kept out two to have copied for his records. "Do you have the file for the boat in St. Pete?"

"I'll have it brought down."

"I want to talk to the guy, but I also want you to come with me."

"I suppose, you need me to drive?"

"If you're offering." Consulting his watch, he said, "Maybe you know a good place to eat lunch as well?"

CHAPTER EIGHT

Fulton's Marine was a small repair shop tucked amongst other industrial businesses on an ocean-connected canal. Uncut weeds grew around old boat hulls, and rusty engines lay half buried in the dirt. An assortment of boat trailers, some with and without boats on them, had tires so flat and dry-rotted Ryan doubted they would hold air. Dirty, white paint flaked off the building's cinder-block walls, and the office door had rust showing through several layers of paint.

"There's your boat." Emily pointed to a forty-foot Hunter sailboat near the back of the lot as they drove up to the garage. The hull was lodged in a cradle of timbers and missing its mast.

She parked the car. They climbed out and crunched across the gravel toward the office door. The smell of salt-water and dead fish hung in the air even though the building was a half-mile from the Gulf of Mexico. Ryan felt sweat on his brow as the sun pounded down on them. Glancing up, he saw a seagull glide on wind currents and heard the distinct screech as it called to its mate.

Ryan and Emily entered the office. No one was in the cluttered room. A window air conditioner ran at full bore, but the office was still stuffy. Piles of papers sat on every surface, and cups of half-drunk coffee sat haphazardly on several stacks.

"A real winner here." Emily's tone let Ryan know she disapproved of the décor along with the stench of stale cigar smoke and mildew.

He pushed past her through a door marked *Employees Only*. Boats, in various stages of repair, lined the interior walls. Outboard engines hung on wooden stands, and big, disassembled V8 motors and their assorted parts were laid out on the oil-stained concrete floor. Hank Williams Jr. blared from a stereo at the rear of the shop.

They walked toward the music until they found a man standing on a ladder, leaning into the open engine bay of a Yamaha jet boat. Only his legs were visible.

Ryan banged on the side of the boat with the palm of his hand and said, "Hello."

It startled the guy so badly, he almost fell off the ladder. He glared at the intruder as he made his way down to the floor. He stepped off the ladder and pushed his trucker's cap back on his bald head, then crossed his arms over a grease-stained red shirt under bib overalls stretched tight by an ample gut.

"Sorry to bother you, Mr. Fulton. I'm Emily Hunt and this is Ryan Weller. I'm from Ward and Young. We'd like to look at the Hunter you got from us."

Fulton's eyebrows rose, and his double chin wagged. "That boat's mine. I paid for it."

"I know, Mr. Fulton, but we want to look at it one last time." She nodded at her companion. "He thinks we might find something that will lead us to the thieves."

Fulton pulled the stub of a cigar from his mouth. "Fine. Look at it all you want, but don't touch nothing."

Ryan asked, "Mr. Fulton, have you inspected the boat?"

"Of course, I did," he retorted. Then his look turned apprehensive. "Why?"

"I just wanted to know if you noticed anything suspicious in or on the boat."

Fulton looked at them as if trying to decide if they were trustworthy. He wiped his hands on a rag while staring at Emily. She gave the man a lascivious smile and cocked her hip.

His tone softened. "Yeah, I found something." He started for the office door they'd come through earlier. "I found a piece of wood in the cabin. Looked like a crate top. Did you know they gutted the lady?"

Ryan shot Emily a look.

"Guess not." Fulton interpreted the look for himself. "Someone gutted her. I mean, not just stripped of everything valuable, but they took *everything* out of her. All the bulkheads, bunks, galley, head, everything. I don't know why I bought the big turd. Guess I figured it was cheap and I could fix it up the way I wanted. Retirement project, so to speak." The whole time he talked, he stood behind his desk, rummaging through a pile of papers, assorted lengths of rope, and several rusty metal objects Ryan couldn't identify.

"Here we go." He pulled out an olive drab chunk of wood with black Cyrillic writing on it. "There was some heavy brown paper stuck to this. It had wax or something on it to make it waterproof. Seemed strange to me."

Ryan took the wood and turned it over in his hands. He couldn't read Cyrillic, but he knew what the wood went to. He handed it back and thanked the man, then asked if they could see the boat.

"Sure, help yourself. Just be careful climbing around on it. I don't wanna be sued 'cause you were careless."

"No problem, Mr. Fulton, the boat's yours. We just want to look at it," Emily reiterated.

The two investigators walked outside and slipped their sunglasses back on. Ryan found a weathered wooden ladder and carried it to the Hunter where he leaned it against the rub rail. He fished a cigarette out of his pocket. Emily gave him a look of disgust as he lit it. As he smoked, he walked around the hull, examining it in detail. There was a fist-sized hole gashed into the fiberglass where the boat had run aground on a coral reef. Then Sea Tow had damaged the keel when they pulled it off the reef. Ryan wondered what the fragile coral looked like after they'd mashed it with their ham-handed tactics.

Ryan climbed the ladder and entered the cabin. Fulton was right, they'd stripped it bare. Back outside, he saw Fulton leaning against the corner of the building, his hands in his pockets, the brim of his trucker cap pulled low against the glare of the sun.

Ryan leaned over the rail and looked down at Emily. "Why didn't you state that they'd gutted the inside in your report?"

"I didn't know." She gazed up at him and placed her hand above her eyes to shield them from the sun. "After the owner reported it stolen, we got the police report, the owner filed a claim, and we paid. Sea Tow brought the boat in four months later. They claimed salvor's rights and sold it off to Fulton. We never saw the boat. The only reason I knew it was here was because Fulton took title, and the HIN, that's hull identification number, came back as one of ours, and we had to release it."

"You said 'police report.'"

"This boat was stolen from its dock in Pensacola, Florida."

"Why didn't you look at the boat?"

"I asked if they wanted me to investigate it, but they told me not to worry about it. They'd cleared the matter up. I noted it in the report and moved on. Ryan, we must get a hundred reports a month that come across our desks."

"All right." He climbed down and put the ladder back where he'd found it. He glanced over at Fulton who took his cigar from his lips and nodded to him.

Back in the car, Emily asked, "You know where that wood lid came from, don't you?"

"Crates of Kalashnikov's finest AK-47s. They line the insides of the crates with the heavy wax paper before they put the guns in."

"Why would there be a crate of guns on the boat?"

"Most likely gunrunners."

"Someone's running guns into the US?"

"It happens every day. In this case, they used the Hunter to fly under the radar. No one bothers to check into customs if the boat's registered in the US. Just swing by some little out-of-the-way dock, throw a few crates of rifles on a truck and poof, disappear into the great American Heartland."

"Or down the Iron River."

"Emily Hunt, ATF slang, really?"

She shrugged and started the car. "I used to be a cop."

Ryan chuckled and thought about the Iron River, the Bureau of Alcohol, Tobacco, and Firearms's slang for the illegal gun trade flowing from the United States into Mexico to support the cartels and gangs.

"What now?" she asked as they pulled into the parking lot of his hotel.

"We fly down to Key West. Come in, and we can find out what time Chuck has us leaving."

They found Chuck Newland lying by the pool, sunning his body, and watching the bikini-clad babes flit about the pool deck.

"Chuck, this is Emily Hunt, the insurance investigator I'm working with. Emily, this is Chuck Newland, the resident DWR pilot."

"Pleased to meet you." He grinned up at Emily. He had on orange swim trunks, a white Stetson cowboy hat and aviator sunglasses. "Take off is seven thirty a.m., boss. Preflight's at seven."

"Okay, Emily," Ryan said. "Pack your dive gear and whatever else you need for a few days in paradise and we'll see you at the St. Pete's airport in the morning."

She nodded. "See you then."

CHAPTER NINE

It was just after eleven o'clock in the morning when Ryan pulled back the throttles on the Fountain 38 LX, one of Fountain's top-of-the-line sportfishing craft. With triple three-hundred-horsepower Mercury Verado engines, the boat was capable of sixty-five miles per hour, fast enough to cover the seventy miles from Key West to the Dry Tortugas in just over an hour. He kept the boat at its recommended cruising speed of forty-eight, which made for a longer journey and conserved fuel. Even though they had a full tank of gas, he felt no reason to push it.

Yesterday, Chuck had set the Beechcraft King Air B200C down at the Key West airport seventy minutes after taking off from St. Petersburg. The three of them had spent the rest of the day checking into the Hyatt Centric Key West on Mallory Square, inspecting the Fountain boat, which happened to belong to Kyle Ward, and picking up the tanks and weights they would need from the dive shop. They followed the arduous work with an obligatory bar-hopping session which had lasted well into the night.

It wasn't every day Ryan had the use of a high-performance Fountain to do a little underwater detective work, and he appreciated every minute. They were northeast of Garden Key, the main attraction in the Dry Tortugas, where the U.S. government had built Fort Jefferson to help suppress piracy and protect vital shipping in the Gulf of Mexico. Obsolete before it was even complete, it fell into disrepair before being handed over to the National Park Service.

They dropped the anchor over the GPS coordinates for a sixty-foot steel-hulled ketch named *Misty*. The wreck was off Pulaski Shoals, just outside the national park boundary. *Misty* had been pirated off Mexico's Yucatán Peninsula and now rested under seventy feet of water. Looking over the Fountain's rail, they could see *Misty* lying on her side at the bottom. Her severed masts now lay in a tangle of rigging off her port side. It was a sad sight.

"Let's gear up." Ryan said, pulling off his T-shirt.

Emily stripped off her shorts and shirt to reveal a bright blue bikini which prominently displayed her figure. She pulled her thick blonde mane into a ponytail and shoved her clothes into a gym bag.

Chuck, leaning on the center console, pulled his sunglasses down his nose and looked at Emily and then at Ryan. Ryan's eyes met Chuck's and Chuck waggled his eyebrows. Ryan shook his head and grinned. His diving partner's bare skin wasn't hard to notice. Ryan averted his eyes and concentrated on gearing up for the dive.

Emily and Ryan strapped their buoyancy control devices to air tanks and hooked up regulators and gauges. Their BCDs would help them achieve neutral buoyance underwater. He tested the wireless transmitter attached to the first stage regulator which sent air pressures to his wrist-mounted computer. They breathed through their primary and spare regulators. Both sets of equipment checked out, and he went over his gear with Emily. Ryan then inspected her gear, so they were familiar with each other's equipment in case of emergency. His final preparation was to have Chuck hoist a dive flag on the flagpole mounted to the half-tower.

"Captain Chuck, you have the boat." Ryan gave him a salute.

Chuck raised a bottle of water in return.

They stepped off the back of the boat into gin-clear water. The water temperature was in the eighties, warm enough for Emily to just wear her bikini, but both divers wore three-millimeter-thick wetsuits and thin gloves. Between the coral and the wreck, they didn't want to get scraped up. Their basic dive training taught that the body loses heat twenty-five times faster in the water than in the air. The thin layer of water trapped between the skin and the neoprene retained the body's heat and kept them warm.

The two divers geared up, jumped into the water, and descended along the anchor line. There was no current, so he let go and drifted slowly down to the wreck. Ryan probed and poked, moving debris and looking for clues to the boat's sinking. He kept an eye on his dive buddy, watching her swim effortlessly through the water. She was neutrally buoyant with her hands clasped together in front of her. He'd seen divers with a lot more dives under their belt still swimming upright, using their hands to help propel themselves and kicking like they were riding a bicycle. Emily's training and technique were a credit to her instructor.

Eventually, he made his way over the transom, into the cockpit, and down the companionway ladder. The thieves had stripped the inside of the boat, just like the Hunter in

St. Petersburg. Ryan checked his dive computer. They'd been down for ten minutes.

Ryan pulled himself into the engine hatch and flicked on his dive light before methodically sweeping it across the floor. His suspicions were confirmed when he saw the seacocks were open, allowing the water to flood the boat. He probed the bilges with the powerful beam of light. He saw no hidden boxes or unusual pieces of plastic piping connected to the plumbing system, which served no other function than as a hiding place.

Backing out of the engine hatch, he saw Emily at the top of the companionway. She motioned to her pressure gauge and then held her thumb up, jerking it toward the surface. He glanced at his gauge. He was down to a thousand pounds in his tank, more than enough to make the ascent and required three minute safety stop at fifteen feet. Ryan gave Emily the OK sign with his fingers and she turned away from the door.

Approaching the ladder out the cabin door, something caught his eye. They hadn't stripped the head. In a book he'd read, the main character stored valuables behind the vanity mirror. He maneuvered himself into the head and surveyed the cabinet. There were no signs of tampering or that it had ever been out of the wall. He swung the mirror open and placed his hands on the top edge. He pulled down. The hinges held, even as he braced his feet on the bulkhead and strained with all his might. Blood rushed to his head from the effort.

He took a deep breath and shook off the pangs of overexertion. It was worth a second look and he would bring a tool kit next time. After floating out of the hull, he lazily kicked across the deck to the anchor line. Emily was already making her ascent and he joined her on the line.

Ryan loved being in the water. It was an old friend welcoming him back every time he dropped in. Diving required total focus to stay alive and it freed his mind of all the daily minutia. Diving provided food for the table, pictures for the wall, and endless hours of enjoyment. Every trip into the deep blue was a renewal of his fascination. This trip was no different as he watched a school of long silver barracuda track his every movement with their protruding lower jaws and rows of razor-sharp teeth. Ryan grinned back at them.

Back on the Fountain, Chuck had the cooler open and was making sandwiches. Water and soft drinks floated in the cooler's ice, and Ryan grabbed a soda after shedding his rig. They hooked up new tanks to their BCDs and tested the regulators.

Emily turned to Ryan, a smile of immense pleasure on her face. "Maybe, I should start investigating these wrecks."

He nodded in agreement while chewing a mouthful of sandwich. He swallowed. "This is a cakewalk compared to some wrecks I've been on. I do think it would be in the insurance company's best interest to investigate them."

The three spent a leisurely hour sitting on the Fountain, taking in the sun and the sights around the Dry Tortugas. Sailboats and powerboats, of all kinds, cruised through the waters of the glassy sea. Seaplanes took off and landed near Fort Jefferson, ferrying their passengers to and from Key West.

Ryan missed the cruising lifestyle he'd enjoyed on his around-the-world sailing adventure. He'd lived on his boat when the Navy had stationed him in Little Creek, Virginia, but it was not the same. He couldn't see this: tiny palm tree-populated islands in crystal clear waters.

Ryan and Emily geared up for the second dive and were

sitting on the gunwales, ready to roll in, when Chuck asked, "Why do divers always fall backward off the boat?"

Ryan was about to launch into a narrative about safety when Emily looked up at Chuck's grinning face and appealed, "Why, Chuck?"

Chuck clutched his stomach as he laughed. "'Cause if they fell forward, they'd still be in the boat."

Everyone laughed at the terrible joke, and Ryan was still chuckling about it as they fell backward into the water and dropped to the sailboat. He swam into the boat's head, where he laid out his tool pack on the tiny counter. Inside the canvas roll was a small pry bar, a sledgehammer, a flat blade and a Phillips screwdriver.

He wedged the pry bar into a gap between the back of the cabinet and the cabinet's frame. Levering up on the bar caused the wooden back to buckle, and a chunk of wood fell away. He took a new angle with the pry bar and forced the panel out of the cabinet. It floated beside him, suspended motionless for a moment, before slowly drifting to the deck.

He examined the frame of the cabinet. Someone had modified it so all they had to do was lift the panel straight up and pull the bottom out. In its slot, it was hard to tell the back wasn't fixed in place. Behind the cabinet was a framed-in space between the head's bulkhead and the boat's fiberglass hull. He shined his light down into the hole. Inside was a black leather pistol case, a box of nine-millimeter cartridges, and a small book in a plastic zip-closure bag. He glanced over at Emily, who was hovering in the doorway. He motioned for her to hold the mesh goodie bag open while he dropped the three items into it. The book had a creased brown cover, worn from much use. Inset letters on the cover read: *Journal.*

Ryan motioned for her to exit the boat and he followed her up the anchor line.

Chuck hauled in their gear and held up the goodie bag. He said with whispered awe, "Treasure."

Emily was first up the boarding ladder and Ryan watched her backside as she climbed aboard. He followed her without the grace and efficiency, and they helped each other tug off their wetsuits. They used the hose connected to the Fountain's fresh water tank to wash the salt from their bodies and gear.

Chuck removed the items from the goodie bag and pulled the pistol out of its case. "It's a Browning Hi-Point, nine-millimeter, T Series made in 1966. My old man carried one of these in Viet Nam." He racked the slide, popping a cartridge high in the air. He caught it deftly with his hand. Then, he dropped the magazine from the handle. "Beautiful piece, too bad it got immersed in saltwater." He used the hose to wash the salt away.

Ryan pulled the journal from the plastic bag. In the hot sun, condensation had formed inside the bag. As he riffled through the pages, five one-hundred-dollar bills spilled out and fluttered to the deck. Chuck and Emily watched him pick up the money.

"Are you claiming sunken treasure?" Chuck asked.

"Dinner and drinks are free tonight." Ryan grinned and tucked the money back into the journal. He pointed to the pistol. "A souvenir for you, Chuck."

Chuck beamed. "I like hanging out with you, Ryan. Fast boats, free guns, and beautiful women." He gave Emily a lecherous grin which she didn't return.

"Let's make the run back to Key West," Ryan said. "We can make it in time for sunset, margaritas, and steaks on the grill."

"More reasons why you're my favorite DWR employee. Next to Greg Olsen that is." To Emily, he said, "He signs our paychecks."

"I've never fully understood why a commercial dive operation is looking at our back cases. Shouldn't law enforcement be working on catching the thieves?" Emily glanced between the two men as she dried her hair with a large towel.

"Don't you worry your pretty little head about it, girl. Ryan knows what he's doing."

"Still, I'd like you to explain to me why you're so interested in sunken sailboats."

Ryan sat down on the Fountain's gunwale. "We have a small group of people in DWR dedicated to working with the government on maritime security issues. We suspect these boats are being used to smuggle guns and other contraband into the US. My job is to track down the group, or groups, of people bringing them in."

"Are you in on this, Chuck?"

"Only when Ryan needs me. Otherwise, I do what Greg Olsen tells me to do."

Emily nodded in understanding then changed the subject. "I'm getting hungry, let's go eat."

They dropped the boat off at the marina, showered, and changed clothes at the hotel. After dinner at the Conch Republic Seafood Company, Chuck took off to find a party, and left Emily and Ryan standing on the sidewalk. While Ryan preferred the laid-back atmosphere of the Middle and Upper Keys to Key Weird, there was a magic about the southern most point in the US. He'd been here multiple times to train at the naval stations on Boca Chica Key and Fleming Island. He and his teammates had performed the Duval Crawl with every trip. It was a right of passage for the happy-go-lucky revelers clogging the streets. Ryan asked his companion, "Shall we join them?"

Emily smiled. "When in Rome."

Ryan laughed, feeling an intoxicating rush of lust. They ended up at a table in the sand, at Lagerhead's Beach Bar. They "oohhed" and "ahhed" at the sunset as it spread vibrant oranges, yellows, and reds across the horizon. Then they returned to their margaritas, laughing, talking, and people watching. Many drinks into the night, Emily asked if he had a girlfriend.

He put down his glass and turned to look at her. Feeling very drunk, he could not gauge the level of her seriousness. He said, "No."

"That sounds awful."

"Yeah, now I'm depressed. Thanks."

"Another drink is in order then." Emily motioned to the waitress for another round then asked, "Any prospects in sight?"

Ryan looked at her again, his vision blurring at the edges. He moved with deliberate slowness to pick up his almost empty glass. She was hitting on him, or maybe he was misinterpreting the signals. "Unfortunately for both of us, I am too drunk to properly answer that question."

The waitress set down the next round. Ryan sipped the fresh margarita and told her it would be his last. She smiled and placed her hand on his forearm before agreeing with him. He gazed at her through beer goggles. She was even more beautiful, and he was too drunk to do anything about it. He fished out his cigarettes, which he'd refrained from partaking in all evening, and lit one.

He finished the cigarette, took a long drink of the margarita, and stood. His legs were rubbery, and he wobbled, steadied himself with a hand on the table, and bid Emily good night.

She rose and took his arm. “You’re not leaving me here alone!”

Arm in arm, they stumbled back to the hotel.

CHAPTER TEN

Ryan's internal alarm clock woke him at six a.m. His mouth felt like someone had shoved cotton balls into it and his head pounded. He glanced at his watch and over at Chuck's bed. The pilot wasn't there. Groaning, he tossed off the covers. Emily stirred. Ryan glanced down to see he was still wearing his clothes. He peeked under the covers. Emily was also wearing her clothes although her bra lay on the nightstand. Ryan rubbed his eyes.

They'd made it to his room, and she'd come in with him. After she'd asked him which bed he was sleeping in, and he'd pointed it out, they'd taken turns in the bathroom. When Ryan had come out, he'd seen her snuggled in the covers. He'd lain down beside her and closed his eyes. She gave him a long, lingering kiss and then rolled over.

Ryan turned on the coffee maker, and stood in the shower, running the water as hot as he could stand. When he walked out of the bathroom, Emily wasn't in the room.

He was pouring himself a cup of coffee when the door opened. Chuck fell through it straight onto his bed. He looked like he'd slept in his clothes.

"Have a good night, Captain?"

"What happens in Key West stays in Key West, boss. Besides, I figured you needed a little room to operate on Emily." Through a yawn, Chuck said, "I take it that didn't work out for you?"

"Worked out just fine. We got drunk and went to our neutral corners." Ryan's thoughts lingered on the kiss as he pulled on board shorts and a DWR polo shirt.

"A wasted opportunity there," said Chuck.

Ryan shook his head. "Just laying the groundwork."

Chuck laughed. "Don't wait too long."

Ryan picked up the thermos he'd filled with coffee and said, "Let's go spend another day in paradise."

They collected Emily, who had bloodshot eyes and wet hair from her own shower. She kept asking them to keep their voices down. On the way to the marina, they stopped at a convenience store for a six-pack of beer, and each drank a cold brew after they were on the boat.

"Oh yeah, baby, hair of the dog!" Chuck grinned and cracked open a second one.

Emily looked pale with a tinge of green. She sat so she could easily lean over the rail.

Operating with a hangover came naturally to Ryan. It was hard to count the number of times he'd stayed up partying with his teammates before hopping on a boat and racing off to blow something up.

"Just the thought of going out today makes me sick to my stomach," she moaned.

"Here, suck on this for a few minutes." Ryan handed Emily a small scuba tank filled with pure oxygen. He kept oxygen on the boat in case of a decompression sickness emergency. Today, it was also a hangover tonic. She put the regulator in her mouth. She stayed anchored to a seat in the shade of the covered half-tower while Ryan idled them out of the marina and ramped up the throttles on the big fishing boat. They ran east toward Marathon.

CHAPTER ELEVEN

Chuck Newland called out the GPS coordinates as they closed in on their target. He looked at the vast expanse of open sea with no land in sight and asked, "How did they find this thing way out here?"

From their vantage point, the top of the lighthouse marking Sombrero Reef was just visible on the horizon.

Emily, who was feeling better with the help of the oxygen and drinking plenty of water, explained, "The story I heard was that some fishermen found it with their fish finder. They started fishing it and told some diver friends of theirs. After they dove the wreck, they reported it to the Coast Guard who ran the HIN and reported it to us."

Ryan idled the boat and had Chuck take over the controls while he went forward and dropped the anchor into sixty feet of water. He paid out most of the anchor rode as Chuck backed the boat up to set the hook. The Fountain was just outside the barrier reef, and the heavy current tore past the hull. Ryan tried to gauge the water's speed. A fully laden diver could swim at three knots. The water looked to be moving closer to four.

He rigged a rope to run from the anchor line to the back of the boat. He pointed at it and said to Emily, "Use the tag line to pull yourself to the anchor line. When we come back, follow it to the back of the boat. Don't let go or you'll be halfway to Maine before we can pick you up."

The current ripped past their bodies as they made their descent. It threatened to tear them loose and was strong enough to carry their legs out straight, like a flag in a stiff breeze. He thought about calling the dive or at least sending Emily back to the Fountain, but she was already halfway down. He should have followed his gut instincts.

The current was much stronger on the bottom than at the surface. Ryan sped up his descent to catch Emily before she reached the anchor. He'd gotten it close to the wreck of the thirty-six-foot Beneteau, but there was still ten feet between the anchor and the stern of the boat. They knelt in the sand, each holding the anchor line with one hand. The swiftness of the water was like being caught in a river rapid. Concern clouded Emily's eyes. Ryan clipped a rope to the anchor line, and he motioned for her to stay low to the sand and to grip his BCD strap. Together, they let go of the safety of the anchor line and the current swept them downstream to the sailboat.

The boat lay on its port side with the cockpit facing the current, and they each grabbed the stainless steel lifeline surrounding the boat's deck. Ryan tied off the line to the rail and shoved Emily down the ladder to the cabin. Inside, they could feel the hull trembling as the water rushed by. The hairs on the back of Ryan's neck stood up. It was an eerie wreck occupied by a five-foot-long goliath grouper, who had taken residence in the forward V-berth. Unlike the last two boats they'd seen, the interior of this one was still intact.

Ryan didn't bother to search for hidden treasures. He wanted to get Emily safely back to the Fountain.

Using sign language, he told Emily to go out to the cockpit. She headed out of the wreck, and he took a last look around before following her. Ryan looked toward the anchor line but couldn't see her flowing, blonde mane. Twisting in a three-hundred-and-sixty-degree circle, he still couldn't locate her. Adrenaline shot through his body as he slowly made a second circle.

Ryan took a deep breath and peered into the down current gloom. He saw flashes of yellow as she kicked her fins. He thrust himself over the railing, kicking as hard and as fast as he could. She was struggling to swim back to the boat, and he knew she was just depleting her air reserves.

When he reached her, it was too late to swim back to the wreck. Emily was exhausted. He could see it in her eyes. Ryan grabbed the shoulder strap of her BCD and hauled her down to the reef. He used a large chunk of coral to block the current and give them some relief. A look at his dive computer told him they'd dropped from sixty-three feet, at the wreck, to seventy-five feet.

Emily's blue eyes were as big as saucers, and her breathing came in quick, ragged gasps. Her gauge showed she'd sucked down most of her air. She was breathing so hard the gauge needle quivered. Ryan felt guilty for allowing her to dive in conditions unfavorable for a diver of her experience. He made eye contact with her to help her regain her composure and used hand signals to get her to breathe slow and steady.

He clipped one end of a six-foot nylon strap to her and attached the second carabiner to his BCD. He would normally secure the Jon Line to an ascent line during long decompression stops or in strong current conditions. Now, he was using it to keep them from being separated.

From a D-ring on his BCD, he took a reel containing two hundred and fifty feet of bright orange line and clipped it to a lift bag. Using his secondary regulator, he triggered a burst of air into the bag. It rose toward the surface, stripping line off the reel. On his wrist-mounted dive slate, Ryan wrote instructions for Emily. She shoved her hands into the cummerbund of his BCD and got a tight grip. He puffed air into his BCD and they slowly rose from the sea floor. The line would help control their ascent and hold their position in the strong current while they did their safety stops. Ryan hoped Chuck Newland was paying attention to the time and had already started to look for them.

It took more time to ascend than Ryan would have liked, because he had to reel in line, control their buoyancy, and deal with a wiggling passenger. Partway through their three-minute safety stop at fifteen feet, to eliminate residual nitrogen from their bodies, Emily began thrashing wildly with her hands and feet. When Ryan pulled her back down to him, she jerked his regulator out of his mouth and shoved it into hers. She knocked his mask askew. Panic clutched his brain as water swirled up his nose and stung his eyes. Involuntarily, he tried to breathe through his nasal passages. He stopped himself just before he sucked in a lungful of water. Ryan squeezed his eyes shut and allowed his training to take over. He grabbed the secondary regulator, hanging on a necklace beneath his chin, and shoved it in his mouth. He took a deep breath, repositioned his mask, and cleared it.

When he looked up from blinking away the saltwater, Emily was staring at him in horror. She was frantically motioning for them to go up. Ryan grabbed the shoulder strap of her BCD and pulled her close to him. They had yet to finish their safety stop. She gesticulated wildly at her pressure gauge. It read zero. He gave her the OK sign with his fingers, looked at his computer and then held up one finger, showing her they had one minute left. The last thing they needed was to get the bends from a nitrogen bubble expanding in their joints or brains. Able to breathe again, she was calming down.

The dive computer beeped. Ryan hit the button to stop the low-pressure alarm indicating there was less than five hundred pounds of air remaining. The air was dwindling rapidly with two divers breathing from the same tank. Ryan kept them down until they had completely drained their air. With thirty seconds left on their safety stop, they kicked for the surface, exhaling on the way up to avoid a lung overexpansion injury.

Emily spat out her regulator and took in deep breaths of air. They orally inflated their BCDs and looked around. They'd surfaced in waves that were two feet higher than when they'd gone under. On the horizon, dark clouds were building, and a bolt of lightning streaked down to touch the water. Wind was blowing the tops off the three-foot waves. An occasional five-footer lifted them higher.

Ryan yanked his weights free and let them drop, then did the same with Emily's.

"I don't see the boat, Ryan." Worry and fright hung on the words.

"I know, Em." He rotated and lined his compass up with the heading he'd taken on the Fountain before getting in the water. He wasn't sure how far the current had pushed them downstream. They were off by a few degrees of their original heading.

He inflated a safety sausage. The six-foot-tall, bright orange marker would give Chuck something to home in on.

"Everything will be okay," he reassured her. "Chuck knows what to do if we don't come up the anchor line. We went over the plan."

"I'm just worried and tired." She leaned her head back and stretched out. "I'm sorry about down there. I panicked when I ran out of air."

"It happens to everyone." Ryan busied himself with folding the lift bag before clipping it and the reel to his BCD. They'd already dropped their weights, and if they were stranded for an extended period, they would have to dump more gear. Ryan wasn't looking forward to that. Some of the gear he'd had for years and was sentimentally attached to. Plus, he would have to buy new tanks and weights for the dive shop where he'd rented them. He was already on the hook for the weights.

Emily asked, "Have you ever run out of air?"

"I was setting up a sidemount rig, where you have two tanks, one mounted on each side of the body, instead of one on the back. Each tank has its own regulator and you swap back and forth to keep the air in the tanks even. Anyway, I was down about twenty feet and changed from the left reg to the right. Before I went under, I'd inadvertently shut off the right tank, and when I stuck the reg in my mouth, there was no air.

"I panicked, thinking the tank was empty and I was going to die. When I finally remembered to stick the left reg in my mouth, I was freaking out and stuck it in upside down. I took a big breath of air and water and almost choked. That doubled down on my panic, and at that point I was holding my breath, which is a big no-no, and thinking about shooting to the surface."

He checked his watch and counted the minutes since they'd surfaced. He'd told Chuck he should look for them forty minutes after they entered the water. If Chuck failed to find them after thirty minutes of searching, he was to radio the Coast Guard on channel sixteen and declare a lost diver emergency.

"What happened?" she demanded.

"I figured it out and here I am." The sea swept them up and dropped them back down in a dizzying roller-coaster ride.

"Really?" She spat out saltwater. "You're telling me this harrowing tale of danger and you end it like that?"

"I got the regulator in right, took a couple of deep breaths, and cracked open the right tank. Everything turned out okay. Moral of the story: don't panic."

"Don't panic," she muttered indignantly.

The half-hour search time was almost over when Ryan and Emily heard a boat motor in the distance.

Emily said, "I hope that's Chuck."

Ryan wrapped his arms around her and pulled her close. She was shivering, and tears rolled down her cheeks. He kissed her forehead. She buried her face in his shoulder, and her arms went around him.

The motor grew louder as the boat came into view.

Ryan felt the first fat drops of rain strike his face. The dark clouds were moving faster than he'd estimated.

Chuck put the engines in neutral and tossed a line to them. Ryan caught it, and Emily let go of him for the safety of the tag line and boat. Chuck lifted Emily and her dive gear out, then it was Ryan's turn.

Chuck wrapped Emily in a blanket and got her some water to drink. The clouds were upon them now, darkening the sky and pummeling them with waves of driving rain. Chuck had taken the time to zip up the clear, plastic window skirts between the windshield and the covered half-tower, so they were mostly dry. Chuck took the helm and pointed the boat toward Marathon to escape the storm. Ryan stripped off his wetsuit and pulled on dry shorts and a sweat shirt. Emily changed into dry clothes, but her teeth still chattered.

Ryan took the wheel, and Chuck and Emily held onto the grab bar behind the captain's seat, standing to absorb the pounding of the boat through the heavy seas. It was a brutal ride with the bow crashing down into four-foot waves. Spray surged off the nose, drenching everything in its path.

"I saw a red bag pop up about fifty yards off the stern," Chuck yelled. "The anchor was stuck on something when I tried to pull it up. I ended up cutting it away. When I got the boat turned around, the red bag was gone. I motored down current trying to stay in a straight line. Lucky y'all had that orange marker or I'd have never found ya."

It wasn't luck. Ryan carried the safety sausage for that exact purpose. It was the first time he'd used it in an emergency and he never wanted to do it again. Between the roar of the motors, the wind, and the waves, it was hard to hear. Ryan shouted, "I'm glad you did. First round's on me."

Forty-five minutes later, the wind was still lashing rain against the windows. The three boaters were warm and dry, hoisting cocktails at Tarpon Creek Bar & Grill. After her near-death experience, and bobbing around on the ocean waiting for rescue, Emily had desperately wanted a drink. Ryan ordered three shots of tequila for them.

CHAPTER TWELVE

The storm raged most of the afternoon. Emily called her boss and arranged for someone to move the boat back to Key West, then the trio rented a car and drove to their hotel.

Chuck left to meet the woman he'd spent the previous night with, and Ryan stepped into the shower. His cell phone rang as he was rinsing off.

He stepped out of the water and grabbed the device. "Hello?"

Emily asked, "Are you taking me to dinner again tonight?"

"Yeah, I can." He looked at his reflection in the mirror. His skin was red from the sun. He ran a hand over his short brown hair and grinned to check his teeth. Crow's feet crinkled at the corners of his eyes. "Give me a few minutes."

"Come open the door, I'm outside."

"I'll be right there." Ryan wrapped a towel around his waist and went to the door. He swung it open and Emily, wearing white canvas shoes, tan shorts, and a red T-shirt, was leaning against the wall.

She looked him up and down with a wry smile. "Interesting dinner attire."

He laughed and shook his head, then turned away from the door. After collecting cargo shorts and a gray camp shirt, he went into the bathroom and pulled on his clothes. When he opened the door, Emily was sitting on the bed with his wallet in her hand. She was looking through his business cards, credit cards, and pictures.

Incensed, Ryan stepped toward her to snatch the black, leather billfold from her, but she tossed it back on the TV stand before he could.

Trying to keep his voice even, he asked, "Find anything interesting?"

"I learn a lot about men by what they keep in their wallets. You, for instance, are well-organized and don't like clutter. You like the basics, just like how you're dressed, and you love your family."

"Mind if I go through your purse?"

She held out a small leather clutch. "If you want to?"

He waved it off and stuffed his pockets with his wallet, keys, a folding knife, and loose change.

Outside the lobby, they climbed into the rental car and headed for one of Ryan's favorite restaurants, Hogfish Bar & Grill on Stock Island. They got a table on the water and ordered beers and hogfish sandwiches.

The couple laughed and talked while they waited for their meals. Emily laid a hand on Ryan's when he made a witty comment. He liked the feel of her touch.

When the food came, they both dug in ravenously and enjoyed the delicious hogfish. They ordered another round of beers after dinner. Ryan slipped off to the restroom, and when he came back, he sat beside Emily. They watched the two-man band play island songs and Jimmy Buffett covers.

He put his arm around her and rested it on the back of her chair. When she turned to look at him, he kissed her.

Thirty minutes later, they were in her hotel room bed. He was glad he'd waited until he wasn't drunk to make love to her as he held her close and kissed her neck. Her skin felt like it was on fire, and he couldn't touch her enough to satisfy his desire.

Afterwards, lying in the dark, he felt Emily's warm body press against him, her leg cocked up on his thigh, warm skin cooling and drying. He could smell her hair as she rested her head on his chest.

"Thanks for saving me today," she whispered.

"There was no other choice."

Emily's finger trailed across his chest and down his abdomen. She reignited his physical response as she slid on top of him.

RYAN DASHED from one room to another searching for a ringing phone. It was impossible to find and gradually, the room he was in faded as he awoke. He pressed a hand to his head to shield his eyes from the bright sunlight streaming through a crack in the heavy curtains, and he had to blink several times to clear the spots from his vision.

The phone on the nightstand rang again. Ryan picked it up and pressed the receiver to his ear. "Hello?"

"Wake up, boss," Chuck said. "We've got an early flight time. I left your bag leaning against Emily's door."

"Thanks." Ryan sat up on the edge of the bed. "You're the freakin' pilot, push the time back."

"I can't. I need to be back in Texas this afternoon."

Ryan set the receiver down in its cradle and felt a hand

on his shoulder. He turned to see Emily, wrapped in the crisp, white sheet, smiling up at him. He leaned down to kiss her. The plane would have to wait.

"What now?" Emily asked as they flew across the glistening blue waters of the Gulf of Mexico.

"I need to do more research to figure out who these gunrunners are."

"How do you plan to do that?"

"I'm not sure," Ryan said. "There have to be more insurance companies who've dealt with the same theft issues as you have. I'll talk to them and see what I can come up with."

"What about the journal you found?"

"I'll read it on the way back to Texas City."

"Will you let me know what happens?"

"I will."

The flight felt like it only took ten minutes as he chatted with Emily. He wanted to see her again. His last relationship had been with a woman in Virginia Beach, two years ago. Since his exit from the Navy, he'd put off dating, even though his mother often asked him when he would settle down and have a family like his brother and sister. After watching too many friends get married and then divorced because their wives couldn't handle the long deployments, or the dangerous nature of their husbands' demolition jobs, he was in no hurry to get tied down. More than one sailor had left his wife on the pier as he sailed away, only to find out she'd been trolling for a new man in the club that same night. Ryan had no use for that kind of drama. He was again in a job where he would become intimate with danger, and he had yet to meet a woman strong enough to carry that kind of baggage.

Chuck refueled the Beechcraft while Ryan accompanied Emily to her car. He smoked a cigarette as he walked back to the plane. He sat up front with Chuck on the way to Texas City and they talked about flying and their prior service. Chuck had joined the Air Force, like his father who had flown Cobra gunships in Vietnam and then for Air America, the CIA's clandestine operation in Laos.

"He never talked about it until I joined the Air Force. He started telling me about some of his operations. Not all the gritty stuff but enough to let me know he'd seen some nasty combat. I found out more when the government declassified a lot of the Air America records."

"Those guys did some crazy shit," Ryan said. "I read a few books about it."

Chuck nodded and stared out the window at the ground rushing by. Ryan pulled out the journal and began reading it from the beginning.

The pilot glanced over at him and said, "Let me know if you find anything interesting."

CHAPTER THIRTEEN

Greg Olsen was on the back deck of his Tiki Island house, parked under the patio table umbrella. He was staring at the screen of his laptop but not getting much accomplished.

Ryan stretched out in a deck chair and lit a cigarette while looking across the West Bay estuary. They had a clear view of North and South Deer Islands and further on, Galveston. Cumulus clouds stacked up on the horizon.

"An apt name," Ryan commented. "Since cumulus in Latin means 'pile.'"

Greg closed the laptop and leaned back in his chair. "This sucks. I hate looking at numbers." He motioned for Ryan to give him a smoke, and Ryan slid the pack and lighter to him. Greg lit one and tossed the lighter on the table. "I've been working for my dad for as long as I can remember. He taught me how to dive and had me working underwater when most kids were playing tee ball. I learned more in those years working for him than I ever did at Texas A&M."

He paused and stuck the cigarette in his mouth. Ryan

let him stew on whatever he was thinking about.

Greg crushed out the butt a minute later. "Damn things make my legs feel weird. Makes them tense." He poured a shot of Cazadores tequila and offered one to Ryan, who shook his head.

Ryan watched him tilt it back, pour another shot and slam it down.

"I was supposed to come home and run this damn crew," Greg said. "Instead, you get to have all the fun. DWR's been running government operations since World War Two. It was supposed to be my turn, Ryan. Now, I'm just a cripple in a wheelchair." He punched himself in the leg. "Can't feel a damn thing."

"You're the man running this operation. I'm still your flunky, just like when we were in the Navy."

"Yeah, well, I'm no operator now," Greg complained. "I'm just another useless fobbit."

Ryan took a puff from his cigarette. "The world needs fobbits too, Greg. Paper pushers, logistics trains, we need them all. Now you're the admiral, and admirals don't go traipsing around in the field with the troops."

"They have a flagship and go to battle with the fleet."

"Your flagship is the DWR office. Your fleet is every boat DWR owns and you get a cushy bed and a hot meal every night. Those of us mucking around at the bottom of the ladder get the MREs and the dirt naps."

Greg shook his head and lit another cigarette.

Ryan grabbed a beer from a cooler and sat back down.

"Where are you with this pirate thing?" Greg asked.

"I've been going through records from several other insurance companies. Nothing ties them together other than there are pirates in the Gulf." He cocked his head and watched a center console boat race by, the chrome rocket launchersfishing pole holderson the T-top reflecting in the sunlight. "I've been reading the journal we found on one of the wrecks. This guy Philip Nagel had a nice trip going until they headed north past the Yucatán Peninsula. I Googled him and found out they kidnapped him and his wife off his boat. He paid the two-million-dollar ransom. He's fighting with the insurance company for pay off on his kidnap and ransom policy. The insurance company claims he didn't follow procedure and notify the authorities, or them, until he was home. They think it's a hoax."

"What do you think?" Greg asked.

"I think they got kidnapped, and he paid the ransom. The guys who run the kidnap racket rarely let their victims contact anybody but the bank. Once they get their money, they let the victims go or just shoot them."

Greg propped his elbows on the table and rested his chin on his knuckles, the smoldering cigarette captured between the index and middle finger of his right hand. They watched two fishermen work their boat along the docks and piers projecting out from Tiki Island. They cast lures into the shade and cover of the structures.

"Is the kidnapping related to the piracy?"

"I'd like to talk to Nagel and find out," Ryan replied.

"Go for it."

"Can I have Chuck fly me up to Peoria?"

"If he doesn't have anything else going on."

"I'm going to call Emily and have her meet me up there."

Greg raised his eyebrows and let out a stream of smoke. "I'm not paying for you to fly up there for a date."

"I want her to get me in the door. Nagel might not talk to me about his boat, but he'll probably talk to the hot-looking insurance agent who held the boat's policy."

CHAPTER FOURTEEN

Arturo Guerrero sat in a leather chair behind his office desk. Three of his trusted lieutenants, Alejandro Vargas, José Luis Orozco, and Ernesto Daniels sat across from him. Professor Ruben Morales listened in on speaker phone.

Guerrero swept his hand over his jet-black hair and turned to look at Orozco. The man would not meet the stare of his *jefe*'s black eyes. Guerrero continued to stare at the man. Orozco squirmed in his chair.

Finally, Orozco looked up and said, "If you insist on this war, they will close down the border and send in the Army to patrol it. We'll never get our product through. They'll figure out who's bombing their cities and they'll bring the war to us. Mexico City will never fight for us and the Americans will destroy us."

Guerrero studied the man. Orozco was loyal and had a respectable record, but Guerrero knew he cared more about money and power than about the business.

Arturo said, "We will continue this battle, José Luis. We'll take down these *Yanquie* dogs and beat them over the head until they give us back our lands. We must reclaim our heritage."

Orozco shook his head. "It's over, *Patrón*. Look around, no one cares about our heritage. They care about feeding their families and getting a job at the Ford plant."

"You do not understand," Guerrero thundered. "The people care about their heritage. We must take back everything those white devils have stolen from Mexico in the name of manifest destiny. You can't see it, but we're already doing this. Look at the population explosion of Latinos and Chicanos who are flooding across the border."

"Then let them," Orozco shot back. "In a few more years, we'll have control and there will be more mouths for our product. Let them be slaves to the needle and to the white powder. Stop this nonsense about armies and bombs and ISIS. We don't need them."

"That is where you are wrong, my friend," Guerrero said. "We need to restore our heritage and reclaim our lands."

Orozco half-shouted, "All we will do is destroy what we've already built. The U.S. Army will tear it down. They'll shatter us. The other cartels will take our place because we have become weak with your ideas of building an army to fight for an imaginary land. We must focus on our core business. Forget about this other nonsense!"

"We are arguing about the same thing," Guerrero said. He glanced at the other two men who had remained silent. "We want to pour our product across the border and put guns in the hands of our people. Forget what you think. I have forgotten it already." Guerrero's voice rose with passion. "I am telling you what you will think, and *la Revolución* will continue. I will discuss it with you no more."

The two men glared at one another for half a second before Guerrero turned to the phone and calmly asked. "Professor, are you ready for the next phase?"

"Yes. Everything is in place."

"Excellent." Guerrero picked up a smoldering cigar from the ashtray beside him. He puffed on it to reinvigorate the flame.

Orozco shook his head as his boss said, "Make California burn."

CHAPTER FIFTEEN

Ryan Weller met Emily Hunt in the arrival terminal of General Wayne A. Downing Peoria International Airport outside Peoria, Illinois. She'd flown commercial from Tampa and he'd arrived on the Beechcraft piloted by Chuck Newland.

They picked up her suitcase from the carousel and walked out the front doors where they headed to the first taxi and climbed in. Ryan gave Nagel's address to the driver who typed it into a GPS unit and started the meter before pulling away from the curb. The cabbie gave them a detailed narrative about the city of Peoria and its history, pointing out landmarks along the way. When he pulled the car to the curb, they were in front of a newly renovated eight-story brick building in the Peoria waterfront district. They skirted the first-floor storefronts to a lobby entrance and rode an elevator to the top floor.

During the cabbie's occasional pauses, Ryan had given Emily a brief on Nagel. Nagel had made it big during the real estate boom of the early 2000s, buying and selling residential and commercial real estate. He'd been an early prophet of the 2008 real estate crash and had divested himself of much of his holdings before the market turned down. He had also advised his clients to sell at lower prices just to get out before the crash.

With a nest of cash, he'd swept up prime properties in Peoria and Chicago at discount prices when the panic selling began. He'd held many of the properties until the market rose again and then sold them off to make an even larger fortune. Nagel had retired three years ago, but he still retained a silent partnership in his brokerages and helped manage a large portfolio of rental properties.

Emily knocked on the intricate, frosted glass inlay of Nagel's penthouse door.

Nagel swung the door open enough to see them and asked who they were.

"I'm Ryan Weller and this is Emily Hunt. She's with Ward and Young, the insurance company for your old sailboat, *Misty*. May we come in? We have some questions for you."

Emily held up a credential pack with a company ID card showing.

He swung the door open for them to enter. Nagel was tall and slim with dark brown hair fringing a balding crown. He had brown eyes and a wide smile, showcasing chemically whitened teeth. He wore a white dress shirt with gray trousers, brown Gucci loafers, and a matching belt.

To Ryan, the apartment looked like a fashion magazine layout with its contemporary decorations. Through the floor-to-ceiling windows, they could see the Illinois River and Lake Peoria.

"She works for Ward and Young." Nagel pointed at Ryan. "Who do you work for, Mr. Weller?"

"I work for Dark Water Research, a commercial dive and salvage business contracting with Ward and Young."

"Are you attempting to salvage my boat?"

"Unfortunately, the pirates stripped her bare, cut off her masts, and sank her."

"After that bloody pirate incident, my wife doesn't even want to look at another boat. You can have her."

Ryan grinned. "Your wife or the boat?"

A sly smile crept across Philip Nagel's angular face. "Since my wife isn't here to defend herself, you, sir, may take your pick."

Emily stepped into the conversation. "We went to the Dry Tortugas to look at your boat. Ryan found some of your belongings while we were scuba diving on her."

From his briefcase, Ryan produced the journal and pistol, which Chuck had thoroughly

cleaned and oiled.

"You may keep the pistol. I took it with us for protection, but I couldn't take it out of its hiding place at most of the ports we visited. When I needed it the most, I was afraid to get it out and use it." Nagel picked up the journal and fanned through its pages. Five one-hundred-dollar bills fell onto the counter. He scooped them up and slipped them back into the book.

Emily glanced at Ryan as he put the gun back in his briefcase. Later, he would tell her Nagel would have known they'd kept the money if it wasn't in the journal. Returning it would create a bond of trust between the salvor and the former boat owner.

"Tell us about your time aboard *Misty*," Ryan prompted.

Nagel sat down on a bar stool at the kitchen island and

ran his hand across the cool white granite. "It was always my dream to sail around the Caribbean, and I talked my wife into it over several years. We bought the boat in Chicago, sailed out of the Great Lakes, down the St. Lawrence Seaway and out to Bermuda. Our first ocean passage." He smiled at the memories. "For two inexperienced sailors, crossing the Gulf Stream was rough. But we made it and we convinced ourselves if we could do that, we could survive just about anything. After Bermuda, we sailed down to the Bahamas and bounced around the Caribbean, enjoying the good life. We decided to head back north. Mary wanted to come home. We planned to sail right up the Mississippi to the Illinois River and complete the Great Loop."

"I've always wanted to do that," Ryan said. He knew the Great Lakes, Saint Lawrence Seaway, Mississippi River, and Intracoastal Waterways formed the Great Loop. Connecting those waterways allowed boaters to circle the eastern half of the United States.

"I would like to complete it one day," Nagel said wistfully. "Perhaps by powerboat." He got up and poured himself a glass of water from a pitcher in the refrigerator. Holding it up, he asked, "Would you like some?"

Both of his guests declined.

"As I was saying..." He sipped the water as he sat back down. "We left Cancún with a full head of sail headed for New Orleans when we saw a boat. I thought it was the Mexican Navy making a patrol. They hailed us, boarded us, and, well, our lives haven't been the same since. My wife is in therapy as we speak."

Ryan asked, "Why did you think it was the Mexican Navy?"

"I saw the Navy operating around Cancún while we

were there. The men who boarded *Misty* had a similar boat and uniforms."

"Can you describe any of the men who took you?" Emily asked.

Nagel shook his head. "They wore balaclavas, and black bulletproof vests with a patch saying *Marina* across the front." He slid his finger across his chest to show where it was. "They had M16s or whatever our troops carry."

"Not AK-47s?" Ryan asked.

With a roll of his eyes and an exasperated tone, Nagel said, "I've seen enough news to know what weapons our troops carry."

Ryan held up a picture of an AK on his cell phone.

"No, not it."

Ryan paged to a photo of an M4 carbine. Nagel nodded. "That's it."

Ryan accessed the search engine again and looked up Mexican Navy boats. They went through pictures, Ryan standing beside Nagel, until they came upon a center console, twenty-five-foot rigid-hulled inflatable boat marked with *Marina* down the inflated tubes. An aluminum tower in the rear, built over twin outboard engines, sprouted a radar dome and several antennas.

"They had a Mexican flag patch on their sleeve," Nagel remembered.

"According to the news, Mexican *Federales* have been finding caches of fake Army and Navy uniforms in some of the drug cartel busts," Emily informed them.

"Was there anything else distinctive about the uniform?" Ryan asked.

"One man had a strange patch on his shoulder. When we returned to Peoria and got everything sorted out, I looked it up on the internet. I couldn't find the patch, but I found something similar."

Nagel told his guests to wait where they were while he went into another room. He came back carrying a three-ring binder. "I made a file of everything pertaining to the incident. As you might well know, I'm waging a war with the insurance company to get back the ransom money I paid." He leafed through the pages. "Here it is. The patch looked like this." He turned the binder, so everyone could see. "I colored in the areas to make it look like the patch." Mexico was in tan, the United States in a light gray. "This portion here." He pointed at an area shaded red. "That represents Texas, New Mexico, Arizona, California, Nevada, and Colorado. There wasn't any wording, just a picture."

Ryan and Emily were both puzzled.

"The red area represents Aztlán," Nagel continued. "Legend has it Aztlán is the ancestral home of the Aztecs before they migrated into Mexico. After the Mexican-American War, the U.S. paid Mexico for the land which now comprises the Southwestern United States. Chicano independence groups are claiming these lands are their ancestral heritage and the U.S. should return them to Mexico to create the *Republica del Norte*, or Republic of the North."

Ryan leaned on the counter. "These groups believe America stole land from Mexico even though we took it fair and square."

"Fair and square have many definitions, Mr. Weller," Nagel said.

"We paid Mexico for those lands and assumed Mexican debt to U.S. citizens. Is that not fair?"

"Not according to these people. Some don't care, but others do, and my wife and I have been caught in the crosshairs of this little skirmish. It appears the two of you are now involved as well."

"Where did they hold you hostage?" Emily asked.

"They blindfolded us and took us to a ship. They referred to it as *buque madre*." Nagel shrugged.

"Mother boat," Ryan repeated to himself. He'd learned Spanish from Mexican construction workers his father had employed at many of his construction sites.

"They took us to a ship and locked us in a cabin. They brought us just enough food and water to keep us healthy. The only time I was allowed out of the cabin was to use a computer to transfer money. When they confirmed the wire transfer, they blindfolded us and took us ashore. They left us on a deserted Mexican beach. We had to walk to a small town to get help. I called the authorities to report the kidnapping and then we came home."

Ryan asked, "Any idea what the name of the ship was?"

"No. I've been over and over this with the insurance company. They even tried to trace the money, but those... pirates... had transferred it out of the account I'd wired it to. From there, it disappeared. My insurance company believes I made this transfer in an effort to defraud them and move money out of the United States. It's a lot of money and I understand what they are saying, but it's the principle of the matter. Miss Hunt's company paid for our sailboat after someone found it in the Florida Keys. I remember speaking to you, and you were more than helpful. Thank you for that."

"I was glad to be of assistance, Mr. Nagel." Emily pulled a card from her briefcase and laid it on the granite. "Call me if you think of anything else that might help."

"Thanks, Mr. Nagel," Ryan said, extending his hand.

They left the apartment, rode the elevator down, and walked out on the street.

"What now, detective?" Emily asked.

"We eat," Ryan said, pointing across the street to another brick building. At one time it had been a train station, but now it housed a barbecue restaurant and a bar. "I'm a barbecue connoisseur. Let's see how this stuff compares to my favorite North Carolina barbecue."

While they waited for their order, Ryan called Chuck and asked if he wanted them to bring him a to-go box. Chuck said he'd already eaten at an airport café, but he would have rather eaten barbecue.

They discussed the case while they ate. Ryan tried to keep his professionalism but could not stop her from holding his hand during the ride back to the airport.

In the terminal, Emily looked at her watch and said, "I wasn't sure how long this would take, so I booked a flight for tomorrow morning. I do have a surprise for you." She set her briefcase down on a counter and opened it. She retrieved a file folder and handed it to Ryan.

He opened it and read the cover sheet. It was another sailboat theft Ward and Young had yet to pay on. According to the incident, the owner, a Mango Hulsey of Port Aransas, Texas, had fought off the pirates when they tried to take his wife hostage. They'd escaped in their dinghy after Mango had shot two of the pirates and then turned the gun on the RIB boat, deflating the tubes and disabling the motor.

"Abandoned?" Ryan asked.

"Ward and Young has classified it as an abandonment since they could have sailed away from the pirates but chose to escape in their dinghy."

"That's harsh," Ryan said. He handed the file back. "Want to go talk to them?"

"Yes," she said, with a nod.

"Do you want to cancel your flight reservations?"

Emily shrugged.

"Did you make flight reservations?"

She struggled to keep from smiling and shrugged again.

Ryan snorted. "Presumptuous, aren't you?"

She grinned as she shrugged.

He pulled her into his arms and kissed her.

In the airplane cabin, Chuck asked Emily, "Are we taking you to Tampa?"

"No, I'm going with you guys to Texas."

Chuck looked at Ryan and gave him a grin that split his face from ear to ear.

Ryan shook his head and handed the Browning pistol to the pilot. "Nagel said you could keep it. He doesn't want it anymore."

"I hate to see a party break up, but this is a lovely parting gift."

"I'll give you a kiss on the cheek, on my way off the plane, for being a good boy," Emily promised, and Chuck blushed.

He glanced at Ryan, who shrugged.

CHAPTER SIXTEEN

Ryan took Emily to his office in Texas City after they got off the plane.

"I thought this place would be bigger."

Ryan smiled. "This is just my office. DWR headquarters is a few miles south of here."

He gave her a quick tour, leaving out the gun vault. Together, they went over what information they'd collected and collated it into a report for Floyd Landis and her employer.

"All work and no play made Ryan a dull boy," Emily said with a lascivious grin.

Ryan stood and walked over to the couch. He gave it a nudge with his knee. "I was just thinking we should test this thing out."

Emily locked the door and then stepped into his arms. "We'll just have to consider this a business liaison."

When the phone rang, Ryan had to untangle himself from his lover and fell on the floor. She laughed as he grabbed for the phone. He pulled the handset and cradle down to the floor to answer the phone.

"Turn on the news," Greg said. "ISIS just set off a bomb in Los Angeles."

Ryan jumped up and found the remote. He turned on the television and changed to a cable news channel he favored.

"Reports are coming in now," the brunette anchorwoman said. Helicopter footage of the smoking wreckage played in the background. "Sources say a van drove into the skyscraper Constellation Place, formerly the MGM Tower, before detonating. We go now to our on-scene reporter."

The footage cut away to show a man standing in a street, the air thick with smoke. Ryan turned off the sound before the man could speak. Both he and Emily remained transfixed on the screen.

"Ryan. Ryan," Greg barked.

Ryan realized he was pressing the phone into his ear so hard it hurt. He eased his grip. "I'm here."

"These are the same guys who killed my mom and dad," Greg growled.

"We don't know that."

"I can feel it. I wish I was still walking around. I'd hunt those sons-of-bitches down."

Ryan said, "I'm sure the FBI is working on it."

"They couldn't find their backside with both hands."

"I agree." He wondered what Greg would say if he knew he was talking to a naked man. But he didn't need to worry as Greg continued to belittle and berate the country's intelligence sources and agencies.

"Greg, I'm shutting down here. I'm going to Corpus Christi to talk to some folks about their sailboat."

"Screw that. We need to find these guys."

"Hey, that's not our job, Greg. You know that. Listen,

let's take *Dark Water* down. You, me, Shelly, Emily, and Chuck."

"Emily? Is she here with you?"

"Yes." Ryan grinned at the woman pulling on her clothes.

"When do you want to leave?" Greg asked.

"Friday morning. We can meet these people for lunch on Saturday."

"Okay," Greg said, resignation in his voice.

"Transfer me to Shelly," Ryan said.

"What, I can't make plans?"

"I know how you are."

Greg punched a button for Ryan to listen to hold music.

A minute later, Shelly picked up and Ryan told her their plans while pulling on underwear and pants.

Emily came over to the desk when he set the phone down. "Are all the files you received from the other insurance companies on a computer?"

"Yes."

"I want to send them to a friend of mine at Ward and Young. Karen's really good at spotting patterns and uses computer programs to analyze and predict patterns."

"Have you had her look at your files?"

"I don't think anyone has asked her to look at the stolen sailboats. If we give her your files and mine, then she'll have more data to examine."

"Sounds good," Ryan agreed.

Emily used the computer to send the files to Karen while Ryan called Mango Hulsey to arrange a meeting.

CHAPTER SEVENTEEN

Dark Water was a gleaming blue-and-white Hatteras GT63 floating beside the other work vessels owned by DWR. After Greg's injury, Allen Olsen had incorporated two custom wheelchair lifts, one to the sportfisher's flying bridge and the other down to the cabin area. They had also modified the V-berth's attached head to accommodate Greg's needs.

With the boat loaded and the diesels quietly idling, Ryan and Shelly pulled the big hull tight against the dock and tied its lines fast. Greg rolled close to the boat and transferred onto the waist-high gunwale. Ryan hoisted the wheelchair over to the boat deck and Shelly stabilized Greg as he swung his legs over the gunwale and transferred back into his chair.

Greg used the lift to the bridge while the others tossed the lines off. Shelly then guided them from the dock slip into Galveston Bay.

Ryan folded up the lift platform and secured it with a built-in clamp before he climbed the ladder to the bridge. Greg sat to the left of Shelly. Chuck Newland spread out on the settee on the right-side of the bridge. The cute, little brunette with big doe-brown eyes, sitting beside him, wore cut off denim shorts and an orange bikini top. Chuck introduced her as Marlene Thorn. Emily sat down beside her, and the two women chatted. Ryan stood to Shelly's right, watching the radar and sonar screens while scanning the high volume of sportfishing boats, pleasure crafts, and massive freighters entering and exiting Galveston Bay via Bolivar Roads, the stretch of water between Galveston and Goat Islands.

Shelly brought the big boat up on plane and set the throttles low, keeping the speed down as they navigated into the open ocean. When the boat was through the heavy traffic, Shelly turned the wheel over to Ryan. He changed headings to the southwest, running offshore toward deep water.

He felt at home on the powerful boat and loved being on the open ocean. His bare feet gripped the deck and his knees flexed with the roll of the hull. He enjoyed having the power of the twin 1,900-horsepower diesels at hand, but he missed the snap of canvas overhead and the quiet rush of water along the hull of his sailboat.

"You guys want to run baits on the way down?" Ryan asked.

Chuck got up to tend to the outriggers. "That's what we came for, right?"

"There won't be any parting gifts like the last trip." Ryan grinned.

"One can only hope," Chuck replied. His eyebrows danced behind mirrored aviator sunglasses. He slapped Ryan on the back.

Ryan shook his head in amusement. "You're hopeless, Chuck. Greg, you want the helm?"

"Sure," he answered and transferred from his wheelchair into the captain's seat.

Chuck and Ryan spread the outriggers and rigged fishing poles with baits to catch mahi-mahi while Greg slowed the boat to trolling speed. Within ten minutes of putting bait in the water, they were hooked up and spent the next few hours catching fish. All six crew members took turns landing the hard-fighting dorados.

It was twilight when they turned into Aransas Pass. A few minutes later, they rounded Cline Point and entered Port Aransas Harbor.

"Where are we going, Ryan?" Greg asked.

"I made reservations at the pier off Virginia's On the Bay." He pointed at the dock extending over the water behind a restaurant on their port side. Greg steered for the dock while Shelly called the restaurant on the VHF radio. They answered immediately, giving Greg a slip number and sending a man to catch their lines.

Greg guided the big boat toward the pier and spun it around by manipulating the engines, the wheel, and the bow thrusters. He then backed up to the dock where a man used hand signals to help guide him in. Greg revved the engines into forward and slowed the boat, so the bumpers Ryan and Emily had hung off the transom just kissed the dock.

The dockhand gave Greg two thumbs-up before catching the line Emily tossed, while Ryan hopped out of the boat and snugged his bow line to a cleat.

Ryan handed the guy a palmed ten-dollar bill. "Thanks."

"No problem. My name's Carl if you need any help."

"I think we're good, Carl," he replied, turning back onto the Hatteras.

Carl walked back up the dock toward the restaurant.

Greg shut down the engines and put the hard covers over the instrument screens. Chuck unfolded the lift and ran it up to the bridge. Greg rode down and went into the salon. Ryan hooked the boat up to the electric and water then helped make a dinner of steaks and mixed vegetables.

With dinner and dishes done, Ryan used a hose to rinse the salt off the front deck, windshields, and flying bridge. He'd learned early in his days as a sailor that a good fresh water rinse went a long way toward corrosion prevention.

As night fell, the men gathered on the back deck. Ryan sat in the fighting chair, Chuck on the settee, and Greg locked his brakes near the starboard gunwale. Chuck produced a cigar case and offered Alec Bradley cigars. They passed a lighter and puffed on their stogies, drank beer, and told war stories.

The women sat in the salon and talked rather than listen to the men tell tall tales.

CHAPTER EIGHTEEN

At 11:30 the next morning, the group walked up to the restaurant. Ryan and Chuck helped the waitress move several tables together on the outdoor patio. After they took their seats, they ordered drinks and waited for their guests to arrive.

The waitress delivered their drinks and at the same time ushered a man and a woman to the table. The man was five feet ten and weighed close to two hundred pounds. It was easy to see he spent time in the gym and was physically fit. His blond hair fell past his ears, and his green eyes evaluated everyone at the table with a quick glance. What shocked Ryan was the below-the-knee prosthetic on the man's right leg. The prosthesis cup was painted to look like an American flag and a titanium shaft ran down to his running shoe. His wife was a full head shorter than him with mid-back-length dirty blonde hair, watery green eyes, and a lean runner's physique.

Ryan rose from the table and extended his hand. "I'm Ryan Weller." He pointed at each person around the table while introducing them.

"Nice to meet everyone, I'm Mango Hulsey and this is Jennifer."

"What kind of chair do you have?" Mango asked Greg as he and Jennifer sat down beside the paraplegic.

Greg pushed back from the table. "It's a TiLite ZRA, all titanium."

"That's a sweet ride, bro. I've got an Invacare aluminum job, not as fancy as yours."

"You're lucky to be walking around," Greg said.

"Indeed, I am." Mango squeezed his wife's hand and she returned his smile.

Jennifer turned to Emily. "Do you work for DWR?"

"Oh, gosh, no!" Emily said. "I'm an insurance investigator for Ward and Young, your boat's insurer."

Jennifer opened her mouth and started to speak. Anger and revulsion spread across her face. Mango put his hand on hers and shook his head.

Jennifer wasn't placated. Irritation colored her words. "It would be nice if you paid our claim."

"That's why I'm here," Emily replied, her smile now plastic. "We're working on your case."

Ryan intervened by saying, "Tell me about your high-seas escapades."

Mango took a deep breath and was about to begin when Jennifer asked, "Why is a commercial diving outfit interested in our sailboat?"

Greg took the question before anyone else had a chance. "Inside the company, we're working on building a new operation for recovering small boats and yachts. We see a niche for salvage of noncommercial craft."

Mango fixed Greg with a stare. "I wasn't born yesterday, bro. I think you're both former military and you're investigating either a drug or gunrunning operation in the Gulf of Mexico."

"Guilty on all counts," Greg replied.

"What branch?"

"Navy EOD," Ryan answered. "Were you military?"

"Coast Guard Maritime Security Response Team."

His answer amazed Ryan. The MSRT was the Coast Guard's equivalent to Special Forces, specializing in direct action counter-terrorism. They were extensively trained to handle any type of maritime security issue and considered by many to be the best in their field.

"We worked with several of the MSRT teams during our time in," Greg said.

"I worked with SEAL teams," Mango said matter-of-factly.

"Great," Jennifer cut in. "If you're done having a pissing contest, what do you need?"

"Tell us what happened," Ryan said.

Mango leaned back in his chair and sipped his light beer. "We left here and sailed down to the Yucatán Peninsula. We spent two weeks in Cancún and Cozumel before we started for the Cayman Islands. A couple of hours offshore, a Mexican patrol boat hailed us. They came alongside, and I tried to wave them off. I realized they weren't Navy even though they wore the uniforms." He glanced over at Jennifer. "They came right alongside, and a guy hopped on our boat and grabbed Jennifer by the hair. That's when I pulled out my gun and shot him. They all pulled out guns and started shooting. I took out the guy I thought was the leader and then pumped lead into their engines and inflatable hull."

Ryan watched Jennifer. She'd been very assertive

earlier in the conversation. As her husband talked, her eyes became glassy.

"Then I grabbed Jennifer and shoved her into the dinghy we kept on the rear davits. I reloaded and kept their heads down while she got the engine going and we took off." He fixed his gaze on Emily. "I chose not to stay with the sailboat because they were continually trying to board us, and our boat sustained multiple hits to the hull and rigging. The dinghy was the faster method of escape."

"Is this the boat they were on?" Ryan took a picture from a folder and spun it for them to see.

Both Hulseys nodded in agreement.

Next, Ryan asked, "What were the Mexicans wearing?"

"They were dressed in black combat gear with *Marina* across the chest of their bulletproof vests," Mango said. "They wore Mexican flags for shoulder patches on the right shoulders and a weird-looking patch on the left."

"This one?" Ryan showed them a picture of the Aztlán patch.

"That's the one," Mango confirmed.

"Did you get a look at the men?" Emily asked.

"They all wore masks," Jennifer said. Ryan saw her eyes had cleared.

"Balaclavas," Mango corrected.

Ryan asked, "Anything else you can tell us that stuck out in your mind?"

"I always thought it was strange a Mexican patrol boat was so far from land. My guess is they were operating off a mothership. I didn't see anything on the radar, ours only had a five-mile limit." He shrugged. "Plus, I've seen that patch before. I was stationed out in San Diego before I joined the MSRT and we had a run-in with what I thought were smugglers. CGIS found a patch and Navy uniforms on their boat. Under interrogation, the men admitted they were taking their wares to a group called Brown Berets."

"What's CGIS?" Shelly asked.

"Coast Guard Investigative Service," Greg, Mango, and Ryan said in unison, and then burst out laughing.

Emily broke up the laughter. "When I was a sheriff's deputy, we had run-ins with Brown Berets. They're a Mexican separatist group advocating for the return of Aztlán. They have chapters in every major city in the US."

"Let me get this straight," Greg said. "The pirates are dressed like Mexican sailors and they're connected to a separatist group? It sounds like they want to place the blame on the Mexican Navy?"

"What good would come from the deception?" Shelly asked.

"If these pirates want to retake parts of the United States, it would be helpful if Mexico and the United States were at odds." Mango picked up his beer and set it down. "If they create friction between the two countries, it might not take long for it to escalate into a war. We're already at each other's throats over a border wall and illegal immigration."

"If someone would supply Brown Berets with weapons, they'd have a readymade army," Ryan added.

"Can someone really do that?" Chuck wanted to know.

"Look what ISIS is doing in the Middle East and in our country," Greg shot back.

Chuck held up his hands in defense.

Ryan said, "It's all speculation until we go out there and find these guys." The group was silent for a minute and Ryan continued, "What if the bombings in Texas and Los Angeles are the work of this Brown Beret group."

"Why would you say that?" Mango asked.

Greg said, "ISIS already claimed responsibility for the bombings, and all the evidence the FBI has collected points to Middle Eastern terrorists."

Ryan shrugged. "I always thought ISIS would follow the same plan as Al-Qaeda, target financial and political centers to do maximum damage to U.S. infrastructure. These targets are in the Southwest, the heart of Aztlán."

"What are you saying, Ryan?" Emily asked.

"Maybe it's a conspiracy."

"Oh no. Here we go!" Greg exclaimed. "These guys aren't grassy knoll shooters and New World Order buffs." He waggled a finger at his friend and employee. "Ryan, here, believes that crap."

Mango laughed. "Some of it's true, Greg."

"Great, another nut," Greg muttered.

When lunch wrapped up and they were leaving the restaurant, Mango cornered Ryan outside. "I want in."

"In on what?" Ryan asked innocently.

"Whatever you're doing to track down these pirates. I got sidelined from the action by this stupid leg. I need a job to get out of the house. Jennifer's driving me crazy. I mean, I love her, but I need some space. You know what I mean, bro?"

Ryan nodded but didn't know what Mango meant.

"I'm qualified to run boats, scuba dive, shoot a gun, and jump out of a plane, if need be. There aren't too many civilian jobs that fit those qualifications, you know what I mean?"

This time, Ryan knew what he meant and said so. He had the same skill set.

"Just keep me in mind if you run into trouble," Mango pleaded.

"I will, Mango. By the way, what's with the name?"

Mango shook his head. "My parents named me after Clint Eastwood's character in the Man with No Name series. In the movie *For a Few Dollars More*, the innkeeper calls Eastwood Manco, but they misheard it and named me Mango."

It was Ryan's turn to shake his head at the craziness. "I'll keep you in mind. If nothing else, DWR could use a good diver, or security man. The Olsens have made a habit of hiring former military to fill positions. I'll put in a good word."

"That would be awesome, bro," Mango replied as he walked with Ryan toward the dock where everyone else had crowded around the Hatteras.

Shelly was showing Greg's bridge lift to Jennifer when the two men walked up. From the flying bridge, Shelly called down, "Do you guys want to go fishing?"

"Absolutely," Jennifer exclaimed.

"Let's go," Mango agreed. "Permission to come aboard?"

"Come on, Puddle Pirate," Greg yelled.

"Hey, Coastie, can you handle the lines?" Chuck called down from the bridge. "These Navy boys haven't unmoored a boat since boot camp."

"Step back, squids," Mango said, "and let a professional line handler show you how it's done."

It wasn't uncommon for service men to hassle each other over their decision to join a particular branch. They believed all other branches were inferior to their own. The service branches had been rivals since their inception, and each service had derogatory nicknames for the other.

"Don't let him fool you, Mango. Chuck was in the Air Force," Greg chided his friend.

"Say it ain't so, a wing nut!" Mango said.

"I am," Chuck replied, "and I'll let you guys do the work while I drink beer,"

"We expect nothing less from the Chair Force," Ryan groused as he tossed off the lines and climbed aboard.

Shelly engaged the drives and they headed for open ocean where the men's good-natured ribbing spilled over to their fishing skills or lack thereof.

CHAPTER NINETEEN

Dark Water had been back at the dock behind Virginia's for thirty minutes when Ryan, who was standing on the bridge, heard his phone ring. He had a brief conversation of yeses, nos, and okays before hanging up. He lit a cigarette and looked over the rail at Mango who was standing on the finger pier, talking to Greg and Chuck.

"Hey, Coastie, got a minute?"

"Yeah." Mango stepped aboard the boat and made his way up the ladder to the bridge. "What's up?"

"I spoke to my DHS contact. He says if you want in, you're in. He ran a background check on you and liked what he saw. I work for DWR, but that's just a cover for doing work for Homeland."

"All right, bro." Mango high-fived Ryan. "I suspected something like that."

"The plan was for Greg to run the show, but he can't do it. DWR brought me in to help, and they told me to be on the lookout for someone I thought would make a good addition to the team. You're it."

Mango looked out across the water and nodded.

Ryan could see he was ready to jump on the opportunity. "Take your time and talk to Jennifer if you need to."

"I don't need to talk to her. I'm in."

"Good. I have an idea about how to track down these gunrunners who stole your boat."

"I'm all ears."

"I want to outline it for everyone."

They climbed down from the bridge and gathered the group in the salon, except for Chuck and Marlene who went to the bar for a drink. When everyone had found a place to sit, Ryan took the stage.

"First for Jennifer's benefit, Greg and I work for Homeland Security through Dark Water Research. I spoke with my contact at Homeland, and he agreed I could hire your husband."

Jennifer looked at her husband. "When did you decide this?"

"A few minutes ago, when Ryan offered me a job."

She nodded, but in a womanly way which said, *we'll talk about this later*.

"We're investigating sailboat thefts in the Gulf of Mexico. We believe they're connected to arms trafficking. Emily's friend just sent us her research, which shows most of the boat hijackings are taking place off the Yucatán Peninsula. Emily has it on her phone if you want to look at the map.

"The consensus is the hijackers are using RIB boats off a mothership. My plan is for me and Mango to take my sailboat into the Gulf and bait one of these RIBs into attacking us. We'll overpower the men and do a little interrogation to figure out what's going on."

Everyone began voicing their objections at once. It took Ryan a minute to quiet the room.

Greg crossed his arms. "I don't like it."

Meeting his stare, Ryan asked, "How else are we going to infiltrate these guys?"

Jennifer said, "I don't like this plan either, Mango. You already lost a leg and we agreed you wouldn't do anything like this again."

"I know." He looked pleadingly at his wife. "This is a job and you wanted me to find something to do."

She crossed her arms and locked eyes with her husband. "Fine."

Everyone in the room knew it was not fine.

"You have a sailboat?" Emily asked.

Ryan nodded. "I have a thirty-six-foot Sabre."

Greg gave his partner the stink eye. "Your boat's still in Wilmington, correct?"

"Yes," Ryan replied. "We'll have Chuck fly us there."

"It'll take two months for you to get into position," Greg said.

"No, it won't," Ryan countered. "It shouldn't take us more than three weeks, tops. We'll run offshore down the East Coast and then cut across Florida on the Okeechobee Waterway to Fort Myers. From there we can make the crossing to Cancún."

"Great, it's settled then," Greg said, throwing his hands up in the air.

Shelly gave Greg a look to tell him to keep out of it and gave Ryan a little shrug to say, *I don't know what his problem is.* Ryan knew exactly what Greg's problem was. He wanted to be in on the action. He didn't want to be trapped in an office, staring at the walls while someone else was out prowling for trouble. Greg wanted to be out fighting and diving and running the show.

"Has Landis approved this little scheme?" Greg asked.

Ryan said, "Not in detail, but he gave me the green light."

Mango asked, "How soon do we leave?"

"That's up to you," Ryan answered. "The sooner the better. How soon can you be ready?"

"I need to pack a bag and I can leave with you from here," Mango said.

"What about you, Jennifer?" Ryan asked. "Want to ride with us down to Florida?"

"I'd like that." She turned to Emily. "Are you going?"

"This is the first I've heard of this plan," Emily said. "I'll need to ask my boss for more time off work."

"Ain't this a party," Greg said with defeat in his voice.

Ryan put a hand on Greg's shoulder. "Buck up, buddy, we need someone to watch our back, and there's no one I'd rather have." He squatted by the wheelchair. "I have a GPS tracker on my boat. If something goes awry, you can track the boat to the mothership and send in the cavalry."

"I still don't like it," Greg huffed.

"I know you don't, but this is the best I've got," Ryan said. "Monday, I'm going up to Austin to meet with a Professor Rueben Morales. He'll give me the scoop on Aztlán. After the meeting, we'll fly to Wilmington and get the boat."

"If your theory is right about these guys building a Mexican army, you better hurry," Greg said. He still didn't like the idea of Ryan and Mango sailing into the sunset after pirates, but he'd come to terms with the idea. It was what needed done.

Ryan said, "We'll do our best."

CHAPTER TWENTY

Chuck Newland set the Beechcraft King Air down at the Austin-Bergstrom airport just after one p.m. Monday. He taxied it to a stop outside a private terminal. The four passengers walked into the terminal while Chuck saw to the plane's needs. Ryan took an Uber northeast through the city. Both Emily and Mango had insisted on accompanying him to the meeting. Ryan told them Landis had arranged the meeting and Morales had agreed to see only him.

When Ryan called Landis to have him check Mango's background, he had also asked him to find someone he could talk to about Aztlán. He wanted a better understanding of what he might be dealing with. During their return to Texas City on the Hatteras, Ryan had used the internet to do more research about Aztlán and the various groups calling for the unification of ancestral lands, but he wanted a professional's opinion. Landis had scheduled an appointment with Morales, a professor at the Center for Mexican-American Studies at the University of Texas. Morales held a PhD in anthropology and had recently published a paper entitled *Historical Heritage and the Legend of Aztlán*. Ryan smiled at the memory of Emily interrupting his research and their not-so-clandestine love-making in his bunk room.

The professor lived in a ranch-style home near the university campus. Morales answered the door and ushered his guest inside. Ryan followed him through a recently remodeled open-concept living room and kitchen to a concrete patio surrounding a clear blue pool, edged with lush flowers. The man wore khaki slacks, brown loafers, and a light green dress shirt. He'd rolled the shirt sleeves to his elbows and left the top three buttons unfastened. He sported a trim goatee and long white hair pulled back in a ponytail. His brown eyes stared at his guest from behind wire-rimmed glasses.

"Please, Mr. Weller, have a seat." He gestured to a chair at the head of the table as he pulled out a chair for himself.

Ryan sat down at the rectangular glass-topped patio table.

"A drink?" Morales asked, leaning forward to pour lemonade from a sweating pitcher into two glasses.

"Thank you, sir."

"Please, call me Rueben."

Ryan leaned forward to examine a medallion nestled in the curls of the professor's white chest hair. "A Spanish *real de a ocho*?"

Morales lifted the coin and chain over his head and laid it on the table. Ryan picked it up.

"It is not a Spanish piece of eight, as you suggest, rather a silver Mexican eight-*reales* coin, minted after Mexico's independence from Spain in 1821. They manufactured this coin until 1918 when the peso was introduced." He took the coin and chain from Ryan and settled it back around his neck. "When I spoke to your supervisor, he said you were interested in Aztlán."

"That's correct."

"You aren't a student at the university. What piques your interest in Chicano heritage?"

"I'm investigating the theft of sailboats in the Gulf of Mexico. Reports show the pirates wore a patch like this." Ryan pulled a paper from his pocket and smoothed it on the table. It was a computer-generated copy of the Aztlán patch worn by the pirates as described by Philip Nagel and the Hulseys.

Morales picked up the printout and studied it for a few moments, while sipping his cold lemonade.

"What do you think?" Ryan asked.

The older man snorted. "What people do in the name of Aztlán no longer surprises me."

"Tell me about Aztlán."

Morales leaned back in his chair and crossed his legs.

"I read your paper," Ryan said. "It was very enlightening."

Morales's eyebrows rose. "Oh, then what do you need me for?"

"I want you to fill in the gaps."

"All right." Morales sipped his drink and set it on the table. Both glasses left wet rings of condensation on the glass top.

A breeze, created by a large fan blowing across the pool, negated the spring heatwave. An umbrella provided shade along with the mature trees clustered around the patio.

"Aztlán means 'the land of the North, the land where we, the Aztecs, came from.' Which is interesting because in the ancient language of Nahuatl, where all these legends come from, no such word exists. You see, Nahuatls stress their words on the second-to-last syllable. When the Spanish began using the word, Aztlán, they placed the accent mark over the second A, shifting the stress point of the word. This is typical of several words the Spanish took from the Nahuatl language."

"Does that negate the whole business?"

The professor chuckled. "Hardly. It is only a mispronunciation. You see, the legend says the Aztecs came from 'the place of the seven caves.' One cave for each tribe of the Xochimilca, Tlahuica, Acolhua, Tlaxcalteca, Tepaneca, Chaica, and Mexica peoples. These tribes left Aztlán for various reasons. According to codices left by the Aztecs and oral histories written by Spanish priests, the Mexicas were the last to leave their homeland between 1100 and 1300 AD because of a heavy drought. Many believe the ancients moved from as far north as Utah to the Valley of Mexico. They've been searching for their homeland ever since. Where it is, or was, no one knows anymore.

"Aztlán, today, is a powerful symbol of spiritual and national unity. Because so many Chicanos and Mexicans believe their ancestors came from what is now the Southwestern United States, they would like to see it returned to Mexico."

"They believe the U.S. government stole their heritage after the Mexican-American War and then with the Gadsden Purchase," Ryan added.

"Correct," the professor replied, running a hand over his pony tail.

"What are your thoughts on the matter?"

Morales squinted his eyes and steepled his hands while he studied his guest. "The Treaty of Guadalupe Hidalgo and the Gadsden Purchase will never be overturned. Those states will never willingly turn themselves over to any

Mexican government. Civil war would erupt before that happens. But I'll tell you a secret, one which should be obvious to anyone willing to look at history. The Mexican people don't acknowledge the border. They believe the border is there to divide and conquer them. Since they don't believe in the border, they'll keep crossing as freely as they please. They'll come to the United States and take jobs and money and benefits because they believe they're entitled to them. This was their land before it became the property of the white men. Manifest destiny means slavery to them."

"What about the Brown Berets and this patch?"

"There are several groups trying to change the geopolitical culture and take back Aztlán, or the Hispanic Homeland, or the *Republica del Norte*." He waved his hands in a circle as if encompassing them in one group. "Brown Berets, *La Raza Unida*, Nation of Aztlán, are just a few who want to move the border back to where it was in 1847. They would settle for an open border if they could get it."

"That's an easy one." Ryan grinned. "Annex Mexico and make it the fifty-first state."

Morales laughed. "Not as easy as you might think."

"It would be difficult."

Morales uncrossed his legs and leaned forward. He spread his hands and looked Ryan in the eyes. "All this information is on the internet, and you read my paper. I'm sure you read many others like it, so, what exactly do you want from me, Mr. Weller?"

"Do you have information on individuals who might want to start a war with the United States to achieve their objectives of a reunited Aztlán?"

"I have my sources, Mr. Weller. None of them tell me of anyone who is amassing an army to sweep across the border and strike fear in the hearts of Americans."

"If you did, would you tell me?"

Morales shook his head as if saddened by his question. "I am but a simple professor."

Ryan now leaned forward. "A professor with ties to the Brown Berets. You give speeches at their rallies and you've been arrested for demonstrating in the streets."

The man's head jerked up, civility wiped from his eyes. "I am a professor who believes in the rights of our first citizens."

"Professor," Ryan asked, "who built the cliff dwellings at Mesa Verde? Who built the ruins at Casa Grande in Arizona?"

"No one knows."

"Could it have been the Aztecs before moving to Mexico City?"

"I don't know," Morales admitted.

"Then how can you call Chicanos and Latinos the first citizens of the United States?"

"Because they were here before the white man!" His eyes blazed with fire as he jerked forward. His face was less than a foot from Ryan's.

Ryan smiled. "Maybe the Chiricahua Apache should revolt against the invaders from the south. Perhaps the Navajo should begin raiding across the border to steal cattle and slaves like they used to. They were here before the white man. If the Mexicans can come freely into this country, then maybe their old enemies should be able to invade theirs."

Morales hissed, "You understand nothing of history, Mr. Weller."

"You're right, I'm just a simple sailor who has fought and bled for my country. What little I know about history could fill a thimble, but I do know this." Ryan stabbed a finger at the ground. "I will fight to protect my country from those who seek to do it harm, whether that's Al-Qaeda, ISIS, or a modern-day Mexican incursion. I'm looking for anyone related to this patch who might be running guns and/or drugs into the United States." He paused to gauge Morales's reaction, then plowed on. "As an American citizen and a staunch anti-Second Amendment advocate, you should be willing to fight anyone bringing illegal weapons into the country."

The professor's gaze locked with Ryan's before shifting away. He refilled his glass of lemonade and leaned back in his chair. "There are rumors of a man named Juan Herrera trying to unite the independent movements." He spread his hands for effect. "I have no idea who he is, or where he's based."

"Could he be behind these sailboat thefts?"

"I don't know. All I have is a name. We hear rumors about him at some of the rallies, but that's all."

"Thank you for your time, Professor."

Ryan stood, and Morales rose with him before leading Ryan through the house. At the door, they shook hands.

"No hard feelings, Professor, I'm just trying to do my job."

Morales' lips lifted in a thin smile, but he didn't say a word.

CHAPTER TWENTY-ONE

Morales watched Ryan Weller step into a midsize sedan. He knew someone would eventually connect the sailboat thefts to the Aztlán movement. He hadn't expected the investigator to drive right up to his front door and tell him of his suspicions.

The professor ran a hand over his head and his fingers wrapped around his ponytail, stroking the thick ring of hair as the car drove away. He closed the door and stepped into a home office. He opened a desk drawer, removed a cell phone, and dialed the only number stored in its memory.

"*Hola, amigo.*" The voice of Arturo Guerrero came over the line.

"*Tenemous uno vecino entrometido.*" *We have a nosy neighbor.*

"What does he know?"

"He suspects the sailboat thefts are connected to the Aztlán movement because of the patch your gunrunners like to wear. I warned you not to let them wear it."

"Relax, Rueben." Guerrero's voice was always smooth

and calm. It took a lot to rile the man. "What does he really know?"

Morales took a deep breath to steady his nerves. "He knows men wearing Mexican Navy uniforms have been stealing sailboats and he believes they're bringing guns into the United States. He has a copy of the patch."

Morales heard Guerrero let out a long sigh. "Rueben, he's fishing for answers. How did he get your name?"

"Through my work at the university."

"He has no way of knowing your part of the movement. If it would make you comfortable, you may have several men follow him."

"Yes, thank you."

"If he knows more than he should, eliminate him."

"*Sí*, Arturo."

The line went dead, and Morales put the phone back in the desk drawer. He picked up a second cell phone and called a number from its memory.

"Fernando, I have a job for two of your men. I want a man followed and, if need be, eliminated."

"*Sí*, Professor."

Morales gave Fernando Ryan Weller's name and emailed a photo he clipped from his home's video surveillance feed.

CHAPTER TWENTY-TWO

Ryan had the Uber driver drop him at Austin's private aviation terminal. He needed time to digest what he and Morales had talked about. He walked around the airport until he found a chair offering some relative privacy. Then he sat and dialed Floyd Landis's number.

"Whataya got?" the DHS man asked as a way of greeting.

Ryan pictured Landis sitting in his rumpled, cheap suit, leaning back in a government-issued office chair with one foot propped on the open top drawer of his desk. His hard eyes would be focused on a notepad while his beefy hand clicked the ball point of a government-issued pen in and out.

"I just spoke to Professor Rueben Morales. He gave me the name of a Mexican national, Juan Herrera."

"Never heard of him. What's he involved in?"

"I'm not sure, but he may be connected to our sailboat thefts."

"What's your supporting theory?"

"I asked Morales if anyone was uniting Chicano independence groups. Our pirates are wearing Aztlán patches, someone has to be coordinating the effort."

"I'll consider it. What else?"

"Mango and I are flying to Wilmington to get my Sabre. Then we're going trolling for pirates."

"Why not use a sailboat already in Houston?"

"Are you authorized to drop a hundred grand on a boat?"

"No," Landis snorted. "How soon will you be leaving for Wilmington?"

"Floyd, was the mansion attack really the work of ISIS?"

Landis chuckled. "Yes, we've found definitive proof our tangos were ISIS affiliates. Keep working the sailboats and the gunrunning, Ryan."

The Texas Governor's Mansion was not a high-value political or military target like the World Trade Center or the Pentagon. It was, however, a soft target, and the hit proved the terrorists could strike anywhere and disrupt life.

To fill the long pause, Landis asked, "Why?"

"What if our gunrunners are tied to the bombing at the mansion? If they're connected to Aztlán and they're bringing in weapons to arm various Chicano separatist groups, they could form a veritable army capable of causing mass disruption in the US. If their goal was to gain control of the border states, wouldn't a bombing campaign be an effective way to start it?"

Landis was definitive. "The guys who did the mansion and Century City were from the Middle East, not Mexico."

"Just something to consider. I don't know how it all fits together and maybe I'm way off base."

"Keep working the sailboat thefts. That's the only way you'll find out."

"Can we put surveillance on Morales?"

"I can't put assets on the guy based on a hunch."

"Okay," Ryan conceded. "Let me know what you get on Herrera."

"I will and keep me updated on your travel progress."

"Will do." Ryan ended the call and Googled Juan Herrera. There were seventy-four million hits with the two most popular being a Cleveland Indians' baseball player and a U.S. poet laureate. He swore and stuffed his phone in his pocket. What did he expect, the man's picture and an X marking his hideout along with a detailed terrorism curriculum vitae?

Mango's comment about the gunrunning Mexicans and the two bombings helped connect dots in his mind. If a group wanted to reclaim Aztlán at gunpoint—which was the only way he could see it happening—they would have to take a page from Al-Qaeda and start a bombing campaign to bring attention to their cause.

"Excuse me, sir," an elderly lady said. Her Southern-accented voice quivered with age. She was staring down at him as he leaned forward with his elbows on his knees, lost in thought.

Ryan looked at the long row of empty seats and then back up at the lady. She wore a pillbox hat with black lace hanging down in front of Coke-bottle-thick horn-rimmed glasses. A black gloved hand clutched an equally dark roll-around suitcase. The rest of her outfit consisted of a black dress, stockings, and shoes.

"Is there a funeral?" he asked.

"Look, sonny, don't give me no guff. Now, ya gonna move or ain't ya?"

Ryan stood and swept his right arm out in a be-my-guest gesture.

The lady looked him up and down and grunted, "Hmph."

"There you are, Mrs. Anderson." A tall man in a flight uniform, with the four stripes of a captain on his shoulder boards, approached.

"What took ya so long, Kenneth?" she demanded as she shoved her suitcase at him.

Ryan shook his head and walked across the terminal to find Chuck. As they walked out to the Beechcraft, Ryan saw the old lady being led up the steps of a Learjet.

Chuck used his head to point at the scene. "That's Thelma Anderson. She's worth about two billion."

CHAPTER TWENTY-THREE

Alex Hernandez and Luis Martinez exited the car and walked along a row of hangars to the small office coordinating all the fixed-base operations for private aviation in and out of Pearland Regional Airport, a light-aircraft commuter facility just south of Houston, where DWR kept its plane. Both men wore business suits and carried Glock 19 pistols in retention holsters on their right hips.

Hernandez opened the office door and held it for his partner. Behind a desk sat an overweight woman with blonde hair held back off her forehead with pink barrettes.

Her voice was nasally. "How may I help you, gentlemen?"

Martinez stepped to the desk and pulled off his sunglasses. He read the woman's name off a desk plate. "Cynthia, can you tell me where the DWR plane went?"

The blonde gave them a suspicious look, glancing at Martinez and then back to Hernandez. "That information isn't available to the public."

"I'm not the general public, Cynthia." Martinez flipped

open a badge and allowed her to look at it for several seconds before he snapped the case shut.

Cynthia yelled over her shoulder without taking her eyes off Martinez, "Tony."

A short, thin man with a wispy comb over appeared in the doorway behind Cynthia. "What?"

"This man says he's a cop and wants flight information for DWR."

"Did you give it to him?"

"Sure, Tony," she replied sarcastically, "that's why I called for you."

"I'm sorry, sir." Tony approached the desk. "We need a warrant to give out that information."

Martinez eyed the small man for a minute then turned and exited the office with Hernandez on his heels. They stood outside discussing their next move. Hernandez kept glancing through an office window to stare at Cynthia. Tony had disappeared back into his office.

"We should ask worker," Hernandez grunted.

Martinez agreed, and they walked across the taxiway, between hangars, to the refueling building. They stepped inside and found a man in his early twenties leaning against a fuel truck with his hands in the pockets of his dirty, blue coveralls.

"Where Dark Water Research plane went?" Hernandez barked.

"Man, you know I can't be telling people about that kinda stuff. Get outta here."

Martinez produced a wallet and extracted a one-hundred-dollar bill. The kid's eyes grew bigger.

"You tell, we give." Hernandez leaned against the truck beside the younger man.

The kid's eyes bounced between Martinez, Hernandez,

and the one-hundred-dollar bill. His feet grew shifty. "Ah, c'mon, man."

"You don't need da money?" Hernandez asked.

"Yeah, hey, man, I could use the extra dough." The kid reached for the money.

Martinez pulled it back. "You tell, you get da money."

"Yeah, okay." The kid wiped his forehead with a rag and looked around the building. He saw no one else. "They, like, flew to Wilmington, North Carolina, man." He snatched the money from Martinez's fingers and shoved the bill into the breast pocket of his coveralls.

"What they do in North Carolina?"

"I don't know, man. All I do is gas up the plane. Chuck, the pilot, wanted some extra fuel and I looked at where he was going, that's all, man, like, I swear." He held up his hands.

"You chur you don't know no more?" Hernandez leaned in closer.

Martinez wiggled another hundred from his billfold.

"Man, I swear." The kid stared greedily at the money. "Like, I don't know no more. Like I said, they went to North Carolina."

"What they do there?"

"I don't know, man, come on." The kid fidgeted with his hands. "Like, I don't know any more." He was almost pleading with the two Mexicans to leave him alone.

"Who else on plane."

"Like, two dudes and two chicks besides Chuck. I never saw them before. That's all."

"When they come back?"

"Chuck'll be back tomorrow, man."

Martinez let the bill slip from his fingers. It fluttered to the floor with the kid's gaze fixed to it.

The two Mexicans walked out of the fuel building and into the sunshine. Martinez pulled a phone from his pocket and dialed Morales.

"Weller and three others took a flight to Wilmington, North Carolina."

"I'll have two plane tickets waiting for you at the American Airlines desk at the Houston airport. Weller has family in Wilmington. I'll text you the address."

"We're on our way," Martinez said.

"Keep me up to date, Luis."

"Yes, sir." The phone line went dead. The two men were already in the car, heading for George Bush Intercontinental.

CHAPTER TWENTY-FOUR

The 1985 Sabre 36 sailboat, *Sweet T*, sat on blocks at the Wrightsville Beach Marina storage yard. Ryan had covered her in tarps, pulled tight around the bottom of the hull with bungee cords and rope, before moving to Texas. To Ryan, she looked in sad shape. Out of water, the boat seemed to flounder awkwardly with her long keel drooping from her belly. In the water, she looked sleek and regal.

Mango and Ryan pulled a tarp back from the hull, so Ryan could access the cabin. He was leaning a ladder against her rub rail when they heard a gruff voice, heavy with Irish brogue, call out, "Who's tryin' ta steal me lad's boot?"

"No one's stealing your boot, Henry," Ryan replied to the old man.

"Come here, lad." The old man grabbed Ryan in a bear hug then held him at arm's length. "You not tell me you come for your boot. What's with you nowadays, Ryan?"

"We're taking her to Houston."

"That's but a wee journey for this lass." He slapped *Sweet T*'s hull.

"Henry, meet Mango Hulsey. Mango, this is Henry O'Shannassy. Mango's helping me crew."

The two men shook hands. Mango said, "Nice to meet you, Henry."

"Likewise, lad." He looked down at Mango's titanium leg. "War souvenir?"

"Got it during a ship-boarding incident in the Persian Gulf."

"SEALs?"

"No, Henry." Ryan laughed. "I befriended a Puddle Pirate."

"I've no beef with da Coasties. Pulled me out of da drink a time or two, they did." He slapped Mango on the shoulder. "Ready to get dis lass in da water?"

"You bet, Henry." Ryan grinned. "Her hull's a little too dry."

Henry unclipped a walkie-talkie from his belt and used it to call for the travel lift. The giant boat lift lumbered over *Sweet T* and took her in its slings. Ryan always held his breath when they moved his boat like this. Even though the men running the lift were professionals, one slip and the boat would be ruined. The lift drove out onto the cement quays and lowered the Sabre into the water. Ryan leaped aboard and pulled the straps free, and once again the sailboat floated majestically in the water.

"Aye, there's none a prettier sight," Henry quipped as Mango and Ryan leaped aboard to move her to a transient pier.

Back at the office, Ryan paid for storage and the boat move.

"Come back to me office, lads." Henry motioned for them to follow him behind the counter to a back room.

"I'm going to grab a cup of coffee, you want one?" Ryan asked.

"No," Mango replied.

"You know how I like it, lad," Henry answered.

"I know. Black like your soul."

"Aye and black it tis." He laughed.

It was a line Ryan had used most of his adult life. Sometimes his soul felt as black as the cups of hot coffee he carried into the office.

Mango listened to Henry tell stories about a young Ryan Weller. After they caught up on their lives and lies, Ryan and Mango bid farewell to Henry and climbed on the sailboat. They sat on the cockpit benches.

Mango, sitting across from Ryan, stretched his legs across the gap and propped his feet on the bench beside Ryan. "An interesting guy."

"I've known Henry for as long as I can remember. He retired from the Navy as a Senior Chief after twenty-five years. He was a diver back when men were iron, and ships were wood. When I was thinking about joining the service, he was the guy I talked to."

"I joined right out of high school," Mango said. "A recruiter came to my school in Indiana. I liked his pitch, so I joined up. I had no desire to go to college. Now, I think Jennifer would like me to use the G.I. Bill."

"What about getting another boat?"

Mango spread his hands and shrugged. "I think she's for it, but we're still waiting on your girlfriend to come through on the insurance."

Ryan lit a cigarette, cupping it in his hands against the breeze.

"I thought you told Emily you would quit on this trip."

"I am." Ryan grinned around the cigarette clamped in his teeth. "Starting tomorrow."

"Sure, that's what they all say." Mango rolled his eyes.

CHAPTER TWENTY-FIVE

Hernandez and Martinez watched the two men lock the sailboat, walk off the pier, and continue down Marina Street to a restaurant. Earlier, when Martinez had seen Ryan putting a sailboat into the water, he'd left Hernandez to keep watch and found an electronics store. He purchased a GPS tracking unit with a six-month battery life. The device came with a tracking monitor capable of pinpointing the sending unit anywhere within a five-mile range.

Martinez carried the hockey-puck-size sending unit in his pocket. It would be best if he could wire it into the boat's power supply, but he knew he wouldn't have the time to do the work, and they could easily detect the device if something went wrong with the boat's small electrical system.

With Hernandez as a lookout, Martinez picked the lock on the cabin door and slipped inside. He placed the GPS transmitter in the engine room, using the adhesive backing on the unit to hold it in place. He verified it was working by checking the receiving unit then slipped out, careful not to disturb anything, and relocked the cabin door. Then he ambled back to where Hernandez waited. They continued to their car and drove to a hotel where Martinez again verified the signal and reported their progress to Professor Morales.

CHAPTER TWENTY-SIX

Bald Head Island slid by *Sweet T*'s port side. The tiny community and lighthouse marked the end of the Cape Fear River and the beginning of the treacherous Frying Pan Shoals where many a ship had wrecked since Europeans first began exploring the eastern coast of what would become the United States.

Ryan, Mango, and Jennifer had spent the better part of the morning traveling down the Intracoastal Waterway, through Snow's Cut and into the Cape Fear River. It was a trip Ryan had made countless times in both sailboats and powerboats, and he still enjoyed it. He felt he would have enjoyed this trip more if Emily had accompanied them. She'd flown back to Tampa, late last evening, at the request of her boss. Before she left, she'd huddled with Jennifer, and the two women had conspiratorial smiles on their faces when they'd come back to the table where the two couples were having dinner with Henry O'Shannassy and Ryan's parents. Neither woman would divulge the nature of the secret, and Ryan had not pressed Emily when he dropped her off at the airport. He was sad to see her go, and he missed her company.

Mango rose to stand on the deck, one hand fingering the mainsail halyard. He, too, had the smell of salt in his nose and was eager to be under sail. The bow rose and fell on two-foot rollers. Mango looked back at Ryan and Jennifer with a grin on his face.

The captain grinned back, feet planted wide against the waves, hands loose on the wheel. "Let 'er fly!"

"Aye aye," Mango cried and ripped the line from the cleat, hauling it hand over hand.

The sail sprang up the mast, snapping open with the breeze. Ryan turned the boat into a close reach as Mango unfurled the jib. The sheet snapped taut. Mango locked the line in a cleat and sat on the bench beside Jennifer and spread his arms across the back of the seat.

"This is the life, bro," Mango said behind sunglasses and a grin.

Ryan tightened the sheet, making the little Sabre heel over further, which increased their speed. "We have a few days to enjoy ourselves before pirate watch. It's a little over four hundred nautical miles between here and Stuart, Florida, where we'll catch the Okeechobee Waterway to Fort Myers."

"Then it's Gulf sailing."

"You ever go anywhere else besides Cancún on your boat?" Ryan asked.

Mango leaned his head back. "We did two short trips over to the Florida panhandle. Then we just went for it. What's it like making it all the way around the world?"

"Incredible. Some days, I wonder why I'm still working. Right now, I'm tempted to finish this job and sail off into the sunset."

"What did you do for money on your trip?" Jennifer asked.

"I had a modest savings account, plus Mom and Dad gave me money they'd set aside for a college fund. Guess it was clear I wasn't going to get a degree. Anyway, I was a divemaster at some Pacific resorts and waited tables for six months in Australia."

Mango said, "I get a little disability money from the VA and we have some savings. We were just going to be frugal, eat from the sea."

"I did that, too. Lots of fish and lobster, crabs, and shrimp. I'd shoot fish with a spear gun and trade it for vegetables and rice if I could. What are you doing now to make ends meet?"

"Jennifer is a nurse, so she's going back to work," Mango said. He squeezed Jennifer's shoulders and she gave a tight smile. "I haven't done much. Like I said, not much call for a one-legged guy with a special forces' skill set in the real world. Thanks to you, I'm getting paid to move a sailboat around and get justice on some pirates."

"Don't thank me yet." Ryan shook his head. "We don't know what kind of trouble we'll get into. You know the saying about best laid plans."

"Yeah, Murphy's Law—if anything can go wrong, it will."

Jennifer groaned, "Don't jinx the trip."

CHAPTER TWENTY-SEVEN

Before leaving Wilmington, Ryan had arranged for a slip at Sunset Bay Marina in Stuart, Florida. The transient marina, at the mouth of the St. Lucie River, required advanced booking because of the heavy water traffic moving along the Okeechobee and Intracoastal Waterway. The office building was a typical Florida stucco construction, painted yellow, with a second-story balcony, white wrought-iron railings, and a green metal roof.

In the office, Ryan paid for an overnight slip and bought cold sodas. He and Mango were sipping beverages while standing in the air conditioning and pointing out clever items they could use from the ship's store when the door opened and an older man in blue jeans, a Hawaiian shirt, Top Sider shoes, and a straw Indiana Jones hat walked in.

He looked the newcomers up and down and pulled off his sunglasses to let them dangle from a neck loop. "You boys just get in?"

"Yes, sir," Mango replied.

"Skip, everybody calls me Skip. You headed up the

Ditch in that Sabre?" he asked, using the local nickname for the Okeechobee Canal.

"That's the plan," Ryan replied.

"Lake's pretty low this year. That Sabre draws six feet, doesn't it?" He had an air of professionalism about him, a confidence born from years on the water.

"Yes, it does," Ryan said. He'd been aground twice in the Sabre, even though he knew her technical specifications. The hubris of youth.

"Had a guy come through yesterday," Skip said. "He told me the lake was kicking up three footers and his keel hit the bottom of the channel more than a few times."

Mango wanted to know if the lake was going to be any better tomorrow.

Skip rubbed his jaw. "Supposed to be the same tomorrow, but the lake makes her own weather. That's the second largest body of fresh water inside the lower forty-eight."

"What's your recommendation, Skip?" Mango asked as they followed the old captain out to the porch.

"My recommendation, son, pray for rain." He lit a cigarette and offered the pack around.

Both men declined. Mango could see the desire in his companion's eyes.

"If I were you boys ..." Skip eased into one of the rocking chairs lining the porch. "I'd slip on down to the Keys and play hooky for a few days. You leave tomorrow morning and sail straight through, weather over in Islamorada or Marathon."

"We can get under Seven Mile Bridge," Ryan muttered, thinking about spending a few days diving in the Keys. They'd brought their dive gear and the Sabre had an onboard compressor to refill the tanks.

"How long will this detour take?" Mango demanded.

"Couple of days, give or take time off for good behavior." Skip chuckled.

"Thanks for the info, Skip." Ryan extended his hand and the man shook it.

Ryan and Mango walked down the sidewalk bordering the marina seawall. Ryan glanced down to see small fish cruising just beneath the water's surface.

When they arrived at the restaurant, Sailor's Return, Ryan asked, "What happened to your wife?"

Mango shrugged. "She said to get a table and she'd join us later."

They did as Jennifer had asked and ordered two beers before being seated at a table.

"What do you think about going down to the Keys?" Mango asked. "Do you believe Skip?"

Ryan shrugged and looked around the room. "Go ask those dudes." He pointed at two white-haired men at the bar.

"What makes you so sure they know about the lake?"

"Look at them, scuffed and worn boat shoes, shaggy hair, leather skin, and clothes that scream, 'I live on a boat.' Trust me, those guys know all the gossip."

"That's what you look like, bro. Just add a few years." Mango left the table, ambled across the room, and took a seat beside the guy on the left. He ordered a round for the three of them.

Ryan laughed to himself. Mango was right, all he needed was the wispy white mustache or beard. He pulled out his phone and dialed Greg's number. Greg didn't answer his work or cell phone, so Ryan called Shelly. She answered on the third ring of her office phone.

"Where's Greg?"

"He's in a meeting. The same one I was in. He told me to talk to you. What's going on?"

"We're going the long way around Florida. The Ditch is too shallow for my boat."

"Okay, this is already taking longer than you thought."

"Take it out of my vacation time."

Shelly sighed. "Do what you need to do. Stay safe."

Ryan hung up as Mango slid back into his seat.

"The lake is exceptionally low this year," he reported.

Ryan grinned. "Nothing we can do about it but go enjoy the Keys."

"You're happy about this?"

"I'm not *unhappy* about it," Ryan replied. "Besides, are you really eager to face down those pirates again?"

"Now that you mention it. No."

"Then we'll make the most of this delay. I called Greg already."

"What did he say?"

"Told me to do what we needed to do."

Mango looked over at the restaurant entrance and smiled. Ryan turned to see what held his partner's attention. His eyes widened, and a smile spread across his face as Jennifer walked into the room, escorting Emily Hunt. Ryan stood as they approached. Emily gave him a hug and a kiss before they settled into their chairs.

"Is this the conspiracy you two were cooking before you left?" Ryan asked Emily.

"Yes." She smiled at him.

"The boat's going to be crowded," Ryan said.

Jennifer shook her head. "We're taking Emily's car back to Tampa. We'll stay at her apartment while you guys make the crossing."

"We had to change plans," Ryan said. "Lake Okeechobee is too low to cross. We have to take the boat down through the Keys."

"Good thing I have an understanding boss," Emily said. She fiddled with her napkin, straightening it across her lap and smoothing out the wrinkles.

"What does that mean?" Ryan asked, narrowing his brows.

"It means," Emily said as she looked up to meet his eyes, "I have to take a few more days off work than planned. Kyle wasn't too happy about this trip."

"Oh, it's Kyle now?" Ryan said.

Emily rolled her eyes, shook her head, and let out a sigh that puffed up her cheeks. "He's my boss, Ryan. He employs me. I have several cases he wants me to finish. I gave two to one of the other investigators, so they could wrap them up while I'm gone. There's nothing personal between us."

"Okay," Ryan said dismissively.

"Can we get a drink at this table?" Emily twisted her body to search for the waitress.

Dinner was a quiet affair after Ryan and Emily's tiff. When it was over, they walked out to the parking lot and stood in the cool evening air. Laughter, snatches of conversation, and the clink of glasses came from Sailor's Return's outdoor patio. Water lapped against the concrete quay, and boats creaked against fenders. Cars roared on the road as they crossed Roosevelt Bridge on U.S. 1.

"Emily, are you staying?" Jennifer asked.

Emily looked at Ryan, her eyes questioning.

He stared into those bright blue eyes and smiled. "She's staying with the idiot."

Laughter broke the tension.

"That's a good thing." Mango put his arm around his

wife's shoulders. "We're looking forward to some alone time."

Ryan narrowed his eyes and screwed up his face. "Gross." To Emily he said, "Make sure you wash the sheets when you get home."

Emily giggled and slapped Ryan on the arm. Jennifer blushed. Mango grinned.

They walked down the transient dock to the Sabre. Emily turned to Ryan. "She's beautiful."

"Thanks." Ryan gave the boat a loving pat. "I think so, too."

Mango and Jennifer lugged their bags off the boat and said goodbye after Emily handed over her car keys. Ryan then stowed Emily's gear in the forward V-berth. Tonight, he was thankful for the shore power to run the air conditioner. With the cabin closed against one of nature's deadliest creatures, the mosquito, the tiny enclosure would otherwise be a sauna. Ryan had managed for many years with screens over the companionway door and portholes, but as he aged, he'd become more accustomed to the finer things in life. Air conditioning at a marina was one.

CHAPTER TWENTY-EIGHT

Ryan awoke to the beeping of an alarm and the glare of a sun sinking low on the western horizon. A glance at his watch told him he'd slept for four hours. Emily stood behind the wheel and had the boat neatly trimmed. He enjoyed the view of the stunning blonde standing at the helm of his boat. The wind blew wisps of hair across her face, and the sun had kissed her glowing skin around the blue bikini. He could never tire of the view. She noticed him staring and smiled self-consciously, then looked away over the light blue water. He sat up and checked the GPS plotter in the cabin. They were nearing their destination.

He returned to the cockpit, two water bottles in hand. He gave her one in exchange for a kiss. An hour later, with Ryan at the helm, they watched the green mangroves of Boot Key slide by. They rounded the island's west end and entered the channel between Boot Key and Key Vaca.

"Welcome to Boot Key Harbor," he said. "I'm going up front to catch the mooring ball."

Emily stood and stretched before she took the helm. Ryan went forward with the boat hook. Five minutes later, they were on the ball and Emily shut off the motor. In the silence, they could hear gulls screeching as they wheeled in the sky, the wind rustled the lines, and water lapped the hull. In the distance, a powerboat screamed at full speed, and cars tooled along A1A.

Ryan walked back to the cockpit and stepped down beside Emily. He put an arm around her waist, and they stood looking at the glistening white hulls of the many boats moored in the harbor. Then he tugged her to him and kissed her. It started gently, then as she wrapped her arms around him, it turned greedy and hard.

"What was that for?" she asked when they parted.

"Lust. A man can only spend so much time around a woman clad in as little clothing as you are before it gets his blood up."

She laughed.

"You're a tease," Ryan said and pulled the sail cover from a locker. She helped fit the tight canvas over the sail. While they worked, he asked, "How about a hot shower?"

"Now who's the tease?"

"We'll take the dinghy up to the marina shower and then grab dinner."

"Ryan Weller, you are a charmer."

He shrugged, fastened the final snap into place and followed her into the cabin. They stuffed clothes and shower items in bags and then took the dinghy to the office. Ryan paid for the mooring ball. The hot shower felt exquisite as it cleansed the salt from his skin and hair. They met back at the dinghy and stored their bags.

"Where to now, Captain?"

"Across the street is Florida Keys Steak and Lobster House."

"Going all out?"

"I have to impress you somehow." He took her hand and guided her up Thirty-Sixth Street to A1A. Crossing the infamous Overseas Highway was harder than most of the things they'd had to do in the last few days. With a steady stream of traffic moving both directions, it took a few minutes for an opening to appear that allowed them to run across all four lanes of traffic without having to stop on the double yellow line.

Emily laughed. "I'm not sure I can do that with a full stomach."

"Don't eat too much."

She nudged him in the side with her elbow.

Inside, a hostess seated them, and Ryan ordered a margarita and a piece of key lime pie. Emily followed suit with a tiramisu and a Long Key iced tea. They discussed what would happen after he dropped her off in Tampa and tossed around various theories about the actions of the sailboat thieves.

While they lingered happily over drinks, Ryan watched two men in suits at a table close to theirs. Alarm bells clashed in his head as he reached for a nonexistent pistol on his hip. Through a fog he heard Emily speak to him, but his focus was on the two men. They were a threat. He worked hard to keep his stress levels in check, but these two had triggered something in his brain, and he didn't know exactly what it was. Emily spoke to him again, this time touching his arm before he answered her. He quickly scanned the room again, feeling sheepish for allowing his combat fatigue to crowd his brain at such a valuable time.

After dinner, they collected their take-out boxes into a bag and Ryan paid the bill. He carried the bag in one hand as they made another death-defying sprint across A1A. Hand in hand, the couple walked back to the dinghy.

"Why did you name your boat *Sweet T*?" Emily asked as they approached the sailboat.

"My high school girlfriend named her."

Emily raised her eyebrows. "Was her name Teresa?"

"No." Ryan laughed. "I had a penchant for sweet tea."

"Did you see her when you were home?"

"I haven't seen her since the night of high school graduation. I heard she moved to Indiana or someplace in the Midwest."

Ryan tied the dinghy to the back of the Sabre and helped Emily up before handing over the take-out containers and climbing aboard. Emily made room in the fridge by pulling out a bottle of wine.

"Might as well drink this." She held it up.

Ryan grabbed glasses and a bottle opener. Outside, he opened the wine and poured it before sitting down on the settee beside Emily. They spent the rest of the evening sipping wine, telling stories from their past, and holding hands in the dark. She nestled close to him with her head on his shoulder. Ryan's thoughts were turning amorous when he heard a phone ring.

Down in the cabin, he pulled the phone from the chart desk. "Hey, Greg."

"What are you doing, Ryan?" His voice had an edge to it.

"I'm moving the boat into the Gulf, just like we talked about."

"No, with Emily. This ain't some vacation you're on."

"Listen, Greg." Ryan's voice got low and hard. "Last time I called you, you couldn't be bothered to answer the damn phone, so don't give me a ration of crap."

There was silence on the line for a long time. Long enough for Ryan to ask if Greg was still there.

Greg sighed. "Yeah, I'm here."

"We good?" Ryan asked tentatively.

"We're good, man."

"Okay, I needed a few days to sail around Florida because the Okeechobee Canal is too low. Emily wanted to ride along. A few days, either way, off the schedule, won't stop us from catching these pirates. I'm going to spend a day or two in the Keys with my girlfriend and then pick up Mango."

"Then you'll hunt the pirates?"

"Yes, but I need you to stay sharp, man. If something happens to us, you need to mount the rescue."

"Stick to the plan, Ryan."

"I am. Anything else you want to pass along?"

"No."

"I'll call you when Mango and I are headed for Mexico." Ryan thumbed the *end* button and dropped the phone in the desk beside his Walther pistol before closing the lid.

CHAPTER TWENTY-NINE

Luis Martinez spoke into the phone. "Yes, I'm sure. We followed them into a restaurant and overheard their conversation. They were discussing gunrunners who are stealing sailboats. The man says he's sailing into the Gulf looking for what he calls pirates."

Professor Rueben Morales mulled this over before he spoke. "I want you to take them out."

"Say again?" Martinez requested. He was positive he'd heard Morales ask him to kill the man and woman on the sailboat; however, he wanted to be sure.

"Luis, you must eliminate them. They cannot continue to pursue the leads they have. Kill them."

Martinez had his confirmation. "Sir"

Morales cut him off. "You have your orders, Luis."

"Yes, sir, but"

Morales hung up the phone before Luis could finish his sentence. When *Sweet T* had left North Carolina, there had been two men and a woman on it. Now there was only one man and a different woman. The man, Martinez knew, was Ryan Weller, the object of Morales's manhunt. He was unsure where the other man and woman had gone, or who the new woman was.

Fortunately, the old man, Skip, in Stuart was as talkative with Martinez as he had been with Ryan and Mango. He told Martinez about Lake Okeechobee and the Okeechobee Waterway. Skip also told Martinez how the last two guys he'd talked to were going to Marathon on their way to Fort Myers. Then he droned on about how the government had once planned to dig a larger canal across the state and connect it to the St. John's River south of Jacksonville. For five minutes, Martinez tried to excuse himself, but the man would not shut up. Finally, Martinez walked away.

The two manhunters had made a beeline for Marathon and set up shop in a small hotel. Martinez found a boat captain willing to charter his long-neglected trawler and would ask no questions. For the right price, the man had offered to commit petty crimes for them. Martinez knew he'd found the right man. Until his quarry arrived, Martinez had plied their new captain, Eddie Mackenzie, with booze and cigarettes. Mackenzie was as unkempt as his trawler. If paradise had a shady side, Eddie Mackenzie fit right into it. Martinez doubted anyone would miss the man if he disappeared.

This evening, *Sweet T* had shown up on the tracker and Martinez had followed it to Boot Key Harbor. He hung around the city docks, waiting for the couple to come to the marina office to pay for their stay. He and Hernandez watched as Ryan and Emily went about their business and took a table close to them in the restaurant.

Now, the two watchers were waiting for their opportunity to kill.

CHAPTER THIRTY

Looe Key was lit up like a Technicolor dream world. The vibrant colors of the coral were outshone only by the fish swimming in and out of the reef's holes and ledges. Emily's hand squeezed Ryan's as they floated on the azure surface of the ocean. The water was flat calm, and the visibility was better than one hundred feet in all directions. Some of their fellow snorkelers marred the waters by kicking up sand as they dived to the bottom.

Never had Emily seen such an abundance of sea life as on this reef. Lobsters poked their spiny carapaces from hidey holes, angelfish flashed and fluttered, moray eels lurked in tunnels and crevices, reef and nurse sharks darted after small prey. Schools of grunts hovered just off the rocks, and barracudas cruised the fringes.

She smiled behind her snorkel, which let water trickle into the mouthpiece. She exhaled forcefully, blasting the water from the breathing tube. Ryan let go of her hand, bent at the waist, and dove straight to the bottom, twenty feet below. She admired the long, lean lines of his muscular body.

He came up holding a conch shell as big around as a dinner plate. Turning it over, she could see the conch retract its foot. Emily held the shell in her hands, feeling the rough horns and the smooth flare of the shell's inside. She handed it back to him and Ryan replaced it where it had been. He motioned for her to join him and she dived to look at the sand-covered body of a stingray with only its straight, barbed tail visible. Waving his hand over the ray to dispel the sand caused the ray to rise from the sea floor, flapping long majestic wings as it glided away. Emily returned to the surface and took deep breaths of fresh air. Ryan emerged beside her and grinned.

She pulled him close and kissed him. This was the best vacation she had been on with a guy. James, her former boyfriend, would take her to beaches and boardwalks. They always had fun, but James didn't have the same adventurous streak as Ryan. The other man in her life was Kyle Ward, and she wondered what he would say when she returned to work. She knew all she had to do was give him the right look and he would grovel on his knees with a marriage proposal.

In the afternoon, they moved to the wreck of the two-hundred-and-ten-foot freighter, *MV Adolphus Busch*, which was purposely sunk to create an artificial reef. Big holes, cut into the sides of the ship, made easy swim through passages, allowing divers access to the hold.

Emily and her beau made two dives. The first one to the deeper hold and the second to explore the bridge and upper structure in shallower water.

Back on *Sweet T*, Emily beamed from ear to ear. "Did you see all of those barracudas?"

"What about those goliath groupers?" Ryan asked.

"They were bigger than a Volkswagen Beetle!" She

threw her arms around him. "Oh, Ryan, it was wonderful, thank you so much."

"You're welcome. I'm glad we got to do this."

"Me, too." She kissed him and then went back to cleaning her scuba gear.

Ryan cleaned his own gear and filled the tanks before storing them in their racks.

Emily stood on the foredeck and used a bucket of fresh water to rinse off her body and do a quick wash of her hair. Ryan joined her and did the same. Finished with their bath, they stretched out in the afternoon sun to dry.

One by one, the other dive boats motored away until *Sweet T* bobbed alone on her anchor ball.

She watched him bait a hook, unspool a hand line over the side, and jig it up and down. In short order, he hooked a fish and worked it to the surface. A few minutes later, he had a ten-pound yellowfin grouper in the boat.

"Good thing we already ate our leftovers from last night. We need room in the fridge for this guy." Ryan held the fish up by the tail.

"I hope you know how to clean that thing. My grandmother once told me, 'Never clean a fish.'"

"Do you at least know how to do it?"

"I never learned."

"Come, I'll show you." He picked up a filet knife. She watched as he cut the fish behind its gills then ran the knife along the backbone to the tail. He flipped the fish over and repeated the cuts. He sliced the meat off the skin and dumped the carcass over the side of the boat. Using the fresh water hose, he rinsed the blood off the filets and held up two hefty cuts of fish flesh.

"Now I know," she stated.

"Next one's yours."

"I don't want you to get out of practice. I'll help you cook though, just so we have an even trade."

Emily carried the filets to the kitchen and poured olive oil into a pan. She felt self-conscious as Ryan watched her. Her grandmother may not have cleaned a fish, but she'd taught Emily everything she knew about cooking them. Emily rifled through the pantry and pulled a handful of ingredients together to make a sauce. While the fish cooked, she sprinkled on herbs and chili powder. The variety of stores Ryan kept aboard amazed her.

When she commented on it, he said, "When you eat fish for almost every meal, you learn to cook it in a myriad of ways."

They ate in the cockpit, plates on outstretched legs and cold beers by their sides. They stacked the dishes in the sink and settled in to watch the infamous Florida Keys' sunset.

In the dying rays of sunlight, Ryan stood and trained a pair of binoculars on a boat at the far end of the *Adolphus Busch*.

"What are you looking at?"

"I swear I've seen that boat before."

"There are lots of boats around here. There must be two boats that look alike. Besides, we're in a popular area."

Ryan brought the binoculars down but still watched the boat. "I've seen it somewhere."

Emily used the binoculars to study the white trawler with a blue canvas top and matching blue stripes down the sides of the hull just below the rub rail. The boat needed a good cleaning, fresh paint, and new canvas. Two men stood on the aft deck using fishing rods to jig baits up and down and a third lounged in the captain's chair on the bridge, smoking a cigarette with his feet propped up on the railing.

Emily looked around at the glassy sea and marveled at

the silence. There was a stillness in the air she had never felt before, and when she spoke, her words seemed to boom across the water. Ryan grinned and held a finger to his lips. She nestled her head on his shoulder and they watched, hand in hand, as the sun set fire to the western sky before sliding below the horizon.

"That was beautiful," she whispered.

"Not compared to you." Ryan grinned and leaned in for a kiss.

"What a cheesy line." She giggled, pushing him away. But a moment later, she reached for his hand. "Come on, sailor, take me to bed."

CHAPTER THIRTY-ONE

The sailboat shifted and Ryan's eyes snapped open. His head was groggy from being awoken from a sound sleep. His ears widened to listen for what had caused the boat to move. He looked over at Emily, tangled in the sheet, golden hair fanned out on the pillow. Ryan closed his eyes and relaxed, willing sleep to return.

He heard the scuff of a shoe on fiberglass. His eyes snapped back open. There was someone on his boat. He held his breath and listened intently over the low ringing of his tinnitus. The boat swayed again. Very slowly, he slipped from the bed and stood. He kept his weight centered in the hull, so he wouldn't give away his movements by causing the boat to rock as the person above had just done.

Eventually, whoever was in the cockpit would come through the cabin door. Ryan moved to the navigation table and gently lifted its top. He grabbed the Walther pistol and eased the top back down. He took three quick steps to the kitchen and tucked himself behind the cabin wall, out of the line of sight for the invader entering the cabin.

A man dropped down the ladder holding a pump-action

shotgun. He moved along the narrow passageway, placing himself between Ryan and Emily. Ryan feared his bullet would go through the man and hit her. A shot in the wrong place could also sink his boat.

He looked down at the filet knife he'd left by the sink after washing dishes last night. He slipped his gun into the waistband of his shorts and picked up the knife. Metal scraped on metal as he lifted the blade from the stainless steel sink basin. The sound drew the man's attention. He spun, leveling the muzzle of the scattergun.

Ryan stepped forward, pushing the barrel of the shotgun away with his left hand. His right hand drove the knife forward. The man used Ryan's force on the muzzle to help him swing the butt of the gun up. Ryan lunged with the razor-sharp blade. It sliced through the man's left shirt sleeve and fileted the bicep open to the bone. Arterial blood sprayed out like a fire hose, coating Ryan. The gunman's finger closed on the trigger of his weapon as he screamed in pain. In the confined cabin, the gunshot was deafening. Ryan's ears rang, and pinwheels of light, caused by the muzzle blast, danced in front of his eyes. His hand burned where he still gripped the barrel. Buckshot shattered a window while Ryan shoved the man backward.

The intruder continued to struggle, and Ryan pulled the knife back to plunge into his chest. Just as he began to swing his arm forward, a spearpoint thrust through the man's torso.

Outside, a searchlight snapped on, the light filtering through the sailboat's cabin windows. Ryan could see his attacker's mouth opening and closing like a fish trying to breathe. Blood trickled from his lips as he sagged to his knees.

Ryan's gaze rose past the spearpoint, and the dead

man, to find Emily kneeling on the bed with a spear gun still in her hands. She dropped the tube-shaped weapon and slumped backward. Ryan looked down at his chest and shorts. They were covered with blood. It ran down his legs and pooled at his feet. It looked like all eight pints of the dead man's gore had leaked out his arm to cover the teak floor, pool in the bilges, and spray across the furniture. The cabin stank of copper and excrement. Ryan could taste it, and it surprised him how well he still tolerated the smell.

Emily pushed herself from the bed and stepped into the salon. Ryan could read the anguish, the anger, and the fear on Emily's face as she stepped over the dead man and pressed herself against him. He held her close, feeling the blood squish between their bodies. He kissed her forehead.

The spotlight swept across the sailboat's cabin. Shafts of light sifted through the portholes, casting an eerie glow on the gruesome scene. It illuminated the shattered porthole and blast pattern peppered into the fiberglass. Ryan tossed the filet knife into the sink, strapped his dive knife to his calf, and pulled his pistol from his waistband. He shoved the gun into Emily's hand.

"Keep it out of sight and distract them. Act like you're hurt since you're covered with blood."

"What are you going to do?"

"I'm going to find out what they want. Go."

Emily went to the stairs and turned, she rose on tiptoes and kissed him. She staggered up the ladder into the cockpit, throwing her arms across her face to ward off the light now focused on her.

Ryan, hunched in the cabin door, heard the *chunk-thunk* of a pump-action shotgun slide open and closed. He leaped into the cockpit and tackled Emily. Their momentum carried them overboard. Buckshot raked the air behind them.

Ryan turned under the water and looked up. The light probed the dark water where they'd gone in. He grabbed Emily's hand and pulled her underwater to the far side of the boat.

Back on the surface, he whispered, "Stay here."

"But the blood will attract sharks."

"We'll have to chance it."

Ryan moved forward to the bow of the Sabre and pulled himself down the mooring ball rope. Fifteen feet down, he cleared his ears and pushed off toward the trawler. He covered half the distance before he came up. He took a breath and dove to the sounds of gunfire. When he came up again, he was in front of the trawler. Grasping the anchor, he pulled himself up to the rail and reached to pull his body all the way onto the boat. Gunfire shattered the wood and fiberglass around his head and hands. As he fell into the water, he heard one man curse a second about the damage to his boat.

He dove under the boat and held onto the propeller shaft to keep his body in place. The boat rocked as men ran back and forth to look over the gunwales. He felt the burn of excess carbon dioxide in his lungs and let himself drift up to the boat's swim platform. He came up underneath the faded teak decking and peered through the gaps between the boards. Turning to look at the sailboat, he saw Emily had moved to the stern.

Ryan felt a bump against his leg.

Shivers racked his body. Sandpaper-rough skin rubbed against his legs. He dared not move. He had to get out of the water. Another bump hit his torso, this one harder than the last. There were two sharks swimming around him, drawn by the scent of the blood coating his clothes and his body. If they smelled it on him, they would smell it on Emily. He kept his gaze on Emily and saw a fin slice through the water.

A ragged burst of light bloomed at the stern of the Sabre. The thunderclap of a gunshot accompanied it, followed by a second and a third. Emily aimed the fourth and fifth shots into the water to scare away the sharks.

Emily screamed, "Get out of the water!"

Ryan felt the water swirl around him. Armed with only a dive knife, he was no match for the prehistoric predators. His only hope was a distraction. He pulled the knife free of its scabbard and ducked below the surface. He grasped the propeller shaft again. The spotlight gave the water just enough illumination for him to see a twelve-foot-long tiger shark flash by. A smaller blacktip shark nosed in closer to him. Ryan set his body and gripped the knife tighter. Just as the blacktip came into reach, he stabbed his knife into the fish's belly and jerked the steel blade toward the shark's tail. Blood stained the water and the shark thrashed in its death throes. Ryan shoved off the hull and reached for the swim platform. He looked back to see the tiger shark flash by, mouth open, teeth almost gleaming as it homed in on the dying blacktip.

Grasping the teak platform, Ryan jerked himself from the water and rolled to his knees. He'd escaped one deadly threat to fall into the clutches of a second. He rotated the knife blade, so it ran along the length of his forearm, and he sprang over the gunwale. The muzzle of a shotgun swung toward him. He dropped to the ground as it exploded.

Ryan lashed out with his knife. The blade sliced into the gunman's leg. The man dropped the shotgun and fell to his knees, screaming in pain. His hands clutched the leg wound. His foot dangled at an odd angle from the severed muscle. Ryan got to his knees and wiped his mouth with the back of the hand that held the knife. He noticed the second shooter lying on his back with a bullet hole in his chest. Ryan leaned forward, putting his hands on his knees. He was out of breath and tired.

"Ryan," Emily called.

The big man levered himself to his feet and steadied himself against the rail. Emily was standing in the Sabre's cockpit with her hand to her face, the searchlight blinding her eyes. Ryan climbed the ladder to the bridge and pushed the light down.

"You okay, Em?"

"Yes, are you?"

"Yeah." He looked at the water. It still boiled from the feeding frenzy beneath the surface. Sharks, too numerous to count, swarmed in a giant ball. Teeth lashed out at the mere hint of blood. He snapped off the light, thankful to have escaped the turbulent waters.

Ryan returned to the man on the deck of the cockpit. He was curled up in a ball with his hands clutched around the leg wound. Dark liquid oozed between his fingers. Ryan searched the cabin and found a first aid kit. He carried it out to the cockpit and placed it on the deck beside the wounded man. He pulled the man's hand from the cut and washed away the blood. Next, he poured antibacterial ointment into the cut and pulled the flesh together with the help of butterfly bandages then covered the bandages with gauze. Finally, he fashioned a splint from two wooden spoons to keep the foot immobile and wrapped the whole thing with an ACE bandage.

"Who do you work for?" Ryan asked his patient.

"I was ..." He panted. "Hired to bring ..." More heavy, ragged breaths. "Those guys out here."

"Why'd you shoot at us?"

"Ah, man... I was paid ... to do a job."

"What's the going rate for killing a man?" When the injured man remained silent, Ryan tried another tack. "You live in the Keys?"

"Yeah." The man grimaced as he rolled onto his back.

The man wasn't going to be much of a threat. He was in pain and his foot flopped around like a piece of rope. Ryan pulled the man up to his good foot and helped him into the trawler's salon. He eased him onto the cushions of the settee and went to the fridge. From it, he retrieved a bottle of water and handed it to the man along with a bottle of Tylenol. The man shook half a dozen pills into his hand and swallowed them with a chug of water.

"You all right? What's your name?"

The man laid his head back on the cushion. He closed his eyes, fighting through the pain. "Eddie Mackenzie and no, I ain't all right, you sliced my damn foot off."

"I'm going over to my boat. I'll be back in a bit. We'll run you into a hospital then, okay, Eddie?"

Eddie nodded. "Get me the bottle of rum from the fridge."

Ryan complied before he climbed up to the bridge. The current had pushed the two boats further apart. While checking out the controls, he found a pack of cigarettes. Not his usual brand, but they would work. He sparked one up and started the engine. By the time he maneuvered alongside the Sabre, Emily had the fenders over the side of the sailboat and helped tie off bow and stern lines.

When Ryan hopped across, he saw Emily had more blood on her.

"I was trying to move the dead guy," she explained. "He's too heavy for me."

Ryan stepped into the cabin and gagged from the smell of cordite, blood, urine, and excrement. In the confined space, it was overpowering. He grabbed a dish towel, wet it, and tied it behind his head to cover his mouth and nose. Together, he and Emily carried the corpse out of the cabin and put it on the back deck of the trawler beside his partner. Ryan used his phone to take pictures of the dead men and Eddie Mackenzie. He realized, as he sent the photos to Floyd Landis, that the dead men had been in the restaurant in Marathon and on the docks in Wrightsville Beach.

Ryan was still in the trawler's cabin when his phone rang. He'd just lit a cigarette for Eddie and one for himself.

"Who are these guys?" Landis asked.

Ryan recounted the night's events, ending with, "What do we do with them?"

"Let me make a few calls. Sit tight."

"Think I can clean up my sailboat?"

"Shouldn't be a problem," Landis said.

Ryan asked, "Can I feed the dead guys to the sharks and sink the trawler someplace nice and deep?"

"Holy ... you can't just feed dead guys to sharks, Ryan. We don't operate like that."

"Call me back soon or that's what I'm doing."

With the sailboat's bilge pumps turned on, they used a hose to spray down the decks, cushions, and cabinets. They used the basic cleaners Ryan kept aboard to scour the cushions. The blood left a nasty stain.

"What happens if someone comes looking for those guys?" Emily asked.

"The only person who's going to miss those guys is the guy that sent them."

Emily sat down on the end of the V-berth mattress and

looked at her boyfriend. "We just killed two men, should we report it to the police?"

"I did. Landis is making some calls." He sat down beside her. "Look, I'm not worried about it. We still have a job to do and I think someone sent these guys to keep us from continuing our investigation."

Emily leaned against him. Her voice shook when she said, "I've never killed anyone before."

He put his arm around her and held her hand. "Em, those guys were here to kill us. We were lucky to get the drop on them. I'm sorry you had to kill them, but we're alive, and we might not be if you hadn't shot them."

Tears rolled down her cheeks.

They lay back on the bed. He stroked her hair and whispered calming words to her. Ryan was unsure how long he held her. His arm ached from being under her shoulders, and he was thankful when her breathing steadied and then slowed into the rhythmic sounds of sleep. He slid his arm out, replacing it with a pillow and climbed off the bed. Careful not to disturb her, he opened a cabinet door and pulled out a pack of cigarettes he'd tucked away at the start of the trip. He lit one in the cockpit and noticed the sky beginning to lighten in the east. If Landis didn't get this straightened out quick, dive boat operators and fishermen would arrive to find a grisly double murder.

He crossed over to the trawler and found Eddie passed out. The empty bottle of rum rolled back and forth across the deck with the boat's motion. Ryan picked it up and set it in the sink. He checked Eddie's pulse and found it beating strongly. The man wouldn't die, but he would never walk right again.

CHAPTER THIRTY-TWO

Ten minutes later, a white center console with a black T-top pulled up beside the two boats. Ryan had watched them come from the west as he sat on the trawler's bridge, smoking another cigarette. He climbed down and helped the two sheriff's deputies tie up.

"You Ryan Weller?" one deputy asked.

"Yes, sir," Ryan said, looking past him to the heavyset guy in a suit. He was already sweating in the early morning heat.

"I'm Sheriff Sam Grady." Grady held out his hand.

"Nice to meet you, Sheriff."

The other man wiped his bald head with a handkerchief. "Dave Ritter, DHS."

Ryan nodded to him and the deputy who remained at the wheel of the patrol boat. He was thankful Landis had gotten cooperation from another agent. Sinking the trawler might have been similar if these men prevented him from leaving.

Sheriff Grady and Ritter stepped over to the trawler. Grady put his hands on his hips. "Suppose you tell me exactly what happened here. Walk me through it nice and slow." He looked beyond Ryan and tipped his head. "Morning, ma'am."

Ryan felt the boat dip as Emily came aboard. They recounted and reenacted everything for the two men. Meanwhile, the deputy used the patrol boat to chase away divers and fishermen. Ritter listened and nodded while Grady took notes and asked questions. When Ryan finished his tale, Sheriff Grady shook his head and put away his notepad.

Perspiration glistened on Ritter's head and ran in rivulets down his face. He nudged the bigger corpse. "That's Alex Hernandez. He's a lightweight in the Austin Brown Berets, does enforcement work and bodyguarding. The other guy was Luis Martinez, a dirty cop fired from El Paso PD. They caught him stealing drugs and money from the evidence locker for the Juarez Cartel."

"What about Eddie?" Ryan asked.

"He's a horse of a different color," Sheriff Grady said. "Eddie McKenzie's a scumbag from Miami. He's well known to the Monroe and Miami-Dade County Sheriff's offices for petty crimes. Has a rap sheet as long as my arm." The sheriff held out his right arm to demonstrate.

"He said he was from the Keys," Ryan told them. He sat on the trawler's gunwale and lit another cigarette.

"Maybe now, but originally Miami," Grady said. "These two probably hired him to bring them out here."

"Are we free to go, Sheriff?" Emily asked.

Grady scratched his chin and studied the pair. "Everything appears to be as you say it was. We have your information if we need to contact you. I understand you're on your way to Tampa."

"Yes, sir," Emily said, her arms wrapped around her chest.

"Good luck." Grady shook hands with Ryan and Emily. "Cast off those lines for me, and I'll take this boat in and make sure Eddie gets medical attention."

"Aye aye," Ryan said as he helped Emily across to the Sabre and went forward to handle the bow line.

CHAPTER THIRTY-THREE

Rueben Morales stared out his home's sliding glass door at the shimmering pool surface. He clutched a cell phone to his ear and listened to Arturo Guerrero.

"You have been irresponsible in your actions. I wanted the man eliminated, and still he is alive. Your men have disappeared, and one is now in a hospital. What do you have to say for yourself?"

Morales sighed, careful not to exhale loud enough for Guerrero to hear. Guerrero had already blistered his ear for the past ten minutes. He'd insulted Morales, Martinez, and Hernandez, and questioned the competency of Morales's operations in both English and Spanish. It was unlike Guerrero to become so agitated over the death of two low-level foot soldiers.

"We can contain this, Arturo."

Guerrero swore in his native tongue then continued in English. "We don't need these problems now."

Morales tried to contain the situation. "We knew someone would investigate the sailboat thefts, and this is one man, one man looking for your ship. What can he do?"

Guerrero snorted. "Plenty. Homeland Security kept the sheriff's office from detaining your investigator. This man is well-connected, and if he finds my ship, he may call the Navy."

"We can do something about it," Morales said. "I sent a man to see Eddie Mackenzie. Eddie gave my man a receiver for a GPS device planted on Weller's sailboat. The tracker has a five-mile radius. If we give the receiver to your men on *La Carranza Garza*, they'll be able to find him."

"Send me the tracker."

"It's on its way."

"Excellent, I will take care of this problem for you, Rueben."

"Thank you, Arturo."

Morales pressed the phone to his ear a minute longer, listening to dead air. He looked at the screen to ensure the phone was off and walked to his office. He placed the phone in his desk drawer and went back to the kitchen, where he poured a glass of water and swallowed two Tylenol.

CHAPTER THIRTY-FOUR

Eager to get across the Gulf of Mexico and find the pirates, Ryan and Mango left the girls in Fort Myers and sailed around the clock. Four-hour watches ground on them, and they snapped at each other out of frustration. Patience was wearing thin after ten days of constant sailing. The interior of the sailboat still stank of copper and excrement even though they'd scrubbed down the cushions with stronger cleaners and repeatedly flushed the bilges. Both men spent more time in the cockpit than in the cabin. They'd run out of stories to tell and books to read.

A call on the satellite phone interrupted a bickering session about who should clean the coffee pot. Ryan snatched the phone from the chart table and pressed it to his ear, allowing his irritability to spill over. "What?"

"I thought sailing mellowed you out," Landis commented.

"These pirates better show up soon," Ryan said, "or we're putting in at Cozumel and getting drunk."

"I was just going to ask if you'd had any luck."

Ryan took a deep breath. "We've been sailing in circles

above the Yucatán. Mango says we're close to where he got ambushed, and we're in the hot spot according to our piracy map."

"I've been watching your satellite tracker. Keep at it. Now, I wanted to tell you about your mystery man, Juan Herrera. He might as well be a ghost. The name is the equivalent to our John Smith. My guess is the professor gave you a bogus name. I got permission to put a detail on Morales in connection with your pirates, but we haven't come up with anything. I only have them for two more days before they're reassigned."

"What about wiretaps?"

"No evidence he's done anything wrong. I can't justify a warrant."

"So much for the NSA spying on American citizens."

"My hands are tied. It's up to you to find something to stop the thefts. We had another report three days ago."

"Then we should be ripe for the picking."

"Be safe out there."

"Thanks." Ryan hung up the phone and poured himself a cup of coffee. Even though he was sweating profusely, he still craved the hot caffeine. He carried a thermos out to Mango and recounted his conversation with Landis.

"Hopefully, we get something to happen soon, bro, because I'm about to go crazy," Mango admitted.

"Better not try to cross the Pacific. Days and days of nothing."

"How did you do it by yourself?"

Ryan shrugged and sipped his coffee. "Easier than you'd think."

As if on cue, the radar chimed. Ryan got up and looked at the screen. The Automatic Identification System designated the radar target as *La Carranza Garza*. The AIS also gave the nine-digit Maritime Identification Number, radio call sign, GPS coordinates, speed, and direction.

"How far away?"

"About seven miles," Ryan said, still staring at the radar screen's sweep. He was unconcerned about a supply vessel running between oil rigs. He straightened and stared at the horizon where the ship would be. Then his ears picked up a buzzing sound.

Suddenly, a black military-style Zodiac RIB, with the words *Marina* emblazoned in yellow down the side of the black inflatable tubes, appeared. It had an aluminum tower in the rear, holding a radar dome and several antennas. Mounted on the bow was a fifty-caliber machine gun. Ryan could barely hear the outboards and knew they were silenced for stealth.

Mango had time to say, "That's the same boat that attacked me and Jennifer."

The machine gunner cut loose with a long burst of automatic fire, sweeping right, and left. Bullets raked the side of the Sabre, splintering fiberglass, destroying wood, pinging off the aluminum mast, slicing cables, and shredding canvas. Ryan jerked his pistol from its holster as he dove for the floor of the cockpit. Mango fell to the deck and covered his head with his hands. Sustained bursts of fire from the fifty cal continued to chew on the boat. The storm of lead ended as the belt emptied and the gun's bolt slammed open.

Ryan raised his pistol and blindly fired all fifteen hollow-point rounds over the gunwale. He dropped the empty magazine and slammed a fresh one home.

The sailboat listed toward the Zodiac, exposing their tentative position. The mast, now unsupported by its rigging, toppled over, taking lines, sails, and running gear into the ocean. A stanchion cable snapped with a sharp crack. Ryan ducked as the cable whipped through the air. It missed his head by mere inches.

Then the machine gun opened up again.

Mango and Ryan were face to face in the cockpit's bottom, gripping the shattered fiberglass, which was poor protection from the incoming fire. Mango looked at his friend with wide eyes. His mouth was slightly open as he took short, rapid breaths.

"Up over the rail. Go!" Ryan shoved Mango and rose enough to bring his pistol to bear. This time, he took measured shots. Two bullets hit the machine gunner while Mango sprang up onto the bench and vaulted the rail. The foot on Mango's artificial limb slipped and he splashed awkwardly into the water. Ryan emptied his magazine. A second gunman dropped his rifle and fell over the side of the RIB.

Ryan reached up to trip the activation switch on the emergency position indicating radio beacon. A bullet had shattered the EPIRB, preventing him from sending a distress message. He cursed as he dove over the rail and swam underwater to the far side of the floundering Sabre. Mango was treading water when Ryan came up beside him. Ryan was heartbroken and angry. These men were destroying his home. The machine gunner concentrated his fire on the sailboat's waterline, chewing a big hole in the fiberglass. Ryan screamed in vain for him to stop. Hot tears burned his cheeks. The boat quickly succumbed to the weight of the water rushing in. It felt like he was losing an old friend.

As it slipped beneath the waves, Ryan told Mango to follow him. They dove toward the boat amid tunneling bullets, which lost energy quickly in the water and fluttered gently to the seabed below.

Through salt-stung eyes, Ryan watched as the boat dropped like a stone into the deep blue abyss. He hovered ten feet below the surface, watching the craft get smaller and smaller, listening to the boat creak and groan as the water pressure slowly crushed it like a boa constrictor crushing an egg.

Above them, the RIB's motor burbled and surged as it circled the site. Ryan felt a tap on his shoulder and saw Mango motioning with a thumbs-up gesture. At the surface, they drew in deep lungsful of oxygen. The RIB charged in. A long string of bullets ripped through the water to the right of the swimmers. They stopped moving and watched as the RIB slowed and came alongside them.

The crew's uniforms matched the descriptions given by the Hulseys and Philip Nagel. The master of the craft braced a foot on the RIB's inflatable tube and smiled.

In heavily accented English, he said, "My orders are to kill you. I think a bullet is too good for you." He leered down. "I wish for you to suffer before you dead." He laughed, and the others joined in.

Ryan stared up at the man. He wanted to lunge out of the water, wrap his hands around the captain's neck, and watch the life seep from his eyes. Instead, he treaded water.

"*Vamos!*" the captain cried, as he circled his hand above his head.

The driver threw the boat into gear and the RIB roared off.

"You think they're coming back?" Mango asked.

"Let's hope not."

CHAPTER THIRTY-FIVE

Emily Hunt walked into her office and set a folder on her desk. The meeting had run longer than planned and she felt exhausted from the endless presentation. All she wanted to do was go home, drink a glass of wine, take a hot shower, and snuggle up with Ryan. But he was a thousand miles away on some adventure and her apartment was empty. Jennifer had gone back to Texas City to start a job as a nurse at Mainland Medical Center.

At her window overlooking the bay, Emily placed her hands at the small of her back. Leaning against her palms, she stretched her muscles and let out a long sigh. After a few minutes, she sat at her desk and wiggled the mouse to wake up her computer. Following Ryan's course at least kept her close to him, and she felt better knowing where he was. There was danger in what he was doing, but she believed he and Mango, both highly trained operators, could handle themselves.

She clicked the tab of the open internet browser, which brought up the tracking page for Ryan's boat. She hit the *refresh* button to update the browser and waited while satellites linked and synchronized before sending the information to her screen.

A white dotted line marked *Sweet T*'s course over an expanse of blue she knew to be the Gulf of Mexico. The dotted line had stopped. The last recorded tracking update was three hours ago.

She hit *refresh* again and waited for the response. It showed the same information. She picked up her cell phone and dialed DWR.

"Dark Water Research, how may I direct your call?"

"This is Emily Hunt calling for Greg Olsen."

"Hold, please." After seven rings, the operator came back on the line.

Emily hung up and dialed Greg's cell phone. It went to voicemail. "Greg, this is Emily, call me back. I think something is wrong with the tracker on Ryan's boat."

She dialed DWR again. This time, she asked for Shelly. Before Shelly came on the line, Emily's cell phone chimed.

The caller ID read: Jennifer Hulsey. Emily's stomach tightened as she answered the phone.

"The tracker isn't working," Jennifer blurted.

"I know. I'm trying to reach Greg or Shelly." Emily tapped the button to join Jennifer into the call she was making to Shelly.

"Greg isn't answering his cell or office number. I'm scared, Emily."

"Me too, Jenn, but we have to stay calm. Maybe the transmitter stopped working."

The ringing stopped, and the phone picked up. Shelly must have heard the last statement because she asked, "What transmitter stopped working?"

Emily explained the transmitter issue to Shelly.

"Did you try the sat phone?"

"No," Emily admitted, feeling sheepish for not thinking of such a simple solution.

"I tried and there was no answer." Jennifer's voice trembled.

Shelly's words were calm. "Okay, maybe they're having some electrical problems or there's an issue with the satellites. We deal with stuff like this all the time. Sometimes it's operator error, or they don't want to talk to us."

The disbelief was evident in Jennifer's voice. "But Mango wouldn't just shut off the tracker and not tell us."

"Maybe the situation changed and has gone, as Ryan likes to say, 'pear-shaped,'" Emily offered.

"Either way, we need to find Mango and Ryan," Jennifer said, her voice carrying the distress the other two women felt.

"OK, ladies, sit tight," Shelly said. "I'll find Greg. We'll straighten this out."

Emily and Jennifer hung up their phones after promising to stay calm. Rational minds were better than panicked ones.

Shelly dialed Greg's office and cell numbers. Both were busy. She got up from her desk and, a few steps later, was standing in front of Muriel Johnson.

"Did Greg leave?"

"I haven't seen him. I believe he's still in his office."

Shelly walked to his office and pressed her ear to the door. She could hear Greg speaking animatedly, his voice rising and falling in pitch to get his point across. "I don't give a damn about schedules. Those boys are lost at sea and we need to mount a rescue op."

Shelly felt her flesh goose pimple with fear as she took a seat across from him. He waved at her and leaned his elbows on the desk blotter. One hand pressed a phone to his ear and the other rubbed his forehead. He was listening intently to the conversation on the other end. Shelly noticed his cell phone was vibrating and the other landline phone receiver was lying off its cradle.

"We sent them out there and now we need to go look for them," Greg barked, then listened. "Yeah, yeah, yeah." He slammed the receiver down in the cradle so hard it bounced out and skittered across the desk.

He rubbed both temples with his fingertips.

"What's going on? I just got off the phone with Emily and Jennifer."

"That was Landis and he can't do anything. All the resources are tasked, and nobody's close to our boys. They're in Mexican waters, and getting those idiots to do anything is like pulling teeth."

"Did they actually wreck?"

"I don't know what happened," Greg admitted. He leaned back in his chair. "I received an alert that the tracker went offline and immediately called the company. It's not a satellite issue and there hasn't been an EPIRB signal meaning the boat sank. We honestly don't know what's going on."

"But they're sending someone to check, right?"

"No, not right now. Since they haven't received an emergency signal, they're considering it a software glitch, which is bullshit."

"I agree," Shelly concurred. She hopped off the chair and paced in front of the desk.

"Stop it, woman, you're driving me crazy."

She plopped back into the chair. "How far offshore are they?"

"Two days. Two *hard* days in the Hatteras."

"Let's go."

"Can you drop everything?"

"We don't have a choice. You can't go by yourself."

"I can take Chuck."

"He's flying Dash's crew to the rigs in Louisiana."

Greg smacked the desk with both hands. "Let's go."

"What can we do?"

"We can go find them. If the tracker comes back on, we turn around. I can't leave him out there, Shelly. He saved my life and I'm going to save his." He pushed away from the desk. "I need to get a few things from our DHS workshop. Meet me at the boat." He glanced at his watch. "In an hour."

She stood. "I need to pack some clothes and make arrangements for work."

"Okay. I'll see you in a bit."

As Greg rolled through the DWR facility, he saw Jerry DiMarco standing by the dive tank. He stopped beside the burly black man. "Jerry, we've got an issue with Ryan and Mango. Can you run offshore with us?"

"Sure thing. I've got a go-bag in the office. Just need to phone the wife."

"Grab it and meet us at the Hatteras in an hour."

"Roger that."

Greg drove to Ryan's office. He grabbed his go-bag, a large backpack equipped with everything from a multi-tool to a week's worth of medical supplies needed to deal with his paralysis. He hung it on the backrest of his chair. In a cross-draw holster, he stuffed a Sig Sauer P226 MK25 nine-millimeter pistol. Two spare magazines slid into a mag holder. A second bag contained several changes of clothes and a shaving kit. He piled these in the car and went back for two more bags Ryan had packed earlier. He also tucked a Walther PPQ M2 into a holster. From the gun vault, he grabbed two Mossberg 500 marine shotguns and a Springfield M1A Socom rifle. Then he raced through town to the boat.

DiMarco met him at the Hatteras. They loaded the gear and pulled the boat tight against the dock. Greg transferred over, rode up to the bridge and fired up the diesel engines.

"What else do you need?" DiMarco asked.

Greg pulled a piece of paper from his pocket and handed it to DiMarco. "These are the last known coordinates for Ryan's boat. Use the computer in the salon to figure out what the currents are like. There should be software to model their movements if the boat's floating or if they're in a life raft."

DiMarco nodded and went below. Greg looked at his watch and then called Shelly to tell her to hurry. Fifteen minutes later, she walked out of the building, pulling a large suitcase on rollers. She stowed her luggage in the V-berth stateroom, gave DiMarco several pointers on the use of the software, and then stepped onto the dock. She cast off the ropes and climbed aboard as Greg backed out of the slip. They idled down Industrial Canal, and as they came alongside the Texas City Dike, he threw the throttles forward and the boat leaped up on plane. They turned south and raced through Bolivar Roads and out into the perpetually brown water surrounding Galveston Island. Clear of the channel, Greg turned the wheel, guiding the boat toward *Sweet T*'s last known coordinates. The seas were building, and the sky was turning the color of lead in the southeast.

Shelly yelled in Greg's ear, "I'm going below to call Jennifer and Emily. I'll be right back."

The boat's wide bow flares pushed most of the waves away, as she plunged through them, yet water still swept over the front deck, ran through the scuppers and out the back of the boat.

When Shelly returned from her phone calls, she closed the rain curtains around the open bridge. She stood beside Greg with her legs spread and her knees bent to take the pounding of the waves.

"I have to run into the waves and it's taking us off course," Greg shouted. "The radar shows it's just a passing thunderstorm and should be over in an hour or so."

Shelly glanced at her watch. They were racing against time, the elements, and their dwindling supply of fuel. She leaned closer to Greg's ear. "NOAA radio says squalls will continue all night and tomorrow."

Greg's face was grim when he said, "That blows our timeline."

CHAPTER THIRTY-SIX

The storm Greg was watching was about to fall on Mango and Ryan. Darkness crept across the horizon and lightning streaked the sky. Already, the seawater had built into three-foot waves and the wind gusted hard enough to send cascades of foam into the air.

The rain came in droves, slamming down so hard it hurt the tops of Ryan and Mango's heads. The drops ricocheted off the water and pelted their skin. When they weren't dodging raindrops, the waves raised them six feet into the air, dropped them into the troughs, and washed over them.

Ryan tried tilting his head back to catch rain water in his mouth. He ended up gargling saltwater. He gave up trying to slake his parched throat. It felt like he was swallowing sandpaper and his tongue ached. Mango felt the same because he'd expounded on it in the last hour as they watched the storm barrel down on them.

Closing his eyes, Ryan tried to relax. After the RIB had driven away, he and Mango had looked for flotsam from the sunken sailboat. They came across a life jacket which Ryan had insisted Mango put on because he only had one leg to kick with. Close to the life jacket, they'd found a water jug Ryan used to keep on deck. It had a length of rope attached to it, and they used the rope to lash themselves together, back to back.

There was no telling how long they could hold out floating in the open ocean. Between their ravenous thirst, inclement weather, and hungry sharks, their chances were slim. Houston was two days away, and the stranded sailors were in Mexican waters below the normal operations of the Coast Guard; not that the Coast Guard would refuse to come down. The Mexican Navy, however, wasn't going to make an appearance because someone might be missing.

These thoughts swirled in Ryan's head as he swallowed dryly and stared at millions of gallons of water that would kill him if he dipped his mouth in to quench his palate. The paraphrased line from Samuel Taylor Coleridge's poem, "The Rime of the Ancient Mariner," came to mind: "Water, water, everywhere, and not a drop to drink." His stomach clenched, and his body tried to curl into a ball as it shook with cold.

If Ryan listened hard, he could hear his old Navy dive instructor, Senior Chief Baker, screaming at the dive candidates from the edge of the pool, "Kick those legs, recruits. This ain't no game! If you want to pass this evolution, you need to stop thinking and just do it. It's mind over matter. If you don't mind, it don't matter."

Ryan's mind switched off as his body became numb. Behind him, Mango was also shaking from the cold. His eyes were closed, and his arms sculled the water. Ryan shut his eyes against the storm.

Throughout the night, they floated in and out of squalls, suffering through the blasts of thunder, hammering rains, and relentless waves, which swamped their bodies and turned their stomachs. They both inhaled seawater and vomited it out. The storm moved on in early morning.

With the clearing clouds came the sun and its glaring intensity. It helped to cure the shivering and the shakes. Ryan knew hypothermia was a real threat if they stayed in the water much longer. They held Mango's T-shirt over their heads as a sunshade. It ended up draped over their eyes and blocked their view.

There was nothing to look at, anyway.

Neither had the energy to speak. Their thoughts centered on survival and home. Ryan's lips cracked and split. He kept running his tongue over them to keep them moisturized, but it was of little use. Dipping them in the water only made them burn from the salt. Mango complained about blisters.

Ryan rested his chin on his chest. He was responsible for this situation. It had been his idea to hunt for the pirates on his sailboat. Backup was a long way away, and he had no way of knowing if they even knew he and Mango were in trouble.

Late in the evening, the clouds built again, and both men prayed they would not bring more rain and storm-tossed seas. Fortunately, the storms stayed to the south, but they still sent ravenous waves to devour them on their march across the ocean. Mother Nature put on a spectacular light show as lightning danced across the horizon. Above them stretched the brightest patch of Milky Way they'd ever seen.

Exhausted, Ryan drifted off to sleep and had strange, vivid dreams. Toward morning, he dreamed of Emily. He was holding her close, one hand around her waist, the other entwined in her thick, blonde mane. She tilted her head back to expose her delicate throat. Ryan gently kissed her neck. She bent her lips to his ear. He shivered as her breath whispered across his skin. "Wake up."

Ryan kissed her neck, working his way from her collarbone to her ear. She pressed her cheek against his, and her lips brushed against his ear.

This time, her words thundered out in Mango's voice. "Wake up!"

CHAPTER THIRTY-SEVEN

Ryan's head snapped up off his chest, and brilliant sunlight assaulted his eyes. He squeezed them shut and gradually worked them back open until they'd become accustomed to the glare. When he finally looked around, he saw a fishing boat on the horizon.

"Untie me," Mango demanded.

With swollen fingers, Ryan struggled with the knot and failed to untie it. They slipped off again and again. "I can't get it."

Mango sliced through the line with his knife. "There are drift net floats about fifty yards away from us."

"Let's go hang on to the net."

"We don't want to get too close. We could get entangled in the ropes or impaled by the hooks. And there's always sharks looking for an easy meal."

"All right, Captain Cautious."

"I've seen it happen. We'll stay close to them and swim toward the boat."

"Let's go." Ryan held on to Mango and began kicking.

On the horizon, the boat turned and worked toward

them. The nets were being drawn in and the buoys created little wakes. If the boat drew the nets in before the captain saw them, they would miss their chance at rescue. Mango found a whistle in a pocket of the life jacket and he began to blow it.

The boat changed directions to come straight at them. It slowed as it approached.

Two weathered men and a preteen boy leaned over the rail. The oldest man gave a broad smile, which creased and wrinkled his skin. He called to them in Spanish. "*Son demasiado feos para ser sirenas.*" *You're too ugly to be mermaids.*

Ryan laughed with relief at being rescued, and at the old man's joke. He replied, "*Las mujeres en un barco son mala suerte. Permiso para venir a bordo?*" *Women are bad luck on a boat. Permission to come aboard?*

The man took a cigarette from his mouth and made a motion for the boy to throw a rope to the waterlogged men. As the young boy helped Mango over the rail, he gaped in astonishment at the stump of Mango's leg.

He cried out, "Your leg, *señor*!"

Mango gave him a devilish grin. "A shark ate it."

"No!" the boy cried and clamped both hands over his mouth. His wide-eyed stare swept up to meet the old man's. The boy dropped his hands and pointed at Mango's leg while shouting a rapid stream of Spanish.

The old man laughed, as did the mate and Ryan. Mango just grinned.

Ryan translated for his non-Spanish-speaking friend. "The boy believes your story about the shark. His grandfather, not so much. He pointed out the leg was healed, and no blood was coming out. Plus, there were no sharks chasing us."

Mango laughed.

"Not a good joke, mister," the boy muttered.

"What happened to your leg?" Ryan remembered seeing Mango's prosthesis jammed into the straps of his life vest. He hadn't thought about it since.

"I had to take it off. It was weighing me down and my stump swelled in the cup, making it hurt. I tried to keep it, but it got washed away last night when I fell asleep."

"I'll get you a new one when we get back."

"You better, I don't think the VA will buy my story."

Joyfully, the rescued men wrapped themselves in worn blankets provided by the mate. The boy brought chipped mugs full of steaming coffee.

Ryan took a minute to examine his body. His toes and fingers were white and swollen from being in the water. His skin was red and blistered from both the sun and the chafing of the rope across his waist and underarms. When he tried to drink the coffee, the liquid stung the splits in his lips. Even though the coffee was some of the best he'd ever tasted, he knew it would only dehydrate him more. After the coffee, Ryan would drink the cold bottle of water the boy had also brought before returning to the business of retrieving the nets.

"We need to call home," Mango urged. "We haven't checked in, and Jennifer will be worried."

"I'll find out if the captain has a phone." Ryan finished the coffee before standing.

The man shook his head when asked about a phone and pointed to a VHF marine radio.

Ryan switched the radio to channel thirty-eight, DWR's preferred channel for radio communication. He pressed the *send* button on the microphone. "Hailing any DWR vessel in hearing range. Hailing any DWR vessel."

His repeated calls went unanswered for the next two hours. The captain gave a shrug of his shoulders.

Ryan asked, "*¿Tienes un una carta marina?*" *Do you have a chart?*

"*Si.*" The man nodded and motioned for Ryan to follow him to the other side of the pilothouse.

He pulled out a dog-eared chart and unrolled it on a small table. Using a coffee cup and an ashtray, he anchored two corners of the map. He lit a cigarette and held the pack out. Ryan took the proffered cigarette and stuck it between his lips. The old man lit his and handed the lighter over before pinning down a third corner of the curling chart with his right hand and pointing to a spot in the Gulf of Mexico with his left.

The Yucatán Channel connected the Yucatán Basin of the Caribbean Sea and the Gulf of Mexico between the Yucatán Peninsula and Cuba. Three currents moved north through this natural funnel and spread out into the Gulf. The Florida Current flowed east between Cuba and Florida. The Yucatán Current wrapped around the horn of the Yucatán Peninsula and swept west then north along the eastern coast of Mexico. The third, Loop Current, rose straight north toward the boot of Louisiana before bending east and south to rush headlong into the Florida Current. In the middle of the Gulf, between the Loop Current and Mexico to the west, the waters swirled in a clockwise eddy. It was in this giant whirlpool Ryan and Mango had found themselves trapped as it pushed them south and west, many miles from the final resting place of *Sweet T*.

Mango squeezed in for a look at the chart, grasping the table for balance as the boat swayed. He waved away the cigarette smoke. "How long until we get to shore?"

Ryan consulted the captain who pointed to the town of

Progreso on the map. The small seaside village sat on the top of the Yucatán Peninsula.

The old man took the cigarette from his mouth, pinching it between his thumb and forefinger, and said, "*Cinco horas.*"

Mango frowned, looked at Ryan, who was about to translate, and said, "I got that part."

"I'll keep trying the radio."

Ryan helped Mango to a chair bolted to the deck in the rear of the cabin.

Every fifteen minutes, Ryan called for any DWR vessel to answer him. He was positive a ship would be in the area servicing one of the numerous oil rigs along the Mexican and U.S. coasts.

At the peak of its circular route, the fishing boat came into radio range of a crew vessel ferrying divers to and from their work site. It answered Ryan's hail, and the captain asked what he could do for him. Ryan requested the ship call Greg Olsen and let him know he and Mango were safe on the fishing vessel *Pescados*, on their way to Progreso, Mexico. The crew vessel captain agreed to call Greg.

Ten minutes later, the radio mounted on the fishing boat's dash crackled to life. "*Dark Water* calling *Pescados*. *Dark Water* calling *Pescados*."

Ryan snatched the mic off its perch and called back. "*Dark Water*, this is *Sweet T*, come back."

Mango's features relaxed into a grin.

Seconds later, Greg's voice came over the air. "Where you at, Ryan?"

Ryan read the coordinates to his friend, who replied, "Hold fast, brother, we're coming to get you."

"Where are you?" Ryan asked, amazed Greg was out looking for them.

"We're about an hour away."

"Roger, boss. See you in a few. *Sweet T*, out."

Greg had underestimated his arrival time because it was closer to ninety minutes before the big bow and tuna tower of the Hatteras became visible on the horizon. *Pescados* came to a stop, turning the bow into the waves. Jerry DiMarco pulled *Dark Water*, its fenders out, alongside *Pescados*. Greg and Shelly were both in the cockpit, beaming.

Ryan gave Greg a salute and a grin. Seeing Greg's mug riding to the rescue seemed like old times, and Ryan was thankful Greg was there.

Mango wrapped his arms around *Pescados*'s first mate and Ryan's necks. Supported between them, he hopped across the gap to the Hatteras. They carried him into the salon and deposited him on the couch.

Outside, Ryan offered to pay the fishermen for their help.

The old man waved him off, and said, "*No es todos los días que recojemos dos sirenas feas que cuentan esas buenas historias.*" *It's not every day I catch two ugly mermaids who tell such good stories.* He laughed heartily and glanced at the boy whose face reddened.

"Shark!" the mate shouted, and everyone burst into laughter.

This time, the boy joined in.

The boats quickly separated as Jerry used a touch of bow thruster. Ryan helped bring the fenders on board. For a moment, he stood in the cockpit and watched *Pescados* head south to work her nets.

He turned to Greg. They clasped hands and gave each other a one-handed buddy hug.

"Good to see you, man."

"Good to be seen. I thought we'd lost you."

Ryan grinned. "You're not so lucky."

"I think I need a cold one. Let's go in the salon."

Mango had hopped over to the fridge and retrieved a cold beer already. He was sitting on a stool at the kitchen island. Ryan cracked open his own bottle of beer and drained it in several quick gulps. He tossed it in the trash and pulled another from the fridge.

"All right, spill it. What happened," Greg demanded.

Mango and Ryan glanced at each other. Mango nodded.

Ryan took the unspoken signal for him to tell the story. "Radar picked up a ship about seven miles out. Then a RIB boat ambushed us. It was running silenced engines and came out of nowhere. They raked us over with a fifty cal and sank my boat. The RIB captain said he wanted us to suffer and left us in the water. We spent a couple rough nights on the open ocean."

"That's an understatement," Mango mumbled.

Shelly sent both men to take showers. When they were back in the salon, she sprayed them down with a liberal dose of aloe ointment to treat their sunburns, then examined Ryan's skin where the rope had chafed, leaving ugly red marks and blisters.

"I think I need a few Band-Aids," he remarked.

Shelly brought out a first aid kit.

Greg asked, "Did you see the mothership?"

"Just on radar," Mango responded. "According to the AIS, it's *La Carranza Garza*."

Greg sat with his arms crossed and his brakes locked. The Hatteras rolled very little as she motored toward the coast of Mexico. "I'll call Muriel and see if she can get some satellite time. We might be able to pick up the AIS signal."

"You can get us satellite time?" Mango asked incredulously.

"We use satellites quite a bit at DWR," Shelly said.

"If he can't get it, Landis might be able to," Ryan added.

"I'll make the call," Greg said. He rolled to a cabinet and removed a satellite phone.

"Hey, can I use that before you do?" Mango asked. "I'd like to call Jennifer."

"No problem." Greg set the phone down beside Mango. "We have plenty of time. We can't do anything until we refuel in Progreso. You guys are lucky the fishing boat picked you up. We used a software program to predict where you might be, and we were way off."

Mango looked surprised. "We thought we were going south and west."

"That's what we thought, too. The storms must have pushed you faster. Plus, the fishing boat tracked north and east."

Ryan grabbed a bottle of water from the fridge and headed to the cockpit.

Shelly called after him, "Don't forget to call Emily. She's really worried."

Ryan half-turned, one hand on the hatch knob. "Get the satellite time and then I'll call her." He'd found a pack of cigarettes in his go-bag, that Greg had retrieved from his office before leaving, and wanted to smoke one in the cockpit.

Back inside, Ryan listened to Greg talk to Landis. DWR couldn't get any satellite time. Landis promised to call back when he had a time slot.

Greg laid the phone beside Ryan. "Call your girlfriend."

Ryan took the phone to his usual cabin and sat on his bunk. After dialing Emily's number, he put the phone to his ear.

CHAPTER THIRTY-EIGHT

Commander Harry Dagnal packed his lip full of chewing tobacco as his copilot, Lieutenant Kelly Benton, spooled up the three turboshaft jet engines on the MH-53E Sea Dragon helicopter. Dagnal spat into an empty water bottle and put the cap back on. He glanced over his right shoulder at his crew chief, Mac Sissler, who gave him a thumbs-up. Benton released the rotor brake and the bird's seven giant rotor blades began to spin through their seventy-nine-foot arc. The dark green helicopter shuddered and swayed and lurched as the blades swept faster and faster, beating the air into submission, until they bent slightly upward to form a shallow cone. The largest helicopter in the U.S. military's arsenal overcame its own inertia and slipped gracefully upward, like a giant insect spewing three long trails of black smoke.

Dagnal, commanding officer of Helicopter Mine Countermeasures Squadron 14 (HM-14), was leading a training detachment from their home base at Norfolk Naval Air Station to Naval Support Activity Panama City. He'd received a telephone call from Commander Naval Air Force Atlantic, informing him of a special operation Dagnal was to perform. Dagnal ordered his favorite aircraft, 555, readied and chose his copilot.

As he and Benton had helped prep the aircraft for flight, they watched maintenance crewmen scramble over the bird, servicing and inspecting the airframe. Dagnal had admired the kids who kept the ancient helicopters airborne. They were a bunch of enlisted airmen, the lowest rank in the service, ensuring he could fly. An adage had come to him and he'd smiled as he'd recited it to Benton, "Takes a high school diploma to fix 'em, a college degree to fly 'em, and a PhD to build 'em."

Fifteen minutes later, the bird was in the air, flashing over the slate-gray waters of the Gulf of Mexico. Dagnal spit into his bottle again and checked the GPS coordinates written on his kneeboard against the GPS screen displaying their position, destination, and arrival time.

Benton had the autopilot on and was scanning the gauges and instruments before looking out the front windshield into the darkness. The bug-like lenses of the night vision goggles made her head look funny in the wash of green light from Dagnal's own NVGs.

The flight was routine, and at the appointed hour, the U.S.S. *Independence*, one of the Navy's new littoral combat ships, came into view. She was stationed out of Pensacola, Florida, for rapid deployment into the Caribbean Basin, and for the new crop of rotor-head students to practice their ship-based launch and landing qualifications. Dagnal took the controls and guided the helicopter over the rear deck of the LCS. A yellow-vested landing signal officer used wands to direct him over the rear of the ship and down to the deck.

As soon as the wheels touched the nonskid deck, purple-shirted crewmen connected a fuel hose to the side of the helicopter and stood under the buffering rotor wash, waiting for the tanks to fill. Meanwhile, a dark group of figures huddled against the ship's superstructure, silent warriors whose sole job was to break stuff, kill people, and blow things up. Dagnal watched them through the green glow of his bug eyes. He wondered what dangers lurked in the Gulf of Mexico that he needed to facilitate the delivery of these men.

Benton motioned to the fuel gauges, and Dagnal signaled the purple shirts to shut off the tap. They retracted their hose, and Dagnal gave the go-ahead for the SEALs to board. Six heavily armed men carried a black rubber Zodiac raiding craft into the rear of the helicopter. Sissler helped strap it to the deck while the LSO held his arms straight out from his side and then lifted them up over his head. He repeated the gesture until Dagnal had his helicopter ten feet off the deck. The LSO held his right arm straight out from his side and repeatedly brought his left arm up over his head. Dagnal slipped the helicopter left, over the port side of the ship, felt the slight drop from the change in air pressure, and then the helo was lifting again. He added power, dipped the nose, and roared down the length of the ship.

The SEAL team leader hopped into the jump seat between the pilot and copilot seats and handed a set of coordinates to Dagnal. The pilot glanced at them before passing them to Benton. She punched them into the GPS unit, and it zoomed into an empty blue spot off the coast of the Yucatán Peninsula.

Dagnal let out a whistle as he adjusted course and speed. "What's going on out there?" he asked, looking over his shoulder into piercing blue eyes.

"Gunrunners."

Dagnal nodded. It was more of an answer than he'd expected. When he looked back, Sissler was in the jump seat. "Got a few hours to relax, Chief."

Sissler pointed at the fuel gauges. "We don't have enough juice to get there and back."

"*Independence* is steaming out to meet us halfway on the return trip."

"Hope that crate doesn't break down," Sissler muttered. He, like most of the fleet, knew about the gremlins plaguing the newest class of ships, everything from cracked hulls to engine failures. It wasn't uncommon for the Navy to tow *Independence* back to port.

Benton glanced at the CO sharply. Dagnal knew she disapproved of the enlisted ranks making disparaging comments about the chain of command and the Navy as a whole. She was a ring knocker, a graduate of Annapolis Naval Academy, an ardent proponent for the rigid strictures of service. Those who didn't conform were subject to counseling.

Dagnal looked back at Sissler and shook his head. Sissler clamped his mouth shut, made a motion of locking it with a key, then tucked the imaginary key into his pocket.

Benton glanced at Dagnal, shook her helmet-clad head, and rolled her eyes behind the NVGs. Dagnal squirmed in his seat to get more comfortable. She would have to deal with his lax attitude toward his crew. It was what endeared them to him.

They settled into an easy silence made familiar from hundreds of hours flying together. Dagnal got up to relieve himself and saw the SEALs slumped in various positions, asleep, reading paperbacks, studying files. He finished and turned back to the scene. The team leader, who had handed him his coordinates, stood five feet away, a hand braced against the roof. He stared at Dagnal and held up his left wrist, so his watch was visible. Dagnal glanced to the GPS screen and then flashed the time remaining with his fingers. The SEAL nodded and sat back down. Dagnal felt unnerved by the icy stare. He climbed back into his pilot's seat, thinking about how comfortable the seat was compared to what those guys were about to do.

The beeping of the GPS unit interrupted Dagnal's constant sweep of gauges, window, and mirrors. He yawned and keyed the mic on the helicopter's intercommunications system. "Ten minutes out."

"Copy," both Sissler and the SEAL replied.

According to his orders, Dagnal knew their target would flash a light. He kept his eyes peeled for the signal. A glance into the mirror, focused on the cabin, showed the SEALs had their gear lashed to the inside of the small boat and they were sitting on its sides, ready for action. Out of the corner of his eye, Dagnal saw the wink of white light.

It surprised him to see a sportfisher with a massive aluminum tuna tower. In the brief glimpse he had of the boat, he saw a light blue hull under a white cabin. Dagnal flew past the sportfisher and turned into the wind. He came to a hover a hundred yards away from the boat and signaled Sissler, who motioned for the SEALs to exit his aircraft.

The boat went first, sliding down the ramp into the water five feet below. Then the men, dressed in scuba diving dry suits, jumped into the frothing waves. Sissler spoke over the ICS, letting Dagnal know their cargo was clear. Dagnal added power. The windshield wipers tried to keep the windscreen clear of the water whipped up by the rotor wash. The big helicopter lumbered higher, and as he gained altitude, Dagnal dipped the nose and raced toward the *Independence*. Behind him, he saw the sportfisher's exterior spotlights were on to collect her packages. The tuna tower was dancing back and forth as the boat rocked in the waves. Dagnal shut off the wipers and mentally saluted the brave men on the tiny boat and wished them Godspeed in their mission.

CHAPTER THIRTY-NINE

Rotor wash lashed *Dark Water*'s spray curtains as the big helicopter came alongside and disgorged its deadly load. Greg kept just enough throttle on to keep the bow pointed into the three-foot waves. Ryan hustled down the tuna tower's ladder to the bridge. A blast of rotor wash tore at his clothing. He saw the rubber raiding craft fall from the helicopter and then six men leaped into the frothing water. The pilot wasted no time hanging around to see if everyone was all right. He added power, gained altitude, and raced away.

The fishing boat idled up to the smaller craft. Jerry had a gaff out and hooked the Zodiac's bow line. All six SEALs were clinging to the lifeline running around the rubber craft. Ryan and Jerry helped the men clamber onto *Dark Water*. Then they all pulled the small boat into the cockpit of the Hatteras. They trooped into the cabin and Ryan's split lips curved into a grin as he shook the hand of Lieutenant Larry Grove. "Welcome aboard, sir. Glad you could make it."

"You can't stay out of trouble, even in the civilian

world," Larry said.

Still grinning, Ryan said, "It's been an interesting adventure."

Greg and Ryan had worked with Larry on several operations before the veteran SEAL team leader transferred to the secretive Naval Special Warfare Development Group, more commonly known as DEVGRU, formerly SEAL Team Six. He was a tall, lean man with a broad smile, blond hair, and ice blue eyes. He'd earned the nickname Iceman. Not only did he look like Val Kilmer's character in *Top Gun,* but he was cool under pressure.

Ryan had called Landis from Mexico and requested Larry's help. Fortune smiled upon them, and the Navy granted their request to allow their shooters to work a dark op.

"This is Senior Chief Roland Jenkins. He works with me at Dam Neck." Dam Neck Naval Base, just south of Virginia Beach, Virginia, was home to DEVGRU.

"Good to meet you, Senior Chief," Ryan said, accepting the man's outstretched hand.

"Call me Jinks, we're not on Navy time."

Larry ran through the rest of the team roster: Andy Vodden, Steve Kellogg, Michael Paddington, and Tyron Kimber.

"You guys get cleaned up and we'll unpack the gear," Ryan told the men.

Out in the cockpit, Ryan unwrapped the waterproof package in the rubber raider. The first thing he found was a spare leg for Mango. He opened the cabin door and tossed the rig to his partner. "Here, make yourself useful."

Mango managed to grin, catch the leg, and shoot Ryan the bird all at the same time.

The package contained silenced Heckler & Koch MP5

submachine guns, pistols, body armor, load-bearing vests, ropes, a collapsible aluminum pole with a hook on one end, and a rolled-up rope ladder. Mango helped Ryan distribute the black combat uniforms, balaclavas, helmets with night vision goggles, and boots also in the loadout.

The men checked their individual gear and weapons before testing them off the rear of *Dark Water*. Back in the salon, Ryan attached a laptop to the forty-two-inch LED television mounted on the salon's forward bulkhead.

"What are we looking at?" Larry asked.

"Landis sent me specs for *La Carranza Garza*. The ship is a one-hundred-and-fifty-foot platform supply vessel once operated by SEACOR Marine. Bollinger Shipyards built *Garza* in Lockport, Louisiana, and she's flagged in the Marshall Islands. She's capable of twelve knots max and cruises at ten."

"How many onboard?" Jinks asked.

Ryan consulted the computer. "Specs say crew of eleven plus two VIP bunks and sixteen passengers."

"Twenty-nine total souls," Jinks added up. "How many do you figure are on the boat?"

"I have no idea," Ryan said. "We saw five on the RIB boat and I killed at least one of those."

Jinks said, "We should expect the max number of men, and for them to be heavily armed."

"You're right," Ryan agreed.

"How do you want to divide up?" the SEAL commander asked.

"Mango, this was your specialty. You make the call," Ryan said.

"We're an eight-man force, and we'll go with teams of two. I'll go with Jinks. Ryan with Larry. I'm sure you guys already know who you'll partner with."

"Everyone okay with that?" Ryan looked around the room and received crisp nods.

Larry asked, "What do you have in mind, Ryan?"

"Landis will provide us with location information. We'll position close to the *Garza* with *Dark Water* and use the rubber raider to slip aboard her. Based on what I'm seeing on the ship's schematics, we can bottle everyone up in the superstructure by locking the outer hatches. With surprise and speed, we can get all the doors locked on the mess deck and the port side forecastle deck before anyone knows we're there."

He pointed to the port side ladderwell running up the exterior of the superstructure. "Larry and I will go straight for the bridge. From there, we can control the ship and secure the inside ladderwell. This will leave the starboard side hatch on the forecastle unsecured. With everyone pinned inside the superstructure, we might have to do some hard close-quarters battle. I think we'll have the upper hand."

For the next two hours, they worked through the battle plan.

Landis emailed more photos of the ship. Ryan pulled up the photos and read aloud the text Landis had written. "*La Carranza Garza* is still flagged in the Marshall Islands, but owned by a dummy corporation registered in the Seychelles. Her home port is Veracruz, Mexico. I have a research assistant tracing the dummy corps. Good luck."

Ryan moved the pictures of the boat to the television. They were satellite photos and others sourced from the internet. The ship's hull was blue with orange trim, and a white superstructure crowded the vessel's bow. Behind the superstructure was a flat cargo deck sitting low to the water line. Side by side on the deck were two rusty green shipping containers. On the port side, a large, yellow crane was mounted at the rear of the ship with its boom pointed forward over the containers.

Larry Grove approached the television and looked closely at the pictures. "Scroll through them again," he said.

The men watched the slideshow again with everyone gathered around the screen.

"Stop," Larry commanded.

Ryan paused on an image of the ship's stern.

"We go up here." Larry pointed to the port side stern. "The crane and the cargo containers will help hide our approach. We'll do like the Somali pirates and latch a ladder onto the handrails. It also gives us a defensible position if we're spotted."

Agreement was unanimous.

"I don't want to step on your toes, Mango," Larry said. "I know this is your specialty, but we do this stuff, too."

Mango shook his head to show his feelings were not hurt. "Happy for the help."

"Okay," Larry continued. "Jinks and Mango will go up the starboard side with Vodden and Paddington. Kellogg, you and Kimber will follow me and Ryan up the port side. From there, we'll follow our battle plan."

The laptop pinged and Ryan checked it. Another email from Landis.

"Landis says the *Garza* has left Veracruz and she's headed out into the Gulf on a southeastern tack." Ryan sat in front of the keyboard and rapidly typed in a website. "Landis says we can use Marinetracker.com to follow the *Garza*." He sent the website up to the big screen. "I'll get Greg to head us in the *Garza*'s direction, and we'll rendezvous with it by nightfall."

CHAPTER FORTY

Senior Chief Roland Jenkins held the throttle wide open on the Zodiac FC 470, a fifteen-foot black rubber raiding craft, ubiquitous to special forces around the world. Ahead of him in the boat, the seven other raiders hunkered against the gunwales. Six-foot waves pounded the little boat, causing the SEAL to rev the motor up the waves and chop the throttle as they dropped down the backside. Spray blasted over the bow, soaking them and their gear.

It was a perfect night for boarding operations. Rain obscured vision and deadened sounds coming off the water. The *Garza* was steaming upwind, which would further conceal any motor noise the Zodiac's silenced outboard made. Ryan hoped the big waves didn't cause a problem boarding.

"Come starboard a degree, Jinks," Vodden said over their wireless communications gear.

"Copy," Jinks replied and shifted the engine tiller. The boat rode up the waves sideways and slid down into a trough. Several times they had to lean hard to starboard to prevent the boat from capsizing.

After running hard most of the afternoon, Greg had located the *Garza* on radar and shadowed the ship until nightfall. The men had gone overboard into the Zodiac while a passing storm front provided perfect cover.

A quarter-mile out, they spotted the *Garza*'s running lights. Jinks turned the Zodiac onto an intercept course to bring them behind the *Garza*.

Five minutes later, Jinks had the Zodiac pressed against the back of the larger boat as they both pitched and rolled. Jinks constantly worked the throttle to keep the Zodiac steady.

Kimber held out the hook with an attached rope ladder, and it banged off the railing as the Zodiac fell away on a wave. He tried again as Jinks brought the boat up close. This time, the young SEAL hooked the railing. He dropped the pole and climbed the rope ladder.

Kimber carried a line attached to the Zodiac and he used it to hold the Zodiac steady while the other men climbed the ladder. When Ryan was over the rail, he and Paddington hauled the little boat tight against the *Garza*'s stern so Jinks, the last man in the Zodiac, could shut off the motor and climb up the ladder. Once he was on board the *Garza*, they used the line to pull the Zodiac over the rounded stern and tied it to the railing. The boat was out of the water and invisible to anyone who might walk by.

Ryan expected guards to step out at any moment. The boarding party had expected roving teams of sentinels as well as lookouts posted on the superstructure. So far, they'd seen no one. He couldn't blame the lookouts for staying out of the driving rain. He licked the water off his scabbed lips and adjusted his grip on the MP5.

Cautiously, they eased forward along the cargo containers. Rubber-soled boots silenced their footsteps and the wind carried away any other sounds. The crew had strung a tarp between the superstructure and the cargo containers to provide shade and a convenient spot for them to get out of the rain. Two sentries huddled under the tarp, smoking cigarettes, with their rifles dangling from slings. Larry shot one and Jinks took out the other from his position on the far side of the ship.

Behind the sentries was a hatch into the mess room. Kellogg stepped forward and slipped a metal bar into the wheel in the hatch's center to prevent it from opening. Simultaneously, Kellogg moved around Ryan and Larry to jam the hatch under the ladderwell. Jinks jammed the galley hatch. Now, the only way into the mess was via a ladderwell inside the center of the superstructure. That same ladderwell ran from the pilothouse at the top of the superstructure to the hold in the ship's bottom.

"Go," Larry whispered. He and Ryan charged up the stairs, past the forecastle deck, to the pilothouse. Larry halted so he could survey the scene. Seeing all was clear, they moved to the pilothouse hatch. Larry ripped it open and held it as Ryan bounded through the opening and braced himself against the roll of the ship.

To Ryan's left were big rain-lashed windows facing the bow. Under them was a console laden with electrical instruments. Just behind the console was the forward navigation station. In the room's center was the ladderwell connecting all decks from the hold to the pilothouse. To his right, the room narrowed to box in an aft steering station, rear electronics console, and windows. Across the room was a second entry hatch, and aft of the hatch was a cabinet with a coffee maker beside a bench.

A guard standing by the coffee maker brought his gun up. Ryan used his silenced MP5 to shoot the man twice in the chest. The guard stumbled back against the bulkhead and slumped to the floor.

Larry leaped into the room to back up Ryan and left the hatch unlatched. It slammed open and shut with the rolling of the ship.

"Secure that hatch," a giant of a man thundered from behind the forward navigation station. Ryan took a second to focus on the speaker while he trained his gun on a man sitting on the bench. The man behind the nav station was six feet six with broad shoulders and narrow hips.

"Are you the captain?" Larry demanded. He trained his gun on the tall man.

"Yes," he replied while Ryan secured his man with zip cuffs on the wrists and ankles.

Ryan had a sudden urge to do the scene from *Captain Phillips* when the Somali pirate looked at Phillips and said, "I'm the captain, now," but he held his tongue. It was not the time or the place for his dark humor. Instead, he secured the pilothouse hatch.

"We're taking control of this ship, Captain," Larry informed him. "We believe you're trafficking firearms into the United States."

"I'm not a U.S. citizen and we're not in U.S. waters," the man retorted.

Ryan made the captain sit on the bench and secured him with more zip cuffs.

Larry smirked. "I'm not here to arrest you. I could toss you overboard for all I care."

CHAPTER FORTY-ONE

While Ryan and Larry commandeered the bridge, Mango and Jinks moved up to the forecastle deck, where they found Kellogg and Kimber jamming shut the port side forecastle hatch. Jinks, Mango, Vodden, and Paddington stacked up at the forecastle's corner and eased around to the front of the superstructure.

On the opposite side of the ship, two of the ship's company rounded the corner of the forecastle holding AK-47s. The roar of a fully automatic rifle nearly deafened Mango and the SEALs, and the brilliant blaze of fire from the gun's muzzle lit up the night.

Mango went flat to the deck behind a kneeling Jinks while Vodden dove behind the anchor windlass. Vodden slid on the rain-slickened steel deck and slammed into the steel windlass with his shoulder. The ship rolled and he crashed into the windlass again. He moaned as he felt his shoulder dislocate. He looked over at his partner Paddington, who had fallen back behind the bulkhead with Kimber and Kellogg.

"Stay down," Paddington commanded and stepped

around the corner. He shot the gunman with a controlled burst of fire. The gunman staggered backward and hit the railing. Jinks shot him twice more and the man fell over the side of the ship.

The second gunman, who had ducked behind the forecastle's steel bulkhead, jumped out and opened fire. Before the four men on the forecastle deck could take out the new shooter, Larry stepped onto the bridge wing and shot the gunman dead from above.

"Secure that forecastle hatch!" Larry said over the communications system. He gazed down at the dead crewman he'd just shot. "Vodden, Paddington, join us up here in the pilothouse, and we'll trap them in a pincer movement."

"I can't," Vodden groaned. "I separated my shoulder."

"Are you good?" Larry asked. "Can you move?"

"I can move." Everyone on the comms network heard Vodden grind his teeth.

"Get up to the pilothouse and stand guard. Everyone else, secure the hatch."

"Copy," came the response from everyone on the forecastle deck.

Vodden held his arm as he and Paddington came onto the bridge. Ryan opened his medical blowout pack and devised a makeshift sling. Vodden leaned against the navigation table. His face was pale and covered with a sheen of sweat.

A bullet blasted up the ladderwell and ricocheted around the bridge before shattering a side window. Rain and wind immediately saturated the bridge.

"Keep their heads down," Larry yelled.

Ryan pulled his MP5 up to his shoulder and loosed a volley of bullets down the ladderwell.

Below, full auto AK fire mixed with the sharper bark of pistols. They could hear no return fire from the silenced MP5s. What Larry and Ryan could hear was Mango, Jinks, Kimber, and Kellogg calling maneuvers over the comms net. Like true professionals, they didn't panic and calmly kept the opposing force bottlenecked in the passageway outside the forecastle.

"OK, Andy," Larry said. "I'm going to set your arm and take some of the pain away."

Andy Vodden nodded and grimaced as his boss jerked his arm. Vodden screamed. Larry wrapped the sling around the man's arm and neck before giving him a dose of pain killer.

"We have to rethink our strategy," Ryan shouted to Larry, forgetting about the comms system. More bullets flew up the ladderwell, and Ryan returned fire.

Larry responded quietly over the comms, "Jinks, can you push those guys back inside?"

"No way, sir. They're pushing us back. Lots of guys with firepower. They'll shoot us like fish in a barrel if we don't do something quick."

"Stun grenades on three," Larry said.

"Copy, I'm throwing a frag out here."

"Do what you need to do, Jinks."

"On three, sir."

Ryan palmed a grenade in each hand and gave one to Larry. They pulled the pins while Larry counted. On Larry's three-count, the grenades flew.

Down in the forecastle deck, Ryan and Larry's grenades bounced into opposite corners. The detonations stunned the men with brilliant flashes of light and deafening sound. Outside, the steel structure shook and rattled as shrapnel ripped through flesh and pinged off walls.

"Advance," Larry shouted.

The former EOD tech bounded down the stairs, followed by the active-duty SEALs. As they descended, a hatch swung open and a man stepped into the room. Ryan dove to the deck and rolled to bring his MP5 up. Their attacker opened fire, and the next instant he pitched over backward with three bullet holes in his chest.

Ryan turned to see Jinks, smoking gun welded to shoulder and cheek, and his stack of gun bunnies coming through the starboard hatch. The next thing he saw was Larry bent over Michael Paddington.

Larry looked up from the prone man in front of him. "Secure the rest of the ship. Now!" His voice had a hard edge to it, and it caught Ryan off guard.

When he stepped closer to Paddington, Ryan saw the man had taken a round through the neck. Larry had lost a SEAL on his watch. He placed a hand on Larry's shoulder.

"Take care of the ship," Larry growled at Ryan.

Ryan pulled up his weapon and turned to help the other men secure the crew with zip cuffs.

Kimber and Kellogg tossed stun grenades into the mess deck below and followed them down. The grenades bounced off the mess door and into the bunk rooms. They stunned the men still moving about in the passageways and open rooms. Part of the crew had locked themselves in the mess. Jinks jammed the door from the outside.

Mango accompanied Kimber and Kellogg to the engine room. They found one man standing watch over the twin 1,175-horsepower Caterpillar diesels. Kimber secured his hands with cuffs and led him to the forecastle. They left Kellogg in the engine room to keep an eye on the power plants.

With the ship secured, the rest of the team began a systematic search of the vessel.

La Carranza Garza's hold was originally built to carry bulk diesel, chemicals, and drilling mud to and from offshore oil rigs. The mud tanks, located amidships on both sides of the central passageway, had been cut open and were now stacked with crates of rifles, pistols, and ammunition. The twin shipping containers held more firearms, including M60 and Browning fifty-caliber machine guns, and a stack of eight Russian-built Strela-3 shoulder-fired surface-to-air missiles.

CHAPTER FORTY-TWO

Ryan climbed up to the bridge, carrying one end of the body bag containing Petty Officer Second Class Michael Paddington. Larry Grove and Roland Jenkins carried the other end. Reverently, they laid him on the bridge deck. Larry stood and saluted the fallen SEAL before turning back to business.

"Your show now, Ryan."

Ryan walked to the rear of the bridge and pulled the comms unit he used to talk to the SEAL team from his ear, switching on an earpiece in his other ear. This one connected him to Floyd Landis, along with a camera Ryan wore that beamed video footage of their ship boarding to the DHS man's office. During the raid, he could hear Landis but not speak to him. Ryan was grateful that the DHS agent had kept silent during the action.

"Do you read me, Landis?" Ryan asked as he adjusted the earpiece and scratched at both ears. The familiar scents of salt air, blood, and excrement mingled with hot coffee. He turned to see the coffee pot full of black brew and Larry Grove pouring himself a mugful.

"I read you five by five."

"Roger." Ryan moved to the large man wearing the uniform of a ship captain. He squatted beside the bench and looked up at the man's blue eyes. "My name is Ryan Weller. You are under arrest and will not be afforded the courtesies of the U.S. court system because the U.S. government has deemed you and your crew terrorists. They have authorized us to take you and your crew straight to Guantanamo Bay where you will be interned in a secure facility until such time when your case can be heard by a military tribunal."

The captain's face went slack, and his big blond head dropped between his shoulders. He slowly shook it side to side. When he looked up, there were tears coursing down his cheeks. In a shaky voice, he said, "My name is Anders Mikkelsen. I am innocent of these charges. I was captain of this vessel when she sailed as *SEACOR Mariner*. The new owner, Arturo Guerrero, offered me a substantial raise. It was much later I realized I was to pilot a pirate ship. By then, Guerrero was having my family watched and he threatened me. He said if I quit, he would kill them."

"Can we verify the threat on his family?" Ryan asked Landis.

Landis whispered in his ear, "We'll work on it."

"They live on Maple Street in Anaheim, California." He gave the house number.

Landis spoke again. "We verified the captain's papers, and his employment with SEACOR. They gave him a glowing review. We're checking out the family."

Ryan extracted a pack of Camel Blues from a shirt pocket and removed a cigarette. He lit it and drew the smoke deep into his lungs.

"May I have one as well?" Anders asked.

Ryan shook another from the package, placed it between the captain's lips and lit it.

Anders took a deep breath. "Could you take the cuffs off, please?"

Ryan cut the cuffs loose and placed a new set on Anders, so his hands were in front of his body.

"Where did the weapons come from?"

"We met a ship off the coast of Belize. I dealt with a man by the name of Jim Kilroy. He is American, I believe."

Larry Grove grunted.

Ryan asked, "What?"

Larry elaborated, "Kilroy is a major arms dealer operating out of Central America. He owns resort properties all over the Caribbean Basin and launders his money through them."

"You've been chasing this guy?" Ryan asked.

"He's well-connected politically," Larry said. "When the winds of fortune blow his way, he gets protection from the U.S. government. When they blow the other way, we go looking for him. The old 'enemy of my enemy is my friend' routine."

Ryan understood all too well. He'd seen it happen many times in Iraq and Afghanistan. "When are you supposed to meet Kilroy again?" he asked Anders.

"Not for a while. Guerrero arranges the shipments. We made a pickup a week ago. That is why we have so many weapons on board."

"Is your only method of smuggling via stolen sailboats?"

"No, we also meet fishing boats and offload guns into their holds. Those fishermen make more money on one run for Guerrero than they do fishing all month."

"Do you move drugs?" Larry asked.

"No, Guerrero likes to keep his businesses separate."

Ryan asked, "Why is Guerrero moving all these weapons into the United States?"

Anders held up his cuffed hands. "All I do is drive the ship."

"I didn't figure a Danish sea captain would be privy to Guerrero's master plan."

Anders snorted. "No, I don't care at all. I'm only trying to protect my family."

"Do you know where Guerrero is now?"

"He has a home in Tampico. He runs his operations from a compound there."

Mango entered the bridge. He made a beeline for the coffee. Kimber and Jinks removed the dead man from the bridge.

"Captain, are there any men you trust to run the ship?" Larry asked.

"Yes, my chief engineer and my first mate. They came with me when Guerrero bought the ship. I believe they locked themselves in the mess. If you didn't kill them during your assault."

"There are men locked in the mess who refuse to come out," Mango said between sips of coffee.

"We made plans, in case someone attacked the ship," Anders informed them. "They were to lock themselves into the mess. You can trust us, Mr. Weller. We have no wish to harm you or your men. We only want to do our jobs and not continue the piracy and gunrunning."

"I'm not letting your men out," Ryan said.

The man next to Anders remained sullen and refused to look at anyone.

"Who is this?" Ryan asked, pointing at the man.

"He's the new chief engineer. Guerrero sent him aboard after he bought the boat."

Larry motioned for Ryan to join him in a corner away from the captain. When they stopped, Larry sipped from his mug and watched Anders Mikkelsen. "You need more than two people to run this ship, and as much as I like Greg, he needs someone to help him on *Dark Water*. The seas are pretty rough for him to be running the boat by himself."

In his ear, Ryan heard Landis. "I agree with the SEAL. Keep everyone confined. You'll have to make do until the Coast Guard gets there. They got a late start."

"Coast Guard," Ryan said. "I thought the *Independence* was meeting us."

"They broke down. Something to do with turbine failure."

"Shocker. How long until the Coasties get here?"

"You have a few hours," Landis said. "We had to reroute a ship out of Galveston."

"Who are they sending?" Mango asked.

Ryan repeated the question to Landis.

"The cutter *Manowar*."

Ryan informed Mango, who nodded and said, "Good guys. Captain's name is Raymond Watson."

"Give me an ETA," Ryan said to Floyd and then to the rest, "I don't trust this guy and I don't think we can trust the crew. Shelly has her captain's license. DiMarco will stay with Greg, and the rest of us will crew this vessel until we can turn it over to the Coast Guard. Mango, you used to be a boatswain's mate, you should be able to do something useful."

Mango crossed his arms and knitted his brows together. "Really, bro?"

Larry grinned, and Ryan shrugged.

Mango's face relaxed into a grin. "I know more about running a boat than any of you squids." Then he turned serious again. Looking at Ryan, he said, "I need to talk to you about something." He motioned with his head toward the ladderwell.

The two men walked down the ladder and stood on the forecastle deck. Standing behind Ryan, Mango tapped him on the shoulder and motioned for him to stay put. He then wrote a note in a small notepad he carried and held it out where Ryan could see it and the camera could not.

"Landis, I need to go offline for a few minutes."

"Ryan, don't you ..."

Ryan shut off the camera and the mic. "What's so important?"

Mango moved into the captain's cabin and crossed to the bunk. He lifted the mattress and a steel lid covering a six-inch-deep locker. The locker contained half a carton of Marlboro Gold cigarettes, a partial bottle of Akvavit, and a random collection of personal possessions.

"I almost overlooked this." Mango pointed to a small catch on the side of the locker tray. He flicked it to the side and raised the tray. Underneath lay stacks of bound one-hundred-dollar bills. Ryan and Mango each picked up a packet of bills wrapped in a white currency band with mustard-colored strips and labeled $10,000.

"I need a calculator, but there's at least a million here," Ryan said.

Mango said, "Closer to five if my earlier count was right."

Ryan chuckled as he fanned the bills with his thumb. He tossed the bundle back in the locker. "I wouldn't be disappointed if those found their way onto *Dark Water*."

Mango scrutinized his friend. "Are you serious?"

"Cliff Olsen told me there'd be occasions when we found ourselves in a situation like this. Think of it as a bonus." He slapped Mango on the back and they both laughed.

Mango tossed his bundle back in the locker. "What did you get from the captain?"

"He works for Arturo Guerrero."

"The pro wrestler?"

Ryan burst out laughing. "That's Eddie Guerrero."

Embarrassed, Mango changed the subject. "What about Aztlán?"

Ryan, still grinning, said, "He says he doesn't know anything about it."

"You believe him?"

"No. He claims Guerrero is threatening his family. He would have quit a long time ago rather than run guns and contribute to high-seas piracy."

"He has to know more."

"We need to interview someone from the RIB boat crew. Did you see anyone you recognized when we were handcuffing people?"

"I saw the guy who ran the boat, but he isn't talking. Jinks put a bullet in his chest right after he killed Paddington. There were several men who are wearing the Aztlán patch."

Ryan pursed his lips. "Let's find someone who knows what's going on."

They stepped back into the forecastle's common area and looked at the men sitting or lying on the deck.

"Let's grab that guy." Ryan pointed at a Mexican kid in his early twenties with a wisp of a mustache and a mop of floppy, black hair.

"No, *señor*, no!" The kid screamed. He kicked and fought violently as Ryan and Mango hooked their arms under his and dragged him into the captain's cabin.

They threw him on the bunk, and he slithered onto his knees. "*Por favor, no, por favor!*" *Please, no, please.* Tears streamed down his face as he sat back on his heels.

"*Cállate,*" *Shut up*, Ryan bellowed. "Stop whining."

The kid shook now. A stain darkened the front of his trousers.

Ryan shook his head in annoyance. He squatted down beside the kid, Walther pistol in hand. In Spanish, Ryan spoke calmly to him. "What's your name?"

"Ernesto."

"I don't want to hurt you, Ernesto, but I will if you don't cooperate."

The boy nodded and sniffed back mucus.

"Good, your friends weren't so lucky. They fought with us and now they are dead. You, my friend, will end up the same way if you don't help me. Who do you work for?"

The boy shook his head.

"You don't know?"

"No say," Ernesto whined.

Mango knelt beside the kid, and Ernesto's eyes darted to him then back at Ryan and down to the gun. They traveled in a constant circle, and when the eyes lifted to Ryan's, Mango smacked Ernesto so hard he left a handprint on the boy's face.

"*Bastardo!*" Ernesto moaned and spat blood on the deck.

"Tell me, Ernesto." Ryan shoved the pistol muzzle against the boy's kneecap.

The boy sobbed again. Tears streamed down his face. "No." He shook his head.

"Tell me!" Ryan grabbed him by the front of his shirt and pulled him upright. "You have the balls to sink my boat and steal from others, yet you cry like a *puta*."

"They will kill me," Ernesto sobbed.

Ryan pressed the gun barrel against the boy's forehead and leaned in until his face was just inches from Ernesto's, then screamed, "I'll kill you."

"Arturo Guerrero," Ernesto wailed.

Still holding the boy's lapels, Ryan asked, "What's Guerrero doing with these guns?"

Ernesto stiffened as if he were proud. "They are for *la Revolución*."

"What revolution, Ernesto?" Ryan relaxed his grip.

The kid backed away and pressed himself against the bulkhead. "We take back Aztlán from *el Norte* and restore our ancestral lands."

"Guerrero is the leader of this movement?"

"He is our high priest. Once the lands reunite, he will be our ruler."

"Was he part of the bombings in Austin and Los Angeles?"

"I hope so." He spat a gelatinous glob of blood and spittle on the deck and wiped his mouth with the back of his hand.

"Where do they take the guns?"

"You should have asked Jorge. He knows the whole operation." The boy wiped his eyes with his palms. "He is dead."

Ryan and Mango left Ernesto bound on the floor of the cabin and went up to the bridge. The air felt good after being trapped in the cabin with the stench of blood, sweat, fear, and urine. Someone had duct-taped a sheet of plastic over the broken pane of glass. It blocked the wind but was flapping at the upper right corner. White-capped waves rolled on the horizon. The rain had ceased, but the seas were still rough. Clouds scurried across a half-moon even though the wind was dying down.

Both men grabbed cups of coffee.

Mango said, "I'll take care of what we talked about when Shelly transfers over from *Dark Water*."

Jinks came onto the bridge. He walked straight to Larry Grove and said, "You need to come with me."

CHAPTER FORTY-THREE

Omar Salam Mansur listened at the door of his hidden chamber. Behind him, Wahbi Rahman Osman murmured a barely audible prayer to Allah.

"Silence," Omar whispered in Arabic.

He'd heard gunfire and detonations he believed were from grenades. Now he could hear two men speaking in English. Omar didn't recognize the men's voices. Most of the ship's crew spoke Spanish. He'd spent enough time listening at the door to recognize most of the crew by their speech patterns. Omar pressed his ear to the thin, metal bulkhead and listened to the conversation. The men had stopped right outside the door. Omar had trouble hearing the conversation over the pounding of his pulse in his ears.

"Hey, LT, I'll be glad when we're done with this op."

"Yeah, me too. I wish Paddington hadn't died."

"It sucked, sir."

"Damn right it does. What did you want to talk about?"

"Do you remember the top-secret intelligence brief about Al-Qaeda using boats to smuggle operatives into the U.S.?"

Omar slipped away from the door and picked up a satellite phone. He dialed the number stored in its memory and listened to it ring. A man answered in Spanish.

"*As-salaam alaykum.*" *Peace be unto you*, Omar said, offering the traditional Arabic greeting.

"Who is this?" the man asked in English.

Omar also switched languages. "This is Omar Salam Mansur. I am on the ship going to the United States. It has been compromised."

"You are on *La Carranza Garza*?"

"If that is the name of the ship, yes."

"What do you mean compromised?"

"I heard gunfire and grenades. Now, there are English-speaking men outside my door. One called LT. I know this is American slang for lieutenant."

"Are you positive?"

The door to the hidden room flew open. Startled, Omar dropped the phone. Two men, clad in all black, carrying silenced machine guns, charged into the room. They forced Omar and Wahbi to sit on the floor, bound their hands and feet with plastic zip cuffs, and shoved gags in their mouths. Omar struggled against his bonds, humiliated at the rough treatment. He swore vengeance on these white Satans.

The leader of the two men in black picked up the satellite phone. He turned to his companion and said, "Let's go."

LARRY GROVE AND ROLAND JENKINS burst onto the bridge. Larry marched up to Anders. "One of your crewmen told Jinks about a special compartment in the forward hold. Please tell us about it, Captain."

Anders Mikkelsen blanched.

The SEAL team commander turned to Ryan. "There's a hidden compartment with four bunks. We detained the two men in there. They're foreign personalities associated with ISIS."

"How do you know this?" Ryan demanded.

"I made a few calls of my own and ran them through a database." Larry held up a satellite phone. "They also placed a call right before Jinks and I found them."

Ryan asked, "Who did they call?"

"I don't know," Larry replied. "My guess would be their handler."

Ryan couldn't keep the anger out of his voice as he addressed Anders. "Why didn't you tell us you were smuggling terrorists?"

"When we put into Veracruz for fuel and provisions, these men come onto the boat. I do not ask questions. I stay on the bridge and allow the Mexican crewmen to load the weapons and other contraband. I thought they went off on the last sailboat."

"You're complicit in bringing Muslim terrorists to U.S. soil," Larry growled. "You lied to us."

Anders appealed to Ryan, "Mr. Weller, I have done these things to keep my family safe."

Ryan shook his head and frowned. "Anders, I can't protect you from this."

"I am forced to do this."

"So you say." Ryan turned away from him. He looked down to see *Dark Water* alongside the *Garza*. Mango tossed a dark green duffle bag across the open water, and it landed near the fighting chair in *Dark Water*'s cockpit. It splashed water off the deck and Ryan could almost hear the thud the heavy bag made. A million dollars in one-hundred-dollar bills weighed twenty-two pounds. The duffle bulged at the seams and strained the top clasp holding it closed. Mango acted like it weighed closer to one hundred and ten pounds.

"Please." Anders's low, plaintive plea hung in the air.

Shelly was on the rail of the Hatteras. A wave caught the boat out of sorts and slammed it against the *Garza*. Rubber fenders saved the fiberglass boat from being damaged. Mango, Kimber, and Kellogg were standing along the *Garza*'s railing, ready to help Shelly across. Vodden had replaced Kellogg in the engine room. Shelly timed the waves and leaped to the *Garza*. The three men caught her at the rail and hauled her aboard.

"What else do you know about Guerrero's operations?" Larry asked Anders.

The captain's eyes dropped. "I have told you all I know."

Ryan doubted it, but short of torturing the man, he wouldn't get any more information from him. He'd scared the piss out of one guy today and that was his limit.

Shelly ran onto the bridge. Between breaths, she exclaimed, "Multiple suicide bombers detonated their vests inside Arizona's State Capitol Executive Building. The building came down."

The men on the bridge stood in stunned silence until Jinks asked, "Who's claiming responsibility?"

"No one has yet," Shelly replied. "It just happened. We heard it on satellite radio. It was breaking news."

Three bombs in key Aztlán states looked more like Guerrero's separatist movement than ISIS. Ryan always figured ISIS would attack Washington, D.C., or key ports to damage infrastructure. These bombings didn't fit the profile Ryan had developed for Islamic terrorists. They did fit the profile of *la Revolución*. The work of a mad man destroying people's lives so he could revise history. Next, there would be an army of Chicano warriors marching in the streets.

Ryan smacked his hand down on the navigation table. "I need to find Guerrero!"

CHAPTER FORTY-FOUR

The door to Arturo Guerrero's study opened and a man stepped inside. Guerrero looked up in anger. No one was to enter this room without permission.

"Get out!" Guerrero shouted.

"I am sorry, *señor* Guerrero. I have spoken with a Muslim man who claims to be on *La Carranza Garza*. He says there has been gunfire and grenade explosions on the ship. He also claimed he could hear two men speaking English, one used the phrase 'LT' when addressing his superior."

Guerrero stood, knocking his chair backward. "Have you tried contacting Jorge?"

"I have tried, *señor,* but I get no response."

Guerrero cursed in Spanish and shouted, "Alejandro!"

A dark-skinned man with a luxurious mustache entered the room.

"*Sí, jefe?*"

"David says someone has captured *La Garza*. I know it is the work of this insufferable Ryan Weller."

"But, *jefe*, Jorge said they killed the men from the sailboat."

"They did not see the bodies," Guerrero seethed.

"How could they have survived?" Alejandro asked.

"I don't know. You will find out about the ship and who captured her."

"*Sí, jefe*," Alejandro said. "I will find out."

CHAPTER FORTY-FIVE

Greg sat wedged into the corner of the settee, behind the dining table of *Dark Water's* main salon. He had a beer in one hand and a white-knuckled grip on the back of the settee with the other. Even though the storm had passed, the waves were still four feet in height. It wasn't a smooth ride on following seas.

Ryan and Mango also sat at the table, braced against the boat's jarring movements, and trying to keep their beers from spilling. They had just finished giving Greg a blow-by-blow account of their search and seizure of *La Carranza Garza* as they motored toward Tampico, Mexico.

Greg shook his head and grinned. "I wish I could have been there with you."

"It wasn't a picnic," Mango said.

"Still ..." Greg sipped his beer.

"How was it over here?"

"Rough as a washing machine spin cycle. Those six-foot waves were killing us. These are killing me."

"You seem to handle it all right?"

"Yeah, I'm just glad Shelly and Jerry were here to help with the driving. I was getting beat up. I need a nap."

"Me, too." Ryan stretched.

It had been a long night which had extended into the early afternoon of the following day as they waited for the Coast Guard. *Manowar* had sent over an armed boarding party as well as a crew to drive the ship back to Galveston. Landis and others at DHS had warned them not to advertise the seizure of the ship and its cargo.

Landis had also given Ryan a brief background on Guerrero. "He comes from an old-money family in Mexico. They started mining silver near Matehuala in the early 1900s and later moved into oil. Now, Guerrero controls much of the drug and weapons trade on the Gulf Coast of Mexico.

"He has a compound outside Tampico. It's on a little peninsula extending into the *Laguna del Chairel*, a large swamp on the western edge of the city. Part of the guard detail is a pack of hungry crocodiles roaming the rivers and canals. I spoke with the State Department and they said Mexico won't touch him. He has too much power and influence in Tampico. Besides, he's brought stability and businesses back to the city."

"What about covert military action?"

"That's a no-go as well, Ryan. If you think this guy is a true hazard to our commerce and well-being, then it's on you to take him out. You're getting paid the big bucks."

"I understand."

"Listen, Ryan, if you go in there, we can't come get you. There's no quick reaction force ready to ride to the rescue. This place is heavily fortified, and Guerrero has a lot of armed guards at his disposal."

"I understand," Ryan had repeated.

"You're going after him, Ryan?"

"Yes. Someone has to."

"Good luck. I'll give you all the help I can from my desk."

"You and every other fobbit," Ryan had muttered.

"I didn't catch that."

"I'll call you when I'm done." Ryan had switched off his comms gear and leaned against the railing, inhaling deep breaths of salt air, and thinking about the men who stayed in the rear with the gear.

Those who went outside the wire to do battle began to loathe the men who never left the base. He understood the need for logistics trains, mess specialists, and security, but there were those who were afraid to step outside the wire and face the enemy. Ryan had chosen a profession where he had to step outside the wire. Now, he was going to cross the line once again. Instead of wrapping himself in duty and honor and country, he harbored hatred and revenge. Revenge for his sunken sailboat, for Greg and his dead parents, for all the people who'd had their boats stolen, and for every wrong he'd ever perceived. Guerrero was the target Ryan was hanging his baggage on.

Greg interrupted Ryan's reverie, bringing him back to the table on *Dark Water*. "What's the plan?"

"I need to get into Mexico undetected."

Mango said, "I'm going with you."

"You've got a bad leg. DiMarco wants to go home and Shelly flew off with the SEAL team when the Coast Guard got here. I don't expect any of you to take on this fight."

Mango leaned closer to his friend. "They took my boat too, bro, and I'm good to go. You guys hired me to be your partner and that's what I am going to be. This leg won't hold me up, bro."

Ryan had his doubts. Mango was already using an ill-fitting backup leg. If something happened to his leg again, he was screwed. Ryan would be stuck with a one-legged man in an ass-kicking contest.

Ryan put an unlit cigarette in his mouth then took it out. "I need to get into Tampico and look this guy's place over. I think it would be best if I went in alone."

"Do you think you're James Bond?" Mango retorted.

"It'd be less suspicious if I went in by myself and got the lay of the land. I'll formulate a game plan and call you in."

Mango crossed his arms and stared at Ryan. "I don't like it, and I know Greg doesn't."

Ryan pointed at Greg. "The boss is right there. It's his call."

Greg shifted as the big boat rolled. "Regardless of what Landis says, Tampico is still dangerous. To get from the U.S. border to Tampico, there are armed convoys escorted by local police and the military. No one travels those roads by themselves if they value their lives, especially U.S. citizens." Mango and Ryan looked at him blankly. "Put it this way, if Batman needed a Mexican Gotham, it would be Tampico. This ain't no Cancún vacation, boys, this is straight into the heart of darkness."

Mango whispered a Marlon Brando impression, "The horror, the horror."

Ryan chuckled.

"Guerrero isn't Colonel Kurtz," Greg said. "I'm just telling you to be cautious. The walls have ears and it won't take long for word to get out that a couple of *gringos* are roaming around the city, asking about the Godfather."

"See, you need backup." Mango pointed a finger at Ryan. "I'm going with you and there's no way you can stop me."

Ryan smirked.

Mango read Ryan's mind. "You're not stealing my leg and hiding it from me, either. That would just be a dick move."

"All right." Ryan held up his hands, palms out, and laughed.

"I ask again, what's the plan?" Greg demanded.

"Mango and I will get a car and recon Guerrero's place. We'll track his movements for a few days and see if we can find an opening to hit him."

"What are you going to hit him with?" Greg wanted a detailed plan.

"Landis gave me the number of a man in Mexico City who can get us whatever firepower we need." Ryan shrugged. "We'll figure something out."

"Ryan, you've always had a cavalier streak about you," Greg said. "If we continue to do these operations together, we need to do more planning. Like we did for taking down the *Garza*."

"That was a straightforward mission with clear objectives. This is more fluid. We don't know the situation on the ground, and we have limited intelligence on Guerrero and his cartel. I plan to recon the area and assess what we need to do. You and I both know the whole thing can go pear-shaped in a hurry."

"I agree, no plan survives the first shot of battle, but we can always modify the plan, and we build in contingencies. You were just getting into operational planning when you left the Navy. I was planning them from day one."

"You were an officer. That was your job. I went through the same training you did to become an operator. I know what needs to be done."

"Agree to disagree."

Mango watched the back and forth with a grin on his face.

"Yes," Ryan said. "You are more methodical than I am, in some areas, and I'll admit, I might not have all the operational skill sets I need." Ryan shrugged again. "It is what it is, and in six hours we're going into Tampico to look around. We need to take this guy down."

"That I agree with," Greg said. "Go get some sleep."

Ryan stood. "I'm glad we're working together again, Greg. I'm glad you have my back."

"Same here, brother," Greg said, and the two men bumped fists.

CHAPTER FORTY-SIX

Alejandro Vargas set down the phone and drummed his fingers on the desk. The news wasn't pleasing. A week ago, a fisherman had pulled two men, one matching the description of the elusive Ryan Weller, from the Gulf of Mexico.

Vargas could only surmise Ryan was behind the raid on *La Carranza Garza*. No news outlets displayed footage of the U.S. military or Coast Guard boarding the vessel and capturing firearms. Normally, they paraded such actions across the cable news networks, newspapers, and internet. The news outlets had all been silent on the subject.

The profile of Ryan Weller Guerrero had handed Alejandro said the American was former military and now worked for Dark Water Research. He may also have a former military accomplice who he called LT. Alejandro was uncertain about some facts. What he did know was the man had the lives of a cat to survive a hit near Marathon, Florida, have his boat machine-gunned from under him, and live through several days of floating in the open ocean.

Alejandro walked down the hallway to his boss's office

and knocked. When summoned, he entered the ornate room and reported his findings while standing on a finely woven Persian rug.

"This Ryan Weller is a thorn in my side." Guerrero leaned back in his chair. He steepled his fingers and looked past Alejandro. "If he's captured my ship, then he will come here."

"I want to send his picture to all of our men," Alejandro said. "They will capture him if he comes to Tampico."

"Excellent idea, Alejandro." Guerrero looked down at the papers on his desk and picked up a pen. It was the signal for Alejandro to leave.

Back at his desk, Alejandro sent Ryan Weller's picture to his lieutenants via text message. His lieutenants would continue to disseminate the photo to other members of the Aztlán cartel.

CHAPTER FORTY-SEVEN

The Hatteras came off plane and idled into the no-wake zone along the Tampico waterfront. Greg steered the boat off the Pánuco River and into *Canal de la Cortadura. The Cut Channel.*

Mango and Ryan slipped over the side of the Hatteras and slowly swam to the woods bordering the canal's mouth, while the boat continued up the Cut. They wore black fatigues and carried backpacks in waterproof bags. After crawling through the stinking mud of a tidal flat, the two men took shelter in the pine trees growing along the riverbank. They stripped off their mud-caked fatigues and put on jeans, T-shirts, and athletic footwear designed to look like dress shoes.

Through the trees bordering Proteins of Tamaulipas, one of the six private terminals forming the Port of Tampico, Ryan and Mango studied the facility. PROTAMSA's four massive grain silos provided storage for corn, wheat, and soybeans. Next to the silos were warehouses holding cement, lumber, and fertilizers. Train tracks ran to and from the facility, and a cargo ship floated under a silo's auger arm at the deep-water dock.

Ryan and Mango watched for armed guards and searched for a likely candidate for auto theft. They skirted pools of light cast by security lamps and stayed in the shadows. Moving past the massive grain silos, they came to a parking lot.

Mango remained hidden in a small grove of trees near the eight-foot-high concrete block wall bordering the property while Ryan ran in a low crouch to the battered door of a mid-nineties Toyota Corolla. He tried the door handle and found it unlocked. The door hinges creaked as it swung open. Ryan eased back and slung his pack to the ground. Reaching for a flashlight, he froze. Cold steel pressed against the base of his neck. The pressure was hard enough for him to feel the barrel of the pistol leaving a mark on his skin.

Ryan lifted his hands.

"Stand up, *pendejo*. Slowly."

As he stood, Ryan scanned the trees for Mango. He saw movement in the shadows. Mango stepped forward with two men flanking him and his arms in the air. When he got closer, Mango gave Ryan a little shrug and a frown as if to say, *What could I do?*

The man who'd gotten the drop on Ryan ordered him to back up against the Corolla. He consulted a smart phone and held it up near his captive's head. When he dropped it down, Ryan saw the man had been studying his picture. Ryan recognized the shirt he'd worn while visiting Professor Morales's house. He shook his head in frustration at the professor's duplicity.

Mango's guards looked like gorillas with broad shoulders and muscular bodies. They held their rifles tight against their chests, one hand on the pistol grip, fingers off the trigger. The leader of the captors was a skinny kid who only stood five feet three. His short stature forced him to look up at Ryan, and Ryan leaned over him for the intimidation factor. It didn't work. Even if it had, he still needed to deal with the two goons, who took no chances and manacled their prisoners' hands with zip ties.

The goons marched them to a small guard shack and forced them to sit inside. Ryan got comfortable and watched the guards to see if he and Mango could escape. One goon took up station just outside the door, the other lounged nearby. Their ringleader, who Ryan called Shorty, paced with a cell phone pressed to his ear. He could hear part of Shorty's side of the conversation when he was near Ryan. Shorty was calling someone to come pick up the intruders.

The two goons seized Ryan and jerked him to his feet. His legs ached, and his left foot was asleep. With the goons' aid, he stumbled out of the building and leaned against a wall. Then they dragged Mango out. Ryan looked up to see Shorty beaming with pride as a black Suburban slid to a stop. A thin but muscular man, with close-cropped black hair and a luxurious mustache, stepped out.

Mustache conversed quickly with Shorty before walking over to the Americans. He looked them up and down, then motioned for them to get into the backseat of the SUV. While they embarked, Shorty threw their gear packs into the rear cargo area.

Ryan watched out the window as they drove. Tampico was a city of contrasts, run by drug lords and gangs while legitimate businesses tried to stay above water. Abandoned buildings stood in disrepair, with trees growing through their roofs and windows, next to well-kept markets and apartment buildings. Nature's reclamation of the concrete jungle was both beautiful and haunting.

For fifteen minutes the Suburban worked its way through the city. They passed broken-down hovels and rich suburbs, some of which looked strikingly like developments in the US. They moved along a freeway before turning onto surface streets again. The driver rolled through stop signs and merely slowed for red lights before hammering through. Ryan believed the driver was going to kill them before they reached their destination. It might spare them the fate of being tortured by a ruthless cartel kingpin. Ryan didn't want to be tortured or dumped in a swamp with a bullet to his head. He hoped these men were taking him and Mango to see Guerrero. It would put them in the lion's den and if he could convince someone to free his hands, well, he was going to kill them all.

Leaving the cramped city streets, the driver navigated onto a road lined on both sides by water and trees. From his studies of the satellite terrain maps while on *Dark Water*, Ryan knew they'd entered the *Laguna del Chairel*, a giant estuary formed by the Tamesí River. The marsh of wooded islands and flowing pools bordered the west side of Tampico. Resorts and housing developments crowded the eastern edges of the Chairel, sharing the water with crocodiles, birds, snakes, and fish.

The Suburban slowed for a bend in the road, and the driver braked, preparing to turn. Water on the north side of the road gave way to a peninsula guarded by a heavy wrought-iron fence. The driver turned the big SUV onto a paved driveway and stopped at a double gate hung from stucco pillars.

Ryan counted four guards, two in the gatehouse and two checking the vehicle. One stood at the driver's door while the other used a long pole with a special convex mirror to check the undercarriage of the SUV for bombs. Waved clear, the Suburban passed through the gate and continued up the driveway. The beds of flowers, pruned trees, and immaculately trimmed grass reminded Ryan of a golf course.

Ten feet off each side of the driveway, the mowed grass ended in heavy stands of brush and trees. Ryan shuddered as he thought about the crocodiles and snakes lurking in the bushes. He hated snakes and always had. He avoided them even if they were caged at a zoo. He got the creeps just thinking about their scaly skin and beady eyes. Military training, in the swamps around Eglin Air Force Base, in the Florida panhandle, had forced him into an uneasy tolerance. He understood their hierarchy in the food chain, but still didn't like them. His motto: the only good snake was a dead snake.

Ryan shuddered again and focused back on the driveway which curled around a ten-foot-high fountain in front of a three-story mansion. At the top of the fountain, an angel mounted on a pedestal poured water from a jug into a basin. Water cascaded over three tiers into a pool below.

The house was a traditional hacienda style with tan stucco, white columns under arches, and a red tiled roof. At the right rear, a round tower overlooked the five-thousand-square-foot palace and grounds. On closer inspection, Ryan saw an armed guard carrying a rifle with a large scope standing in the tower's window. The perfect sniper's nest.

"Out," Mustache prodded when the Suburban came to a stop. He led the Americans inside the three-story grand entryway, flanked by stairs leading to the second level.

Mustache's shoes clicked on marble tile. Paintings and tapestries adorned the walls. A ten-foot-diameter crystal chandelier hung from the ceiling. It tapered down in consecutively smaller circles until the bottom was almost level with the second-story balcony.

Mustache led the Americans up the right-side flight of stairs and then down a hall, marching them to a closed door. He knocked.

"*Adelante.*" *Come*, a deep voice called.

Mustache opened the door and motioned for Ryan and Mango to enter. Ryan glanced around the room. To his right were floor-to-ceiling shelves stuffed with books, framed photos, model ships, and ancient Aztecan and Mayan cultural pieces. A Persian rug covered dark hardwood planks. At one end of the rug was a large wooden desk and at the other sat two leather high-back chairs. On the wall opposite the bookcase, between a bathroom door and the open French patio doors, hung a framed map of Aztlán. Under the map was a liquor cabinet with heavy crystal decanters as well as crystal glasses and other drinking accouterments on its marble top. A cedar humidor rested beside the liquor bottles.

Ryan licked his scabbed lips. He could use a drink.

Through the patio doors, they could see a man standing on the balcony, smoking a cigar. He was lean and tall, dressed in black pants, black dress shoes with square toes, and a black button-down dress shirt with the top three buttons undone. He used a hand to sweep his black hair to the left, a prominent part on the right. High cheekbones offset a thin nose and lips. Black eyes danced under thick brows. Around his neck hung a Mexican eight-*reale* coin and chain, identical to the one Professor Morales wore.

Ryan swore and muttered, "I knew he was in on it."

The man stepped past the door's heavy curtains and removed the cigar from his mouth. "Ah, Mr. Weller." He extended his hand to shake and then waved it dismissively in the air after realizing his guest couldn't reciprocate.

Ryan narrowed his brows. "I haven't had the pleasure."

"I am, how do you say ..." The Mexican gave a little bow. "John Smith."

"Arturo Guerrero," Ryan said with disdain. "High priest of Aztlán."

"I see my men talk behind my back." He took a long draw on his cigar. "Alejandro, you may go."

Mustache disappeared out the door.

"If you want to try something evasive, I have many men outside who would love to place a bullet right here." He put his index finger between Ryan's eyes.

Ryan shrugged, more to ease the pain in his shoulders than to offer a disaffected air.

"Please sit. Did you find the accommodations aboard *La Carranza Garza* satisfactory?"

"Your cook needs a better repertoire," Mango retorted.

"I have not had the pleasure of learning your name, *señor*."

"Mango Hulsey."

"Ah, yes, the man with the name of a fruit." Guerrero chuckled.

"How about turning us loose? I could use *el baño y cerveza*." Ryan turned so Guerrero could see the cuffs behind his back. He did need to use the bathroom, and he really wanted a cold beer. More than anything, he wanted the cuffs off. With his hands free, he could wring Guerrero's skinny neck.

"Alejandro," Guerrero called.

The door opened, and Mustache stepped in. Guerrero made a scissoring motion and Alejandro spoke rapidly in Spanish. His boss shook his head in displeasure and rebuked his lieutenant. Alejandro stepped forward, flipping open a folding knife. Ryan recognized the CRKT tactical knife the Mexican had pulled from his pocket: it was his. He figured Shorty had kept it. A minute later, Mango and Ryan were rubbing circulation back into their wrists. Alejandro accompanied them to the bathroom one at a time.

When Ryan came out of the bathroom, he stopped at the liquor cabinet and looked at the map. Small red dots marked multiple cities in the southwestern United States. Three of them were now blue: Phoenix, Los Angeles, and Austin. Beside each dot, in neatly printed Spanish, were names, addresses, and dates.

Guerrero stepped over beside him and gestured to the table. "You wanted a drink, Mr. Weller?"

Ryan nodded. "A beer would be great."

"There is a refrigerator built into the liquor cabinet. Please, help yourself." He pointed to the cabinet door before pouring himself a shot of tequila. He carried his drink to the desk. Ryan bent and retrieved a beer.

Mango stepped out of the bathroom and Alejandro exited the study.

Guerrero asked, "Would you like a beer, Mr. Hulsey?"

"Yes." Mango took the beer Ryan handed him.

Ryan opened his bottle and remained standing by the liquor cabinet. "Where did you go to school in the States? You've lost most of your accent."

Guerrero smiled around his cigar and spoke with a haughty air. "I am a proud alumnus of the University of Texas."

"Is that how you met Professor Morales?" Ryan asked.

Guerrero removed his cigar and sat in his desk chair. "Yes. Rueben and I went to college together."

"He has a matching medallion," Ryan said. "Can I get one of those, or do you have to join a secret club?"

Guerrero's words were a scathing retort. "I give these medallions to men who have been influential in establishing a new Aztlán."

"Care to share your plan for Aztlán domination?" Ryan figured he might as well learn as much as he could while he was at the feet of its designer. If he could escape, he'd get the details to Landis. He felt like he was in a Bond movie talking to the evil villain. While he could kill one or two men with his hands, he needed weapons to facilitate their escape.

The cartel leader placed his cigar in the crystal ashtray. His calm demeanor had returned. "I could wait another thirty to forty years until the Latino population outnumbers the whites and we are firmly planted on the government's payroll, but that takes too much time. We are sending waves of, as you say, 'illegal immigrants' across the border to aggregate the population. They take your jobs and fill your schools and vote in your elections. No other country in the world is so easy to infiltrate. Mexico would put you to death for sneaking in." He leaned forward. "I will put you to death for sneaking in."

Guerrero laughed as he leaned back in the worn, brown, leather chair. "Yes, you will die because I must carry out my plan. I do not need my ship anymore. She has served her purpose well, bringing guns and weapons through your porous border. It also brought my partners so they could distract your law enforcement agencies from the truth. Your police force is reactionary and only sees what they want to see. Those bombings were not the work of ISIS, but of my agents."

Mango looked at Ryan, who had a *see, I told you so* expression on his face.

"I see you do not believe me." Guerrero chuckled. "You are as gullible as your peers."

Mango's anger spilled over. "Explain it to us then, genius."

Guerrero laughed deep and loud. "It's right in front of you. I partnered with the leader of ISIS, Abu Bakr al-Baghdadi, to bring over his trusted men. They are more than willing to die for their cause. We both hate the Great Satan, and both want to bring it to its knees. For different reasons, obviously, but the means to an end is, how do you say, mutually beneficial." He spread his arms wide then dropped them.

"We smuggled Abu Bakr's men into Mexico and put them on *La Carranza Garza*. We took them and a load of weapons into the States on stolen sailboats." Guerrero held up a hand, palm out. "I'm sure you figured this out."

Ryan nodded, took a long chug of beer, and wished he had a cigarette. They were in his confiscated backpack. "So, you'll use these ISIS ragheads to blow up the cities you labeled on your map." He jerked his thumb at the wall behind him.

"You are observant."

Ryan lifted the lid on the humidor. Thick, dark cigars packed the Spanish cedar-lined box. He flared his nostrils to take in the rich aroma.

"You would like a cigar?" Guerrero smiled around his own stogie. "Pick one. I will grant a dying man his wish."

"I'd like the pack of cigarettes in my backpack."

Guerrero summoned Alejandro, who brought the backpack. He produced the pack of Camel Blues from a side pocket as well as a plastic lighter. After testing the lighter to ensure it was indeed a lighter, he laid the cigarettes and lighter on the cabinet and retreated from the room. Ryan lit a cigarette and let out a long stream of smoke before leaning on the sideboard.

"What happens after your bombing campaign?" Ryan asked.

"I won't divulge all of my secrets." Guerrero waved dismissively.

Mango rose to Guerrero's bait. "Do you really think the American people will stand idly by as you try to force the government to hand over half of the US? You may have some die-hard fanatics in sombreros and dishdashas, but there's at least eight million armed U.S. citizens willing to bring the fight to your doorstep."

Guerrero held up his hands in defense. "I have an army waiting to rise as well."

This time Ryan intervened. "According to the papers he wrote, Professor Morales envisions a socialist utopia where everyone has a job and the government is responsible for the care of the people. If you run Aztlán like you run Tampico, your subjects will beg the U.S. to take them back and extend the Treaty of Guadalupe Hidalgo all the way to Guatemala."

"Enough," Guerrero shouted and slammed a palm against the desktop. "You don't know what you speak about." He stood abruptly. "Morales told me you were an insufferable man. I have work to do. Alejandro!"

Mustache stepped back into the room. He trained Mango's Glock on the Americans. Guerrero strode onto the balcony and motioned with his hand. Another armed man ducked into the room as Guerrero disappeared.

The second man leveled an AK-47 at the Americans. Ryan picked up the pack of cigarettes and pulled out another. He put it in his mouth and cupped his hands to shield the flame of the lighter. After a deep drag, he slipped the lighter and cigarettes into his pocket.

"*Vámanos.*" Alejandro motioned with Mango's pistol toward the door.

CHAPTER FORTY-EIGHT

Ryan held the cigarette in front of his face with his thumb and index finger. He let out a stream of smoke while studying it. Then he brought it down and glanced over at Mango and flicked his eyes at the guard holding the AK. Mango closed his eyes. When he opened them a second later, he gave an almost imperceptible nod.

Ryan took a long pull of the cigarette and held it out to study again. The cherry smoldered close to a line he'd drawn half way down the white paper. The line indicated where he'd placed an explosive charge. He took a deep draw, pulling the cherry almost to the line.

"Let's go," Alejandro demanded.

Ryan slowly exhaled the smoke, stalling for time. Then he flicked his cigarette at the guard and spun toward Alejandro.

Mango leaped toward the guard. His artificial foot slipped on the carpet. He fell face first onto the floor at the same instant the cigarette exploded in the guard's face. The guard dropped his rifle and brought his hands to his face to assess the damage. He let out a wail of anguish. Blood coursed down his cheeks and neck.

The blast tore Alejandro's gaze from Ryan, who stepped inside Alejandro's outstretched arm. He grabbed Alejandro's wrist with his left hand and pushed the gun away. Ryan's right elbow came up as he spun. The elbow slammed into Alejandro's jaw. Shock reverberated up Ryan's arm as he kept turning into the busted mouth. Keeping Alejandro's gun up with his left hand, he grabbed it with his right and used Mustache's finger to fire two shots into the guard. The silenced shots drove the already injured guard backward, sprawling him on the balcony.

"Get the AK." Ryan pulled the pistol from Alejandro's limp grasp as the unconscious man crumpled to the ground. He placed the silencer to the Mexican's head and pulled the trigger.

Mango scooped up the rifle and looked over the balcony to see if anyone had reacted to the explosion.

"How many guards?" Ryan whispered.

Mango crouched by the railing, using his finger to point and count.

Ryan opened the hallway door and shot a guard running down the corridor. He spied their packs sitting on a table. Dashing out to grab them, he came under fire from another guard. Bullets stitched along the marble floor and up the wall in front of him. Shards of marble and plaster exploded into the air. He dropped to the floor and shot his attacker in the foot sticking out from behind the door jamb where the guard had taken cover. The man fell forward to grab his ruined appendage and Ryan drilled him in the temple.

When he stepped through the office door with the packs, Mango had his AK-47 pointed at Ryan's head.

Mango brought the gun down from his shoulder when he recognized his partner. "Sorry, bro."

Ryan closed the door and tossed the silenced Glock to Mango and rifled Alejandro's pockets for his knife. "How many men outside?"

"I counted six," Mango replied.

"Not a lot of guys to guard his compound."

"Guess he feels safe," Mango said. "He owns the whole city. I'm sure he can call in reinforcements."

Ryan used his smart phone to take pictures of the map. Each caption received a close, detailed photo. Working the keypad with both thumbs, he composed an email to Landis and attached the pictures. He hit *send* and pocketed the phone.

"Any idea where we are?" Mango asked.

"We're on a peninsula in the *Laguna del Chairel*. From here, it's a straight shot to the Pánuco River by a canal."

"Call Greg and let's get out of here."

"We need to stop Guerrero. If we only dismantle his network, he'll just build another one." Ryan looked up at Mango. "Guerrero's already destroyed three buildings and he'll destroy a lot more if we don't end this now." He picked up his MP5 and hung its three-point harness over his shoulders. The gun hung sideways across his chest.

Mango frowned. "How do we do that?"

Ryan shrugged. "We have to find him first."

The sound of a helicopter, passing over the house, drowned out his words.

"There's his ride," Ryan yelled and bolted left through the double doors and sprinted down the length of the balcony. The balcony ended just above the tiled roof of a gazebo. He glanced down to the pool patio and his brain made an instant decision. Ryan vaulted the railing and landed on the gazebo roof. His feet slid on the barrel tiles. Before he could fall, he launched himself into the air.

Gunshots echoed all around. The firefight was underway. Adrenaline surged through Ryan's veins. He was back in the game. Everything else washed away in the periphery. He was a combat machine, back in his element.

Thick cushions kept him from busting through the heavy wicker of a chaise lounge. His feet slipped out from under him and he slammed hard into a second chaise. His ribs caught the edge of the chair, driving the wind from his lungs.

Bullets ripped through wicker and chirped off the concrete. Ryan rolled off the lounge and tried to breathe. He felt like he was suffocating as his muscles spasmed. Finally, he was able to draw a deep breath. His bruised ribs shot pain through his body with any movement. Just breathing was mind-numbing. This wasn't the playground, he couldn't call time out. He gritted his teeth as he pulled the MP5 to his shoulder and loosed a three-round burst at a guard across the pool. Pain flared through his body with each buck of the gun.

The report of the sniper rifle echoed above the automatic fire of the *cuerno de chivos*, or *goat's horn*, Mexican narco slang for the AK-47, named for the curve of the rifle's magazine.

A sniper's bullet struck the concrete inches to the right of where Ryan knelt. Concrete fragments peppered his leg. He continued to shoot at two men who were engaging him from across the pool deck.

Under the cover of his own fire, he dashed toward the woods on the far side of the grounds. The sound of the sniper's rifle burst in his ears again.

Ahead, the helicopter flared above the treetops.

Gunfire chased Ryan into the woods, and he hoped Mango was all right. Brush and scrub tore at his clothes and skin as he ran. He spilled through the trees onto a gravel path. The wash of the helicopter's rotors tore at his clothes and sent sand and leaves hurling through the air as it came to a hover. Running made his ribs ache, and his breath came in shallow, ragged gasps. The only way to survive was to shove the pain into a far corner of his mind and push on.

CHAPTER FORTY-NINE

Mango followed his partner onto the second-story balcony. He couldn't make the same leap Ryan had just made to the gazebo and down to the chaise lounges. Instead, he turned right to look for stairs to the ground level. He found them inside the tower. The second and third-story balconies connected to the tower which had a spiral staircase built against the inside walls of the circular structure.

Mango eased to the railing and peered down through the open center to look for guards. When he saw none, he started down the stairs. Two men burst through the tower's door and charged up the steps. Through windows cut into the tower, he could see four more men racing toward his position. He pressed his shoulder blades to the cement wall and fired at the two men below him. He hit both in the chest, starting with the trailing man and letting the muzzle of the MP5 rise to the first.

Mango turned and ran up. He didn't know how many men were rushing to greet him at the base of the tower. The tower would be easy for him to defend if he could eliminate the sniper. At the top of the tower, the sniper's rifle boomed. Approaching the third-floor landing, Mango brought the gunstock to his shoulder and focused through the holographic sight. Pressed against the wall again, he moved slower and twisted his body, and therefore the barrel of the MP5, to check for Guerrero's cartel goons. There was one standing with his back to the stairs, staring down the balcony as he changed a magazine in his AK. He hadn't heard Mango's suppressed shots over the din of fully automatic gunfire and didn't hear the shot Mango fired into the back of his head.

Stepping out on the balcony, Mango looked down the length of the house. He saw no challengers, so he squatted by the dead man and relieved him of his AK and spare magazines. He slung the Russian-made weapon over his shoulder and stuffed the magazines into his cargo pockets.

The sniper rifle boomed again. Mango ran up the stairs toward the top of the tower. Bullets hammered the wall. Mango blindly fired his MP5 down the stairwell then darted for the top floor where the sniper triggered another round. Mango used the big gun's report to mask his final steps. The sniper's back was to Mango as he lined up a shot on a figure sprinting across the lawn on the far side of the pool deck. Mango recognized the fleeing man as his partner and put a three-round burst of bullets in the back of the sniper's head.

More gunfire sounded from below and bullets smacked the roof of the tower, sending a shower of stucco raining down. Mango dropped to his knees and grabbed a grenade from his backpack. He ripped the pin from the device and let it fall through the center of the tower. He laid flat and covered his head and ears with his hands. The tower shook violently with the explosion.

Dropping more grenades inside the tower would only weaken the foundations and collapse his perch of refuge. Shouldering the sniper rifle, Mango slid to the lip of the window and began picking off cartel members. When the narcos got close to the base of the tower, he switched to the AK and pounded them with automatic fire.

CHAPTER FIFTY

Ryan burst through the underbrush onto a grass path and turned toward the helicopter. A man sat in the driver's seat of a golf cart guarding the landing pad. The guard jerked his rifle up. Not bothering to shoulder the AK, the narco pulled the trigger. Ryan dove to the dirt under a stream of lead and cursed as the MP5's stock jammed into his ribs. Rolling to his knees, he guided the stock to his shoulder and fired. Three rounds stitched up the guard's chest and he slumped over the golf cart's wheel, then fell out of the cart.

Rising, the American saw Guerrero on the far side of the helicopter pad. The Mexican drug lord was using both outstretched arms to motion the pilot down to the ground. Ryan ran to the golf cart and knelt behind it to shield himself from the flying debris kicked up by the rotor's downwash. Using the cart as a brace, he centered the sights on Guerrero.

On the other side of the clearing, Guerrero glowered at him. He jerked a pistol from behind his back. With one arm, he continued to flap like a bird, directing the pilot to land. With the other, he aimed the pistol at Ryan.

Guerrero's bullets crashed into the golf cart, splintering the fiberglass. Ryan dove to the ground. He scrambled to the back of the cart to put the engine between himself and Guerrero. Ryan leaned around the bumper and fired.

The Bell Jet Ranger pilot swiveled his head between the armed attacker and his potential passenger. Ryan's poorly aimed bullets had little effect other than to make Guerrero duck while still frantically motioning for the pilot to land.

Ryan rattled a half-dozen rounds off the bottom of the helicopter. The pilot jerked the collective upward and the bird lurched ten feet higher into the air. Ryan trained the gun on Guerrero and pulled the trigger. Without the cover of the helicopter and the wind deflection from the rotor, the bullets found their mark. The man staggered backward and toppled over as the pilot added power, increasing the force of the rotor wash. The helicopter dipped its nose and raced away.

Without the thunder of the helicopter, Ryan could hear a gun battle raging around the house. Grenade explosions punctuated the cacophony then silence followed. Ryan had left Mango to fend for himself. He hoped the pitched gun battle indicated Mango was still in the fight. He hoped the former Coast Guardsman hadn't been wounded.

Ryan checked the magazine on the MP5 and slammed home a fresh one. He stood, clutching his left arm across his ribs and stumbled across the clearing. Guerrero lay with arms outstretched. His legs had folded and tangled when the bullets had torn through his body. Dark blood seeped from his back and discolored the sandy soil. Ryan placed the barrel of his MP5 against the cartel leader's forehead and put a round between the man's eyes. He wasn't getting up. Now it was up to Landis to dismantle the cartel leader's networks inside the US. Ryan had been right all along. And as good as it felt to put an end to this mad man's reign, all his pent-up aggression didn't magically disappear. Arturo Guerrero's quick death seemed too easy for him after all the people he had killed with his bombs and guns and drugs.

On the way back to the golf cart, he glanced down another cart path and saw a gleaming white skiff sitting at a long T-dock. He pulled the guard the rest of the way off the golf cart, climbed on, and raced toward the house.

Before he made it fifty feet, bullets tore through the plexiglass windshield. He ducked behind the wheel and jammed his foot down harder on the pedal. Ryan cursed the machine to make it go faster than the maximum speed it was already traveling. Out of the corner of his eye, Ryan saw a man dart from the brush and run toward the cart. He swerved away from the man, jerking the steering wheel so hard the cart went up on two wheels. The cart traveled off the path and into the yard while Ryan madly sawed the wheel to turn into the lean. The cart slammed back onto all four wheels. Fresh waves of pain washed through his body, and his breath caught in his chest.

The cart's suspension bounced as the assailant jumped aboard.

Ryan whipped the wheel hard left. The front wheels plowed through the grass before they caught and violently jerked the heavy machine to the right. Centrifugal force took over and the cart began a slow roll onto its side.

Just as the cart reached its apex, Ryan twisted the wheel hard right. The counter-steering failed to work this time and the cart continued over. He tried to jump free. His MP5 tangled in the wheel and he fell hard into the cart's footwell, screaming as his ribs crashed into the edge where one would normally step aboard. The cart came to rest on its right side. Ryan's movements were slow as he tried to extricate himself.

Guerrero's guard yelled, "*No se mueva.*" *Don't move.*

Ryan looked up and groaned when he saw the barrel of the AK-47 pointed at his head. He hung half in and half out of the cart. His body weight trapped the MP5 between him and the cart, and the Picatinny rail, foregrip, and holographic sight stabbed painfully into his bruised ribs. He moved slightly and the gun swung free. A burst of AK fire raked the bottom of the cart. Ryan glanced to his left and saw four neat little holes six inches from his head. He looked back at the guard and dropped his head in defeat.

This was how he was going to die. Painfully, on a golf cart in a third-world country.

And he didn't even play golf.

CHAPTER FIFTY-ONE

A sound like a wet melon exploding filled Ryan's ears and wetness covered his face. The sniper rifle's report reverberated across the grounds. The guard fell forward, the left side of his head missing.

Pulling himself out of the cart, Ryan groaned through gritted teeth. He cried out in pain when he flopped onto the hard earth. Climbing to his feet, he clutched his rib cage with his left hand and aimed the MP5 with the right. He peered around the cart to evaluate the situation. Guerrero's men now concentrated their gunfire on the tower at the far end of the house. Perched at the top of the tower was Ryan's fair-haired friend.

Mango gave him a little salute, pointed at his chest, and then held out his hand to make a gun with his thumb and forefinger. Ryan could almost hear him say, "Saved your ass, bro."

Ryan ran for the corner of the garage, using trees and flower beds for cover. Staying close to the wall, he moved around to the driveway. A garage door was open, waiting for the Suburban parked in the driveway.

Inside the garage, he passed a Porsche 911 Carrera and a Toyota Tacoma parked beside a Chrysler minivan. Staying close to the floor, he pushed open a door just enough to see in. Most people expected to see a head at normal height and would shoot into the middle of the door. By staying low to the ground and off to the side, Ryan could keep his head intact and still return fire.

The door opened into a massive kitchen with an island big enough to land a fighter jet on. Stainless steel and granite shielded him from the adjoining living room where a grand piano stood beside shattered sliding-glass doors. He was sure the fireplace at the far end of the room was a fake.

"Who needs a wood-burning fireplace when the temperature rarely gets below sixty? Egocentric narco *pendejos*, that's who," Ryan muttered.

He wiped sweat from his brow and eased toward the busted patio doors. The aluminum rails of the doors were twisted and bent by grenade explosions. Torn and shredded curtains hung limp in the heavy humidity. His feet crunched on broken glass.

Outside, the gunfire had died down to sporadic pops. Ryan kicked the largest shards of glass out of the way before lying on the floor. He slid his head out past the door jamb. Three men were stacked up in a gun train at the base of the tower with their backs to him. He wiped sweat from his eyes and aimed the MP5. He shot the third man of the train in the head. Number Three slumped forward into his companion as Ryan put a round in Two's head. Number One turned as Two and Three fell into him. One jerked his gun up and staggered forward, trying to get free of the dead weight. Ryan ended the struggle with a shot to One's neck followed by a second round to the head.

The muscles around his rib cage stiffened when Ryan

got to his feet. "Mango," he called while he braced his ribs with his arm.

"Where you been, bro?" Mango stuck his head out the tower window. Gunfire from the front of the house drove him back under cover.

In the distance, Ryan could hear sirens. "We got company. Can you get down?"

"Did you get rid of those guys at the bottom?"

"Yes." Ryan scanned the grounds, looking for more of Guerrero's *sicarios*. Reinforcements would most likely come from the road. They could also come over water via the dock Ryan had seen at the northeast corner of the thumb-shaped peninsula.

Mango appeared at the bottom of the stairs and leaned against the tower. "We gotta get out of here, bro. I'm low on ammo and there's more bad guys coming."

"Nice shot back there." Ryan gave him a fist bump.

"Saved your ass, bro."

Ryan grinned, grateful for Mango's help and the chance to be alive but also because he'd called it. "Where's the gunfire coming from?"

"The woods to the east and south. I think the gate guards stayed home to defend their territory. They were sniping at me the whole time I was up there. I picked them off with the sniper rifle until it ran out of ammo."

"How's the leg?"

"Sore. What's up with you?" Mango watched his companion hug his chest with his left arm.

"Smacked my ribs when I jumped off the roof."

"That was a crazy stunt, bro. No way I was doing it. I tried to take the stairs, but they ran me up the tower." He pointed upward. "Had to take out the sniper anyway."

Ryan sucked shallow breaths and nodded. The sirens

were louder. "If we don't want to be run up there again, we better move. Come on."

They ran along the cart path to the helicopter pad. When they came abreast of the pad, Mango paused and looked at Guerrero. The bullet hole between his eyes had wept blood and left a trail down his nose and cheek.

"Shit, bro," Mango said. "We *really* need to get out of here."

"Stop wasting time. Let's go!"

"Where are we going?" Mango asked.

"There," Ryan pointed at the dock and a white, center console Carolina Skiff. He took off running with Mango right on his six. Mango ran with a painful limp each time his artificial leg crashed into the ground.

They stopped before reaching the dock and took cover in the heavy brush just off the path. Mango dropped to his knees, his chest heaved. Both men breathed through gritted teeth.

Ryan took in his friend's pale complexion and heavy sheen of sweat. "You good?"

"I'm not used to this leg and it's killing my stump."

Ryan glanced at the boat and then down the path to the house. The sirens were louder. He guessed reinforcements had arrived. He told Mango, "Go check the boat. If you can't get it started, we might have to swim for it."

"I don't think so, bro." Mango pointed at a crocodile eyeing them from a nearby sandbar. Another opened its mouth in a toothy grin.

"Guess you better start the boat."

Mango ran down the dock while Ryan remained in the underbrush to provide security.

A heavily armored truck barged through the underbrush and onto the path. Welded metal plates formed a pointed boat bow. The same thick plating covered the rest of the vehicle, effectively forming a tank. Three small slits in the steel comprised the windshield, and they'd cut firing slots where the side windows had been. A turret, over the cargo area, sprouted a machine gun. Its barrel swept side to side in search of targets.

Ryan's insides went cold.

Then he heard the skiff's engine start.

Forgetting about his aching ribs and tired body, Ryan prepared to run. Adrenaline once again hammered his veins. He rolled two grenades into the path of the tank and sprinted down the dock, yelling, "Cast off!"

Mango looked up to see Ryan barreling toward him. His eyes went wide at the sight of the tank crashing through the woods. He quickly tossed off the bow and stern lines.

Ryan heard the grenades detonate. They must have been ineffective because bullets whipped the air all around him. He glanced back to see the tank stop at the edge of the water. The M60 turret-mounted machine gun belched fire. Splinters flew off the dock boards as bullets chewed through them at his feet.

Ryan leaped for the boat. He landed on the front casting deck. Centrifugal force from the boat's acceleration slammed him against the center console in a heap of screaming pain. The skiff shot away from the dock, heading south.

Chairel Channel necked down to flow under two bridges, one on each side of Guerrero's compound. Ryan eyed the bridge they were flying toward. It was low and narrow. The Carolina Skiff should slip right through, minus the T-top. With enough speed, they'd knock it off and keep on trucking.

Two police cars slid to a stop at the head of the bridge,

lights flashing and sirens blaring. Four men piled out and aimed their automatic rifles at the skiff. A pickup truck screeched to a stop beside the cars.

"Turn around," Ryan screamed. "They have a technical!"

Mango saw the technical, a pickup truck with an M60 machine gun mounted in the bed, at the same time as his companion. Ryan, who had gotten to his feet and was standing beside Mango at the center console, almost fell on his face when Mango chopped the throttle and spun the wheel. The boat heeled over dangerously on its port beam and Mango threw the throttle forward halfway through the turn. Ryan latched onto a grab bar on the side of the console to keep from being thrown overboard.

They couldn't hear the guns firing, but they could see the geysers the bullets made as they impacted all around them. Ryan turned to look and shouted, "Cut left!"

Mango jerked the wheel, and a line of seven-point-six-two caliber bullets ripped through the water where the boat had just been. The maneuver brought them back within range of the tank and its machine gun. It began firing again. The heavy rounds punched three holes in the port side of the boat. Mango cut hard right and moved to the far bank to get out of range.

"Where to?" he shouted and swerved the boat again to avoid a flotilla of kayakers who suddenly appeared from foliage along the bank and were racing back to the Corona Yacht Club.

The center console's wake caused two kayaks to flip over. The rest of the paddlers screamed obscenities in Spanish.

Ryan opened his phone's map application and directed Mango to stay straight. They flew around an island and turned to the right into a canal paralleling Route 700.

In the distance, more police cars and another technical sprinted up the road.

"Think they'll catch us?"

"We can't outrun a two-way radio," Ryan replied, concentrating on the phone screen. "Anywhere we come off the water they'll be watching, and we'll have to get off the water to meet up with Greg."

"Does this go to the Gulf?"

"No." Ryan watched the dot moving on his phone, indicating their real-time GPS location. "Get ready to make a hard right. We'll go around this island and head straight past the point with all the houses."

They rode in silence while Ryan glanced between his phone and the scenery ahead.

Rounding the island, which turned out to be part of a golf course, Mango said, "Dead end, bro."

"Head for that hotel." Ryan pointed at a Fiesta Inn. "Slow down and enter the channel to the right of it."

Mango guided the little boat up the narrow channel. He gunned the motor to make the boat slide over vegetation and into a wider section of what turned out to be a drainage ditch. Past the bridge, it was a trash-choked concrete-lined chute.

Under the Mexican Federal Highway 80 bridge, Mango beached the boat and both men jumped out. Ryan tied the bow line to a bridge pier to keep the boat out of sight.

Above, traffic rumbled across the bridge. Ryan grabbed the packs and pulled out his pistol. He cocked his head to the side, so he could hear better, while staring up at the undercarriage of the bridge. A car had slammed on its brakes.

"What is it?" Mango whispered. He crouched beside Ryan and pulled his Glock from his waistband.

Two car doors slammed, one after another.

Ryan held a finger to his lips and pointed to the far bank of the creek then held up two fingers.

Mango gave him a puzzled look by squinting his left eye and curling up the same side of his upper lip. He moved his gaze to the bridge abutments as a conversation in Spanish between two men grew louder.

"Get behind the boat console," Ryan whispered before shoving the boat's stern across the creek to form a bridge. He ran across the boat and jumped the last few feet over the water. He landed on his feet but slipped to his hands and knees. Scrambling to the far side of the bridge, he hid behind the concrete abutment. He wiped the stinky mud off his hands onto some grass. A little mud was better than wading through crotch-deep water and having wet blue jeans and sewage caked to his skin.

Two men dressed in black combat fatigues and skull facemasks came down the embankment. Silk-screened white jaws and teeth stood out on the black fabric, giving them a menacing look. The men cursed about having to check the mud and reeds at the water's edge.

Mango whistled, and the two men stopped to look at him, one man standing behind the other. They brought their weapons up and screamed at him in Spanish. Mango held his hands up. A red dot appeared on the second man's forehead and he crumpled to the ground. The first narco whipped the muzzle of his gun toward the sound of the silenced gunshot. Ryan's next burst of fire caught the *sicario* in the chest.

Ryan poked his head above the bridge, looking for more bad guys. A dark-green Nissan Xterra idled at the entrance to an IHOP parking lot. He walked over to the gunmen lying in the mud under the bridge and ripped off the least bloody mask. After wiping it off on the dead man's shirt tails, Ryan slipped it on his face.

Properly disguised, he climbed the embankment and walked toward the car. Staying in the driver's blind spot, he circled the SUV and opened the driver's door. A skinny black man with yellow, decaying teeth looked up in surprise. Ryan shot him twice in the chest. Ryan whistled for his partner to let him know he was alive and pulled the guy from the car before the dead man could bleed all over the seats.

Mango jogged up behind Ryan. He'd tied a bandana around his face. "Wish we had time for pancakes," he muttered.

"Me too." Instead of eating pancakes and eggs, they rolled the dead guy down the embankment to join his compatriots.

Back at the SUV, they took a second to scan the surrounding area to see if anyone had observed them. If they had, no one seemed to care they'd just dumped a dead guy in a ditch. Maybe the populace was used to such occurrences?

Ryan sat in the blood-splattered driver's seat. The man had been a bleeder. *Two to the chest will cause that,* Ryan thought as he backed the Xterra around and stopped to wait for some oncoming traffic.

A white four-door Toyota Hilux pickup truck slowed and turned into the parking lot. It pulled up beside the Nissan. Men with guns jammed the truck's seats. In the truck bed, two men with AKs slung on their backs held onto a roll bar. Bolted to the bed was an M60 machine gun. The Hilux stopped beside Ryan's open window.

"Hey amigos, has visto a estos pendejos yanqui?" Hey, friends, have you seen these Yankee assholes?

Mango didn't speak Spanish, but he could understand a few curse words and asked, "Did he just call us assholes?"

"No, he called us friends," Ryan corrected. "He asked if we'd seen any assholes."

"I think we're surrounded by them," Mango muttered.

"Hold on." Ryan cranked the wheel to the left and Mango braced himself. Ryan stomped on the gas and the Xterra leaped out of the parking lot.

"Wrong way," Mango shouted as two cars came at them on the access road.

White painted arrows showed both lanes of traffic flowed against them. Ryan straightened the wheel and the Xterra ricocheted off another curb and into more oncoming traffic. Mashing the accelerator, he went careening between two palm trees in the median before he got the truck going in the direction he wanted. As he sped away, the M60 chattered its death song.

Both men ducked as the side windows shattered. The big slugs slammed into the vehicle's metal skin. It felt like they were taking punches from a heavyweight boxer as the vehicle shuddered with each hit. The further they got away from the gun, the less of a target they became.

Mango twisted sideways in the seat to watch their pursuers. "They're backing out of the IHOP."

CHAPTER FIFTY-TWO

Horns blared as the Toyota Hilux cut off traffic and bounced over the curbs to follow the Xterra north on Avenue Miguel Hidalgo, Tampico's name for Mex 80 through the city. Ryan wanted to call Greg and make arrangements for him to pick them up, but if they didn't shake the Toyota, there would be no rendezvous. Plus, there was no time to formulate an escape plan. Ryan hunched over the wheel, feeling like a racecar driver as he wove through traffic.

"We gotta ditch this truck and get rid of the Xterra," Mango said. "Those guys are going to call everyone they know to come get us."

"Do we have anything in the car to stop these guys?" Ryan half-shouted over the wind pouring in through the shattered windows.

Mango climbed into the backseat and rummaged in the storage area. "Couple AKs and grenades."

"If I can draw them up close, maybe you can roll a grenade under their chassis."

"Copy that, bro."

Ryan's eyes shifted from the rearview mirror to the road ahead numerous times to gauge distances and look for escape routes. This time, when he looked forward, he had to slow for bunched-up traffic. He saw Mango pick up one of the AK-74s, a smaller caliber gun than its big brother, the 47.

The technical closed quickly, and the M60 began to fire again. Mango triggered a short burst from his AK and sent brass spinning around the inside of the SUV's cab. A scalding, hot casing hit Ryan's neck and slid down his shirt. He wiggled around, trying to get the burning brass out of his shirt, and swerved across both lanes of traffic. Horn blasts accompanied his maneuvering, and the rear window of a red Hyundai ahead of them shattered into pieces as the technical continued to fire. The Hyundai spun to the left, leaped over the median, and hit a car in the oncoming lane.

Ryan pumped the brakes to avoid a collision as a car in front of him locked up its brakes. Mango fired another stream of lead out the rear window. Ryan stomped on the gas. Centrifugal force drove Mango against the rear seat. The action caused him to fire a burst into the floor of the SUV.

Ryan smelled gasoline. "You hit the gas tank!"

Mango yelled back, "Hit the brakes now."

Ryan did and watched in the mirror as Mango lobbed two grenades through the broken rear window.

"Hit it," Mango shouted.

Ryan mashed the gas pedal to the floor board and cranked the wheel to the left. They bounced up on the median and drove around four cars before dropping back into the roadway. Behind them, the technical exploded in a ball of flames.

"Hell yeah, bro." Mango gave a fist pump and sat down in the seat.

Just as Mango got settled, Ryan looked in the driver's-side mirror and saw flames licking up the side of the SUV.

"Grab our gear and get ready to bail. We're on fire!" Ryan sounded like a little girl when he shouted fire.

Mango stuck his head out the window to look at the flames and then grabbed the packs. Ryan looked for a place to park the SUV. If there was more ordnance in the back and it caught fire, he didn't want it to do a lot of collateral damage when it detonated. They passed car dealers, tire stores, strip malls, and houses. Traffic became more congested. He was getting desperate. He'd seen people trapped in burning vehicles and it wasn't a pretty sight or smell.

Ryan spied an empty parking lot between a restaurant and an office building. He jerked the wheel and the Xterra jumped over the curb separating Mex 80 from the access road. Little flames fell off the vehicle, and fire licked at the gasoline trail they left on the pavement.

The engine sputtered as Ryan cut in front of a semi. The driver blasted his horn in warning, and the big tractor-trailer barely missed the Xterra's rear bumper. On its last gasp of fumes, the SUV's engine caught and powered into the parking lot.

Without waiting for Ryan, Mango kicked open a door and tossed packs and guns out before following them. The SUV coasted on its own momentum. Ryan shoved open his door and jumped. He landed on his feet, tucked his chin to his chest, and covered his head with his arms. His body rolled forward in an awkward heap. The rough blacktop tore at his clothes and scraped his elbows. Using the momentum of the roll, he popped to his feet. His elbows stung and his ribs screamed, causing him to double over in pain and stagger forward. All he wanted to do was lie down and sleep.

Holding his ribs, Ryan staggered over to where Mango was sitting on the pavement. Each step jarred Ryan's aching body and sent fresh waves of pain to his brain.

Mango was readjusting his fake leg. Ryan gathered the packs and guns, and when he looked back at the SUV, he saw it had come to rest against a chain-link fence.

Ryan helped Mango get to his feet. They slipped the H&K MP5s into the packs and shouldered the bags.

"What now, *jefe*?"

"Let's walk over there." Ryan gestured with his head toward the back of the restaurant, afraid if he raised his arms he would cry out in pain. Fire burned brightly in the Xterra's rear seat and storage compartment. Black smoke poured out the windows, carrying the stench of burning plastic.

Ryan and Mango walked around the back of what could pass for a steakhouse in the States. Ryan turned to his friend. "Do you suppose Mexicans go out for Mexican food, or do they just call it 'getting food?'"

Mango gave him the stink eye. "What the freak, bro? We're getting chased by Mexican drug gangs, because you killed their leader, and you're thinking about what Mexicans call food in Mexico?"

"It's a valid question. Do Chinese call it Chinese?"

Mango shook his head.

They crossed another parking lot and turned up a side street into a residential neighborhood. The homes were more upscale. Ryan watched the vehicles as they walked. They were either in locked garages or behind bars in small courtyards.

In the distance, they heard AK rounds exploding in the back of the Xterra. The Nissan's metal skeleton would contain the projectiles. Without the chamber and barrel of a gun to focus the pressure of the expanding propellant, the bullets merely popped out as their casing shattered from internal pressure. It still made a lot of racket.

"I'm waiting for the grenades to cook off."

Mango held up his pack and grinned. "There were only two left, so I kept them. They might come in handy."

"Nice."

An ancient Datsun pickup truck chugged up the hill beside them. They moved over to the edge of the road and watched as the dusty and dented pickup with a metal ladder rack stopped at a construction site of a new home. The driver was a heavyset Mexican with greasy hair, cowboy boots, dirty jeans, and a black T-shirt with a company logo on the left breast. He left the driver's door open and the engine running when he climbed out and walked into the framed walls of the two-story building.

Mango and Ryan ran to the truck. Ryan slipped his pack off as he rounded the driver's side. He slid into the driver's seat as Mango jerked open the passenger door and climbed in. Ryan jammed the stick shift into gear and sped away before the doors were closed. Behind them, the driver half-ran, half-waddled out into the street, shouting for the thieves to stop.

Ryan turned left at the bottom of the hill and had to make a sharp right because the road dead-ended into a concrete wall. He gunned it up another hill and coasted down the backside. At the bottom was a cross street. If he continued straight, they would run into a house. To the left of the house was a gravel track leading up the hill into a stand of trees. To Ryan, it looked like an alley or a shortcut for drivers who didn't want to circle the block. He turned into it and shot gravel from his tires as they charged up the lane. He was right. The lane ended at a street, but it exited onto pavement between a concrete post and a utility pole, a gap too small for the truck to fit through. He hauled the wheel left around a big tree and squeezed the Datsun between a smaller tree and a post. The truck bounced onto Avenue *Faja de Oro*.

Ryan asked Mango to bring up Google Maps on his smart phone. Mango pulled the phone out of Ryan's pack and turned it on. Ryan explained that he thought the narcos would patrol the main roads and they should try to avoid them. Neither man was sure how Mexicans reported stolen vehicles. Today, Ryan figured every incident would receive intense scrutiny as a possible lead to Guerrero's killers. Their truck would be on the list of suspected vehicles.

Mango showed Ryan the screen with Google's satellite view enabled on the map application. They were at the south end of Tampico International Airport, and if he kept working north and east on side streets, they would eventually run into Manta-Tampico Road which joined Mex 80, the fastest and most direct route out of town. If the cartel shut the road down and began a vehicle search, they would back traffic up for miles. Ryan suspected the narcos would set up roving patrols on Mex 80 to look for the two *gringos*.

They decided to continue down *Faja de Oro* and get back on Mex 80. After he turned onto the main route, Ryan pulled into the parking lot of a grocery store. He backed into a spot under a tree, and they watched the road and lot. Neither saw anything suspicious.

Ryan got on Google Maps and looked for a place to extract from while Mango kept watch. He located a spot at the end of Aldama-Barra del Tordo Road. On the map the little port town did not have a name, so he assumed it was Barra del Tordo because Aldama was at the other end of the road. Multiple docks projected into the Carrizal River for Greg to bring the Hatteras alongside.

Mango pulled a screwdriver from the glove box. Ryan watched as he swapped license plates with another truck. When he was back, Ryan showed him the map and told him to call Greg. He shoved the transmission in gear and headed north.

CHAPTER FIFTY-THREE

Greg Olsen chewed on a fingernail while staring at the dazzling surface of the deep blue Gulf of Mexico. It was a nervous habit he'd developed since his accident. He'd chewed off all his nails and spit the clippings over the side of the boat. DiMarco climbed the bridge ladder and found him drumming on the console, one hand within easy reach of the satellite phone.

"No word?"

Greg drew a deep breath before answering. "No."

DiMarco handed Greg a glass of sweet tea and stretched out on a padded bench.

Greg remained silent, staring at the now calm water. It always amazed him how quickly the ocean changed. One minute the water was placid and the next, a raging torrent. He took a swallow of tea. Waiting for word from Ryan was agonizing. Glancing at his watch for the third time in the last minute, he realized there was nothing he could do, and he felt powerless. Two years ago, he would have jumped up, grabbed a gun, and led Ryan into battle. Now, his injuries regulated him to the sidelines like some useless fobbit.

"I hate this," he grumbled.

"You should be used to it." DiMarco lay with his hat pulled down over his eyes and his hands folded on his chest. "Hurry up and wait. The military motto and the motto of government ops."

Greg knew DiMarco was a solid operator and a valued employee of DWR, but the man grated on him and he couldn't explain why. He turned his thoughts inward and recounted their actions since dropping off Ryan and Mango.

He'd continued up Cut Channel and found a fuel dock. With a full load of fuel on board, DiMarco had gone through the steps of checking engine oil levels, thru-hull fittings, and pumps. He'd also drained the water from the fuel/water separators and checked the oil filters.

Chores done, they motored back into the Gulf to await news from his employees. Greg didn't want to be sitting at the dock if the city went on lockdown. It was better to be at sea than under lock and key.

Ryan and Mango had planned to be in the city for several days, exploring the area and watching Guerrero's compound. Greg hadn't expected them to call. Still, he would have liked a progress update.

Greg jumped when the satellite phone rang. He snatched up the receiver.

"Change of plans on the exfil," Mango said. "We're headed north out of the city. We'll meet you up the coast."

"Where?"

"Pull up Google Maps."

Greg powered up the computer tablet built into the Hatteras's console and opened the map application. "I've got it."

"Scroll north, up the coast. There's an unmarked town at the end of the Aldama-Barra del Tordo Road."

"Okay, I found it." Greg felt DiMarco come up beside him.

"There should be a marina there. If not, we'll meet you at the end of a dock."

"We're on the way."

"Greg." He heard Ryan yell his name. "Keep your head down, I shot Guerrero. There are police and cartel technicals everywhere."

"Will do." Greg hung up and looked toward the Mexican coast where he could see the twin one-hundred-and-eighty-foot towers of the Tampico Bridge. The massive arch bridge linked the states of Tamaulipas to the north and Veracruz on the south bank of the Pánuco River. The towers were beacons for incoming ships.

He turned to DiMarco as he started the boat's twin diesels. "Ryan shot Guerrero."

Surprise registered on the older man's face. "Bet that stirred up the hornet's nest."

"I wouldn't want to be in their shoes," Greg said. But he wished he was the one who had put the bullet in Guerrero's head and was now on the run for his life. He wished with all his heart for the use of two good legs to carry him back into battle. He missed the adrenaline, the intensity, and the laser-like focus of disarming a bomb in the middle of a firefight. "God, please," he'd begged so many times he'd lost count. There was no answer and there never would be. That didn't stop him from pleading his case.

DiMarco leaned forward to look at the map application. "Where are we going?"

Greg pointed. "Can you put Barra del Tordo in the chart plotter?"

DiMarco entered the coordinates as Greg throttled the engines up and headed north.

CHAPTER FIFTY-FOUR

Mex 80 wound through densely populated urban areas. Strip malls, businesses, and houses pushed in on the street. Small stands of trees and brush grew everywhere someone neglected to prune them. Vines crawled along every fence, bringing shades of green to the already vibrantly colored buildings. Ryan thought it looked cool, but despite the beauty of the city, he and Mango were antsy, losing time in stop-and-go traffic. Beneath their face masks and ball caps, they were sweaty. Ryan's arms ached from the lack of power steering. He guessed the truck was from the eighties when stereos and air conditioning were optional. Neither of which the truck had. Every time Ryan shifted gears, his elbow hit the packs stacked on the seat between him and Mango.

Between the suburban towns of Miramar and Altamira, they'd turned onto Altamira Road by the Petrotemex chemical plant. All around them, police vehicles and armed cartel trucks patrolled the roads.

Altamira Road changed names a few times before it began paralleling the Gulf Coast. Getting off the main road made them less visible and it would be a nicer drive. Ryan enjoyed seeing something new when he drove. Since he'd never driven through Mexico, everything was new.

Leaving the suburbs behind, they headed through mesquite-covered hills, passed lagoons, and crossed rivers. Suburbs gave way to smaller houses, and then they became the rundown shacks of poor farmers and peasants. They pulled off their disguises and tucked them away.

In two hours of driving, the terrain changed from marshy to long, flat plains. A few farms dotted the land, but mostly the countryside was desolate. It was a beautiful drive. Mango navigated with the map application. Lots of little unpaved two-track trails snaked off the main road. Before they reached Barra del Tordo, Ryan turned off onto a small paved road leading east to the Gulf.

"Where are we going?" Mango asked.

Ryan downshifted and slowed for a speed bump on the roughly paved road. "We can't be this close to the ocean and not take a look. Besides, we can find us a taco stand with a view."

Mango brightened. "I'm all for that, bro. I need to eat something." He patted his belly.

The road ended at a small public beach with picnic table shelters and palm trees swaying in the breeze. A small restaurant in a weathered shack had Tecate beer and Coca-Cola signs plastered on it. Ryan parked the truck. At the restaurant, they ordered tacos and cold beers then ate at a picnic table while watching the surf roll in.

Mango was in the middle of biting into his taco when he stopped and said, "Mexican food in Mexico is just tacos."

They both laughed.

Ryan chewed his taco and tried to calculate the time it would take for Greg to arrive. The drive from Tampico had taken two hours, including the running gunfight and stealing a truck. He mused out loud, "If Greg runs the boat hard, he can make almost forty-five miles per hour."

"And burn a serious amount of fuel," Mango interrupted.

"So, he'll run a little slower, knowing we won't be able to get fuel until we get to Texas, which isn't too far away." He took a bite, chewed, swallowed, and continued. "Best scenario, he runs at thirty-five knots and gets here in just over two hours. He might be looking for a dock up on the Carrizal River right now."

"We might have missed him passing by. We should call him."

Ryan pulled the sat phone from his pack, dialed the number for Greg and listened to it ring. He swiveled his head and body to watch the few people walking around the small beach and parking lot. Sun shone on colorful umbrellas, and small children laughed at a picnic table as their harried parents tried to corral them for lunch.

"Hey, buddy," Greg said. "We're almost to El Tordo."

"We're a little south of the village on a public beach. How close to shore are you running?"

"Close enough for you to see us."

"We're watching for you."

"What are you doing at the beach?"

"Eating Mexican," Ryan replied and grinned at Mango, who shook his head in consternation.

Ten minutes later, Ryan and Mango helped a young fisherman push his wooden *panga* into the surf. The kid motored them past the breakwater to a blue-and-white sportfisher with a gleaming aluminum tower. They were going home.

EPILOGUE

Floyd Landis watched as the breaching team formed up outside a small ranch home in a wealthy suburb of Austin, Texas. The team leader counted down over his radio and the breachers bashed in the front door with a heavy steel ram. The Homeland Security Special Response Team didn't fire a shot as they piled through the door and cleared the house.

Landis listened as the SRT agents shouted for several people to surrender. He waited until an agent approached and told him the house was clear. Then he lumbered inside and found Professor Rueben Morales lying on his stomach, hands cuffed behind his back and his feet shackled by zip cuffs. When Landis squatted beside him, Morales screamed and thrashed, demanding to be released.

"Scream all you want," Landis said. "No one cares."

Morales stared up with furrowed brows. "I am an American citizen. You can't raid my home without a warrant and just cause."

With his fingertip, Landis touched the medallion hanging from Morales's neck. "This is a just cause."

Ryan's email with the map of targets and the list of Aztlán cartel and ISIS cell addresses had created a firestorm at Homeland. But typical of government, nothing moved quickly. By the time Ryan and Mango had escaped Tampico and were eating tacos on the beach, word of Arturo Guerrero's death had reached the U.S. cells. In retaliation, several suicide bombers detonated their vests inside Caesar's Palace in Las Vegas, a car bomb exploded in San Antonio, and the Brown Shirts mustered for war.

DHS had finally coordinated with various local police and sheriff's departments to round up the cell members when the cartel attacked the border patrol station in Brownsville, Texas. The Texas State Guard, Highway Patrol, and local units rallied to suppress the invaders.

Landis had demanded the Austin SRT team help him arrest Morales and search his home. Morales had several prepaid cell phones he'd used to coordinate the cartel's attacks on U.S. soil. They also found a large cache of documents linking Morales, Guerrero, and several Mexican-American politicians to Guerrerro's plot to retake the Desert Southwest.

While standing in Morales's study, Landis's phone rang. He answered it with his typical gruff fashion.

"Good to talk to you," Ryan said.

"Word on the street is that two white devils assassinated cartel kingpin Arturo Guerrero. Do you know anything about that?"

"Not a thing," Ryan lied.

The sun-dappled waters of the Gulf of Mexico sparkled like winking diamonds. An occasional wave broached in a whitecap, and a gull wheeled and screamed in the sky. Ryan Weller pulled the salt air deep into his lungs and stared up at the peak of the mast seventy feet above him. The stretch of white sail was almost blinding in the sun.

"This is the life, bro," Mango called to him.

"Yes, it is," Ryan replied, looking back at him. "Mighty nice boat you bought for yourself."

"We like it," Jennifer said.

They were well offshore, sailing from New Orleans to Texas City. The young couple had purchased an Amazon 44 sailing vessel to replace the boat stolen by Guerrero's men. They had used their share of the five million dollars recovered from *La Carranza Garza* that Mango had tossed over to the Hatteras in a big, green duffle bag.

They'd divided the money evenly between Ryan, Jerry DiMarco, Mango, and several charities after they took out the expenses of running the big sportfisher, *Dark Water*, and Ryan's lost sailboat. They tried to give some to the active-duty SEALs, but they wouldn't accept it, so the DWR men had split their portion between the EOD Warrior Foundation, Navy SEAL Foundation, and Coast Guard Tactical Law Enforcement Foundation to give aid to families of deployed, fallen, or injured EOD techs, SEALs, and Coast Guard Special Forces.

When Ryan had told Larry they'd donated the money, Larry had said, "I couldn't think of a finer thing to do."

Ryan made his way back to the cockpit where Jennifer and Emily Hunt lay stretched out on the padded benches. He stopped to admire his voluptuous, blonde girlfriend. She wore a bright-red bikini top with white shorts over her bikini bottoms. She'd fanned her blonde hair out across the white vinyl. Ryan smiled, happy she'd snuck away from work to hang out with him.

Mango set the autopilot and picked up an acoustic guitar.

"I didn't know you could play," Ryan said.

Mango shrugged. "I never told you."

"All that time we spent together offshore, and you never mentioned it?" Ryan said.

Mango shrugged again. "It wasn't important."

"Play us something boaty," Emily said, sitting up so Ryan could sit beside her. He grabbed two beers from the cooler and handed her one.

Mango sat on the bench beside Jennifer and tuned the flat top. Then he strummed out a few cords before singing a Kenny Chesney cover about pirate flags and island girls.

As the words drifted away on the wind, Ryan's thoughts turned to a different pirate. One selling guns to the highest bidder and willing to supply a Mexican drug cartel who'd tried to start a war with America. Ryan took a swig of beer. International arms dealer Jim Kilroy might be protected by the U.S. government, but he wasn't immune to one man on a mission. Ryan Weller was that man.

ABOUT THE AUTHOR

Evan Graver has worked in construction, as a security guard, a motorcycle and car technician, a property manager, and in the scuba industry. He served in the U.S. Navy, where he was an aviation electronics technician until they medically retired him following a motorcycle accident which left him paralyzed. He found other avenues of adventure: riding ATVs, downhill skiing, skydiving, and bungee jumping. His passions are scuba diving and writing. He lives in Hollywood, Florida, with his wife and son.

WHATS NEXT:

If you enjoyed *Dark Water* or any of Evan's other books, please consider leaving a review on Amazon, BookBub, or Goodreads.

If you would like to follow Ryan Weller's adventures, and learn more about him, visit www.evangraver.com. Sign up for my monthly correspondence and receive the free Ryan Weller Thriller Short Story, *Dark Days*. I send out an update around the 15th of the month about what I'm writing, reading, or listening to. I'll throw in some things happening in my daily life and let you know when the next book is coming out.

Follow me on Facebook at Evan Graver Author.

Made in the USA
Lexington, KY
31 August 2019